THE BONE DRAGON

ALEXIA CASALE

faber and faber

First published in the UK in 2013
by Faber and Faber Limited
Bloomsbury House
74–77 Great Russell Street,
London, WC1B 3DA

A CIP record for this book
is available from the British Library

ISBN 978-0-571-29561-6

FSC
www.fsc.org
MIX
Paper from
responsible sources
FSC® C101712

2 4 6 8 10 9 7 5 3 1

THE BONE DRAGON

I rise up, towards the surface.

Through velvet blue into grey dimness.

Up towards the light.

And sound starts to penetrate now. Low echoes, vibrating through the water.

But I'm not ready to leave yet. I'm safe here, floating in the shadows. The pain is distant, belonging to the light and the warmth and the air.

My hands scull uselessly, trying to cup the water: trying to hold myself down. It eludes my grasp, flowing between my fingers like silk. And still I rise.

Beneath the surface now, I look up into daylight. A face appears above me, wide and distorted: pink with heat that can't touch me here in the cool shadow of the water. Her mouth opens and words ripple across the surface, dim and uncertain.

For a breath I rise, breaking the surface. I feel a tear slithering down, curving over my cheek. Sound echoes in my throat. I reach out, fumbling to grasp: her wrist is fat and warm. Another face appears, peering at me, bending down. Fingers close over my own. A hand pats mine and eagerly I grip back, finding purchase, then push away.

I sink back under the water.

The world becomes distant.

The shadows are calm, unhurried. The darkness beckons me down.

'Evie?'

Amy's voice. Soft and warm, like the blankets, like the bed.

Amy, not Fiona.

A sigh. My own. The air is hot and sharp with the smell of chemicals. My feet stir against the blankets, the sheets moving cool and stiff across my legs. And my fingers flex, tightening, loosening on cotton, starched and grainy.

'Evie sweetheart?'

My head turns towards her voice, towards the gentle fingers moving my hair away from my face. Amy.

When I open my eyes it will be Amy, not Fiona. Not that blank face, those staring eyes. But love. And comfort. Safety.

My lips are dry, my tongue fat and clumsy. I swallow, and feel the movement travel down my body. I become aware of my throat, my shoulders, sunk heavily into the pillow, my back into the mattress. My fingers twitch and my forehead spasms into a frown. Pain echoes dully around my ribs, into my spine, up my breastbone, catching my breath in my throat.

'I think she's in pain. Paul . . .'

'I'll find a nurse.'

I open my eyes.

'Evie sweetheart.' Amy smiles down at me with relief and concern and tenderness: all the things a parent should feel. Everything a mother should show.

Amy, not Fiona.

Her hand finds mine, squeezes. 'Are you OK? Are you in pain?'

I sigh again. Again my breath catches. The pain pulls up from my chest and sharpens the room into focus. My arms, legs, are clumsy as I twist, trying to turn towards her. As if I am still dreaming, thoughts form lazily after my attention has drifted away to something new. *How strange for my eyes to be out of step with my thoughts: to be recognising one thing while looking at another*, I find a voice in my head comment wonderingly. I float along on this strange, slow time, registering sensations, unable to make anything of them, out of time with myself.

'Dr Barstow says the operation went wonderfully. You're going to be absolutely fine, darling. Better than ever,' Amy is saying. Her forehead tightens in sympathy, lines drawing down into a fan of arrows above her nose.

I blink and even this is slow, eyelids descending, rising again. The room sways dizzily away as if on a pendulum: swings, settles.

I swallow again, tasting the air.

The door opens before my thoughts have time to coalesce – something about the hospital room, how dry my mouth is, the lingering memory of an earlier awakening.

'Hello, Evie.' Dr Barstow is crisp and smiling: all sharp lines. No nonsense. No fuss. None of the horrible sympathy of the nurse before the operation, injecting both the anaesthetic and enough pity to drown me in.

My gaze drifts to the frieze of teddy bears marching around the top of the walls, then to the multicoloured balloon print on the curtains. An echo of my initial indignation when the nurse first showed us into the room washes through me, but I am too weary to be irritated afresh. Tomorrow. Tomorrow I'll wish they had put me in a normal room, not a paediatrics one. I mean, I can't be the only teenager they've ever had here.

'. . . very well, though I'm sure it has set your parents' minds at ease to see you awake again,' Dr Barstow is saying, casting one of her tight little smiles in Amy and Paul's direction. 'Can you rate your pain for me, Evie?'

I open my mouth to answer, but my tongue is too dry to work. I swallow then grimace.

'How about a little bit of water?' Dr Barstow asks as she bends to work the controls of the bed. I feel it shift beneath me, levering me slowly into a half-sitting position.

Amy leans over with a glass of water, guiding the straw to my lips. 'Better?'

'Yah.' On a breath, a thin quiver of sound. But Amy smiles anyway, her eyes liquid with relief and love. Paul leans in, smiling at me too. His hand moves to Amy's shoulder. Hers automatically reaches up to cover it.

'And the pain?' Dr Barstow asks. 'Where is it on that scale of one to ten we've talked about before, with ten being the worst pain you can imagine?'

'Maybe . . . a six?' It's almost a whisper this time. And I feel the strange, dull pull radiating up and around my chest. My hand flutters over the blankets, touches the edge of a thick, padded dressing through the hospital gown.

'Gently, gently.' Amy catches my hand and moves it away.

'I'll order something extra to help get the pain under control,' Dr Barstow says as she turns a page in my chart, adds a note. She closes the file, returning it to the foot of the bed, then glances at the monitor to the left.

My eyes follow the cable down in a long loop towards the floor, back up, over the edge of the bed, to my finger, encased in a flat clip: oxygen, that's what the nurse said it measured when she first attached it. I don't like thinking about the IV line, the way it snakes across the back of my hand, the strange stiffness in my wrist from the drugs pumping through it.

With an effort, I shift my drifting, lazy thoughts back to Dr Barstow. 'If everything continues like this, your parents will probably be able to take you home the day after tomorrow,' she is saying.

Amy beams at me. 'We're all set up, aren't we, Evie? Lots of nice new DVDs.'

'We'll need to get you up and walking first,' Dr Barstow says but she is distracted, fishing for something in her pocket. 'The nurses will be by to talk to you about that in a bit. But here, I thought you might like to keep this.'

And she puts a little pot down on the wheelie table at the foot of the bed. I register clear plastic. A marigold-yellow lid. And something an odd mix of grey, white and pink sitting inside. Almost like a finger. Mine flex unconsciously in response. All accounted for.

Amy and Paul are frowning. Bewildered. A little worried.

'*That* is the rib that's been giving you so much trouble. Well, a piece of it anyway.'

Amy flinches, drawing back into herself, while Paul jerks oddly, his face twisting. I see his mouth open as if he is about to say something – something angry. Then he shrugs very slightly. His eyebrows and the corner of his lip twitch, but he closes his mouth, flicking a glance at Dr Barstow.

'This piece was completely avascular – completely dead. So there was no chance of it healing. Because it is – was – so low down in your ribcage, you don't really need it. Not a good idea to have it hanging around in there unattached. Much better to take it out. Even better, it should stop your chest hurting. Well, after the wound heals up. I'm going to go and order that painkiller for you now. See you in a bit.'

She, Amy and Paul exchange polite smiles. I turn my attention back to the little pot. And my rib sitting inside it. The thought that I should feel sick, horrified, surfaces. But I don't. I just feel curious. And a little sad. Looking at another thing I've lost.

I smile, drawing my feet up to make space on the sofa, as Uncle Ben comes back into the living room. He pats my ankle as he sits, perching on the edge of the seat so that he can lean over to the table crowded with drinks and pills and tissues that Amy has set up beside me: everything within easy reach of where I lie, propped up with five pillows and snuggled under my quilt.

'Comfy set-up you've got here,' he says as he peers into the pot holding my rib.

'Apart from the great big hole in my chest and the eight staples, you mean?'

'Yeah, apart from that,' he answers casually. That's one of the things I love about Uncle Ben. He's never thrown by these things. And he never tries to drown me in sympathy. But I still know he cares. He's just smart enough to know that sometimes you don't have to be serious, even about serious things. He's holding my rib up to the light now. 'Pretty good specimen,' he says.

And he should know. He's a pathologist. Which is really odd: he's such a nice person it's a pity he isn't a doctor for living people. But I suppose I can understand it: he says he doesn't want to have to deal with people who spend all their time whining about having a pimple at the end of their nose. I wouldn't want to have to listen to people whining about that either.

'Amy says it's morbid and disturbing.'

'I never could figure out how I ended up with such a squeamish sister,' Uncle Ben says, shrugging. Then he grins. 'But it was great fun when we were kids. She had the most amazing squeal.'

I grin too, reminding myself not to laugh. 'What did you do?'

'Oh, nothing too horrible. The odd slug on her toast . . .'

'Ew!' I grimace, but I'm grinning still, wanting to laugh. But it's going to be another six days before I can laugh – after the staples come out.

I hate the staples. It's not so much that they hurt; it's the way my whole left side feels so stiff and heavy all the time. I can't understand it really. They're only little. The wound – the bit where they cut my chest open during the operation – is only about four inches long. Which is big, but not so big that it should make it this difficult to move. I have to move very slowly when I do things like getting up: anything that involves twisting or bending. Amy has to help me in the shower. I thought I would mind that. A lot. But I don't. Because it's Amy. And she loves me.

And I'm not at all afraid of her. Besides, nothing bad ever happened in a shower. I think that helps.

'So, Squirt,' I stick my tongue out at Uncle Ben, 'your Uncle Ben, being a man of stunning genius,' I roll my eyes, 'has had a brainwave! A moment of unsurpassed brilliance.' He grins at me, waiting for me to encourage him.

'What?' I ask, annoyed at myself for giving in, but not really. Annoyed in that good way. Because I like it when Uncle Ben teases me. As if it's been like that since I was born. As if we really are family. Uncle Ben's great that way too. He was never awkward with me. Never seemed worried about what to do or what to say or . . . anything. Auntie Beth, Paul's sister, is lovely but she's still so . . . careful. As if I'll break. Or bite. Or both.

'I'll give you a clue. It has something to do with this impressive specimen.'

'But what?' I plead. 'Come *on*! You have to be nice to me! I'm sick!'

Uncle Ben sighs dramatically. 'It's going to be a terrible struggle, you know, being nice to you for another fortnight. I don't see how I'll manage it. I'm far too wicked.'

I grin and nudge his thigh with my toe. 'You are! You always make me wait!'

'Well, I suppose I'll just have to come clean. So, my idea of amazing brilliance is . . . Well, no. Let's start from the other end.'

I roll my eyes, heave a dramatic sigh and feel the air jerk out, pain catching in my throat. I lever my left knee up towards my chest and breathe through the ache. Uncle Ben's hand comes down on my leg and squeezes gently.

'What's the other end?' I ask. My voice is a little flat, but Uncle Ben doesn't mind.

'The other end is a story. People say – well, Jews and Christians say – that after God made the world and all that, he made Adam ...' As the name passes his lips, I see his thoughts go to Paul and Amy's Adam, his Adam: the pain ripples across the muscles of his face and through his eyes.

But Adam is gone and I am here and, as I watch, I see him lavish his grief back into love to offer it where it's needed.

'So,' he says, just a little too briskly: moving along, moving on, 'God put him in the Garden of Eden. But,' a breath for courage, 'Adam wasn't too keen on kicking about in there by himself, so he asked God for a companion. Well, God thought that this was a pretty reasonable request, so he put Adam to sleep and, while he was asleep, God took out one of his ribs and made it into Eve. So, really, all of womankind came from just that one rib.'

'God's never been very interested in me.' There's something nasty in my voice. I can't stop it.

For a moment, Uncle Ben frowns. Then he squeezes my knee again. 'You know I don't believe in any of this stuff either, Evie. I'm just like Amy and Paul: a hopeless heathen.'

I try to swallow away the nastiness that stings my throat, makes my chest pull around the staples with the weight of the air in my lungs. 'Yeah.' My voice is hoarse, like a whisper. But it's not so nasty this time.

'I just thought it was a funny sort of idea that if all of womankind came from one of Adam's ribs then, theoretically, we should get something pretty amazing out of yours, right?'

I shrug. I used to believe in God. I was quite good at it, even if I didn't go to church. I used to pray every night. But it never did any good.

And if God hadn't done anything to help me back *then*, there wasn't much chance he was going to be interested now. And if he'd wanted one of my ribs, well, why couldn't he have taken it the way he took Adam's? If it had just been an operation, just a matter of going to sleep and having it taken away, that wouldn't have been so bad. Even with the staples.

'Think of it as one of those myths and legends about the Norse gods. You know, like in that project you did at school last year,' Uncle Ben says, but his voice is losing the laughter that it had before.

And I know I am frowning, pulling my face down into that look that made my ... made Fiona's mother call me 'an ugly, sullen little beast'. I try to breathe it away, smooth it away just like my hands straightening the creases in the quilt.

'How about this,' Uncle Ben says, almost urgently, 'if you could have a pet – any type of animal in the world, or even out of the world, even things that don't really exist – what would it be?'

I don't even have to think about it. 'A dragon!' I say, breathless at the very thought, seeing in my mind a picture from a book about Chinese art from school: a serpent-dragon, red and gold, twisting and circling, smoke and fire wreathing from its nostrils. I focus on it, making it as real as I can in my mind, willing myself to forget about God and prayers never answered and the bitterness of worthless hope.

I make the dragon realer and realer, clearer and clearer.

Uncle Ben laughs. 'I can see that,' he says. 'A dragon. That would be a pretty amazing pet. What colour would it be?'

The dragon in my mind – from the book – is red, but I say, 'Any colour.' It wouldn't matter. If there really were a dragon, if I really could have one, I wouldn't care what colour it was. 'And any size. A little one would be perfect too,' I say out loud.

This time my chest is tight with longing. If I had a dragon, I'd never be powerless again ... But I can't let myself think about that.

'So long as it could breathe fire,' I whisper, forcing my thoughts away. I imagine the dragon sitting there, on my lap, looking up at me. 'It would have to breathe fire.'

'Of course!' Uncle Ben says, the laughter back in his

voice. 'Anyway, I thought that we could have a little project together. We could take that rib of yours out of the formaldehyde and dry it out and then carve it into a dragon. Not quite as good as a real one, but I'm afraid I'm all out of magical powers. Besides, maybe if you did a spell on it or a wish or something . . . Who knows, right? It's a nice thought at least.'

'Wonderful.' I sigh, closing my eyes and seeing the dragon. I smile at the picture in my mind. 'There's this book at school with a picture of a dragon. Do you think we could try to carve it like that? All twisty and stuff.'

'Well, we could have a look and see,' Uncle Ben says, undaunted. 'I'm sure we can come up with something.'

Scales are really difficult: they're so fiddly. I keep making little holes in my finger with the weird tool that Uncle Ben is letting me borrow. It looks a bit like one of the things the dentist has so I haven't asked Uncle Ben about it: I figure it's better not to know what it's normally used for.

Amy was really angry with Uncle Ben when he gave it to me. But he talked her around. He usually does, though this time he did it by telling her the tool was brand new and hadn't gone near any dead people yet, so he wasn't as successful as usual: Amy keeps on coming in from the kitchen, hands coated in flour from the biscuits she is making, to check on me. She's going to have to hoover soon or it'll get ground into the carpet.

I've been working on scales all day – it's nearly five o'clock now – and I've still only done the dragon's tail. The tail is so cool. It's got a point almost like the spades suit in playing cards and a whole line of ridges that go all the way up the dragon's back. Only little ones of course, but the bone isn't as smooth as I'd expected. I suppose that's because it was too broken to mend in the first place. But I'd rather not think too much about that. I think about the dragon instead.

Yesterday, Ms Winters brought over the book with the picture of the Chinese dragon, even though it's still the holidays. She and Amy pretended that she'd just come to drop it off, but I knew they were up to something even before Ms Winters directed the conversation to the fact that I'm going to miss the first three weeks of autumn term.

She's offered to come over one evening a week to make sure I don't get behind. And that's great because she's far and away my favourite teacher, but somehow I can't help feeling that there's something more to the whole thing. For now though, I'm busy with the dragon.

After Uncle Ben and I got the bone dried out, he did the first bit of the carving. Well, to be honest Uncle Ben did all the real work making the shape of the dragon. We couldn't really make it curly in the end. But Uncle Ben did sort of manage to carve little feet into it. And because the bone is thicker at one point, he made it so it looks like the dragon is curled over on itself there. And it does curve a little bit anyway, just with how the bone curves naturally.

And when I've finished the scales and made the eyes and everything – Uncle Ben says they should be slitty eyes because dragons are like snakes or cats – it's going to be beautiful. It only makes me wish even more that it was real.

I keep catching myself about to pray that it will turn into a real dragon. But I don't. I won't. I'm never going to pray for anything again.

Amy comes out of the kitchen to check on me for the twenty-seventh time. 'How's it going?' she asks, wiping wet-clean hands on her apron.

I sigh – carefully. I'm getting used to the staples now. 'Slowly.'

'Why don't you have a little break? It might be nice to go and listen to some music in bed for a while.'

What Amy really means is that she wants me to have a nap. But it's nice that she doesn't tell me to do it.

I yawn reflexively. She smiles and I grin, putting the tool and the dragon down on the table, then starting to push myself up. I've only got as far as throwing the quilt off my legs before Amy is there, her anxious hovering reminding me to go slowly: push myself up with my right arm, swing my legs down to the ground, move to the edge of the couch, push myself to my feet, staying bent at the waist until I am standing. Amy gathers up the quilt.

'Can you bring the dragon for me?' I ask. 'I don't need the tool. I just want to take the dragon up with me,' I add before Amy can suggest – only a suggestion – that I'm meant to be going up to have a rest.

'How are the fingers?' She hovers behind me, quilt over one arm, dragon safely ensconced in the pot in her left hand. Her right is outstretched, almost touching my elbow as I shuffle towards the bottom of the stairs.

'It's not any worse than sticking a needle in myself in one of Mrs Poole's awful textiles projects "to explore the applied aspects of Art",' I say, rolling my eyes. It's impossible to truly dislike Mrs Poole, but I wish she wouldn't make us sew. I mean, I get that it's a useful skill and that she's trying to slip it into class so that we all know how to fix a button at least. The fault in her thinking is that some people just aren't destined to sew.

'Do be careful, darling,' Amy says. 'It's better than cutting your fingers open, but try not to treat yourself like a pincushion if at all possible.'

I'm concentrating too hard to answer as I lift my right foot on to the first step, then draw my left up. Right foot on to the next step, then left, hand on the banister to help with my balance because I seem to be very clumsy since the operation. Uncle Ben says that's probably still because of the anaesthetic. But the staples don't help either. At least it's only another two days until they come out. I can't wait.

I have to pause halfway up. Amy waits patiently behind

me. Touches my elbow lightly. A couple of years ago, that would have made me jump. But I don't now. After nearly four years, I can *feel* it's Amy. Even that bit of me that sometimes gets scared of silly things that I know aren't really there knows that it's Amy. So I don't jump. I don't even look back to see for sure. Instead, it's nice to feel her hand – soft, cool – reminding me that she's there to help me if I need it.

When we finally make it to the landing, I shuffle down the hall, hand trailing along the doors of the big cupboard at the head of the stairs, across the wall, the door to the bathroom, the moulding around my bedroom door.

Reaching the bed, I reverse the procedure from downstairs to get from standing to lying down: turn and sit on the edge of the bed, wiggle backwards, use my right hand for balance as I twist and swing my legs up. Amy fluffs my pillows as I lower myself on to my side and finally turn on to my back. She pulls the quilt up over my legs and puts the pot with the dragon down on the table by the bed, then passes me the remote control for the stereo.

'Call if you need me,' she says, kissing my hair. 'I'll come and find you when it's time for dinner.'

She turns and smiles at me from the doorway before she leaves.

I sigh – carefully, of course – and turn on the stereo. *Howl's Moving Castle* is in the machine. I always play audiobooks when I'm in bed: they seem to fill up the silence better than music and stop my thoughts from wandering, in the quiet, to things that I don't want to think about. When it's a really bad day, I repeat the words in my head, forcing out the not-real sounds and the not-now voices and the things that aren't really there, filling my mind up so that they can't fit: so there's no room for them and they get tired and go away again. Sometimes I have to play the whole book and then start it over again before that happens.

But not this afternoon. This afternoon I've got the dragon to think about, and I let the story wash over me as I sink into sleep. The room is warm and the sheets are cool. It's still sunny outside and the dragon is safe on the bedside table.

I come awake slowly, feeling groggy and confused, hot and stiff. I ball my fists into my eyes and yawn, throwing back the covers with a careless sigh that quickly becomes a grimace. *Must remember to be careful with the sighing, with the yawning, with everything*, I grouse to myself. I'm tired in that unpleasant, irritable way you get when you sleep somewhere too warm.

Sighing, I get slowly out of bed, putting the pot with the dragon in my dressing-gown pocket. It's still sunny outside so I know it can only have been an hour or so, but it's probably enough to make Amy happy.

As I shuffle down the hallway, I hear Paul and Uncle Ben's deep voices murmuring below, and I cheer up as I think about showing Uncle Ben all the scales I've done.

But as I put my foot on the first step I hear Paul say, '. . . all afternoon with the lawyer,' and I stop.

'I can't believe they're not going to take the case forward! You'd think with something like this they'd be pushing like crazy.'

Amy says something I struggle to catch.

'Yes, I know all that,' Paul snaps irritably. 'All this rubbish about how the evidence doesn't prove it was *them*. How they wish the system acknowledged the difficulties – was less slanted towards the burden being on the victim to prove the case. I know all that. It just doesn't make it any less . . .'

'Disgusting.'

That's Uncle Ben. And he really does sound disgusted. And angry. And fed up.

Gripping the banister, I sit – slowly, carefully – down on the stairs, clenching my teeth and pressing my lips together. I know they will tell me about this later. Not right away probably, because of the operation. It probably *would* have been better not to have heard it now. But I have. So there's no point going back to my room now: I can't pretend I don't know. I curl my fingernails into my palm. It hurts and I'm glad. I try to focus on that instead of the other pain: the sense that my throat has closed up, and the hot-cold feeling like I might be going to cry.

'And that useless woman from Family Services! You'd think that if any case were possible, this would be it. I mean, what more evidence can there be than the operation and the doctor's testimony? At least Dr Barstow was willing to write a statement about the operation, not like that stinking little weasel . . .'

'Sh, Paul. Evie's asleep,' Amy interrupts.

Paul gives a sigh I can hear even from the stairs. 'I can't believe that cow had the nerve to say that it's complicated by the fact that all this has come out so late in the day. As if we were such terrible parents that we didn't ever take Evie to the doctor, even before we knew about all this! And why Social Services didn't give her a proper medical check-up when that pitiful excuse for a mother abandoned her I'll never know. How could no one have *noticed* she was walking around with her ribcage in pieces?'

'Paul!' But this time Amy isn't telling him off. She just doesn't want him to say that: doesn't want him to say any more. She doesn't want to hear it. I don't want to hear it either. I feel the tears from her voice in my throat.

I miss what they say next as I close my eyes. Clenching my hand around the pot with the dragon in it, I try to think about that and nothing else, try to breathe around the pain of holding myself stiff so I don't break.

'. . . important thing is that Evie is getting the help she needs now. You should both be proud that she finally trusted someone enough to tell them about her . . . injuries.'

'And it only took three years,' Paul says, his voice full of teeth.

Then no one says anything for a long time.

There's nothing to say. I didn't tell them sooner. The case is over before it started. The only thing next is the staples coming out and going back to school and the world going on. Because it always does. Even when it shouldn't possibly be able to because no one should have to keep on living when it's beyond unbearable. But the world doesn't care about that. And somehow hearts don't stop, even though it isn't possible they should keep on beating. And people don't just stop breathing. Instead they find out there are infinite places beyond unbearable.

My teeth ache. My throat aches. And my fingers are cold, though my face is hot. I close my eyes and force the pain down. Holding on to the pot with the dragon, I swallow and breathe, and swallow and breathe. Sooner or later, I'll have to open my eyes and see that the world is just the same. There is no stopping, no refusing to let time go on. It will anyway.

I keep my teeth clenched as I pull myself up on the banister, right-handed, curling my body over against the pull of the staples, against skin that can't stretch and the deeper ache of *wrongness* underneath, in the place where my rib was.

'You'd think, sooner or later, there would be a limit to unfairness,' Paul says suddenly and I freeze, still hunched over. 'I don't want to have to tell Evie that there isn't any fair for her.'

'I don't want to tell her we've failed.' Amy's voice doesn't sound like that. Like everything has been stripped out of it.

'Then maybe we should ask her . . .'

'Paul.' The word snaps out like the click of teeth, sharp as a bite.

'Now that's a tone I've not heard for a while,' says Uncle Ben, offering just the right mix of coaxing and teasing and curiosity to carry them past the moment. But Amy doesn't answer his kindness with fondness, nor Paul with his usual good humour.

I straighten in the silence.

'So what shouldn't Paul ask Evie?' Uncle Ben's voice is light, but there's something hard and heavy under the words: a demand I'd never understood until I came to live with Paul and Amy. But I recognise it now: that rare thing you can only bring out with family. A refusal to be denied that can't be rejected because there's too much history and future between you. So whatever question you ask, if you ask it that way – and only once in a very rare while – you'll get an answer.

'Paul . . . Paul thinks we should hire someone to deal with them.'

'No,' interrupts Paul, even more anger and frustration in his voice than before. 'I think we should offer Evie the option . . .'

'Which is even worse than just doing it,' Amy hisses. 'As if Evie needs to have that decision thrust on her!'

'So not another lawyer, I take it. A detective?' Uncle Ben asks.

There's an angry pause, then Amy says, 'Someone who could make them go away.'

'Just "go away", huh?' says Uncle Ben. But something ugly in his voice tears anything musing and playful from the words.

'I wasn't suggesting that,' Amy says. Her voice is still empty. The words have no inflection.

'I was.'

The words are so soft I can't make out whether it is Uncle Ben or Paul who says them.

There is nothing for a while.

'Even if you *did* – Evie's thoughts on the matter aside,' Uncle Ben starts, then stops. 'She wouldn't be any better off with one or both of you in prison, and I'm ... not a brave enough man.'

I love him for that, even as my eyes burn, burn, burn. I take the dragon-pot out of my pocket, pass it into my left hand and press it into the middle of my chest while I climb back up the stairs. I try to think about the dragon but I have to stop. I can't bear to imagine having a part of me that's as powerful as a dragon right now because a dragon *would* be powerful: it would be more powerful than any of them – the lawyers, the courts, Fiona's parents ... But there's no dragon. And even with Amy and Paul and Uncle Ben, Fiona's parents are still invincible.

I fix my eyes on the handles of the big cupboard at

the head of the stairs and fill the ringing spaces in my head with chanting – 'blank, blank, blank' – so I can't hear anything else. I think about the wardrobe part at the bottom of the cupboard where Amy keeps extra coats and board games and blankets, balls of wool and knitting needles, a box of buttons and different coloured threads. And when I've listed all the things I can think of there, I think about the top of the cupboard – two long, deep shelves – where Amy keeps old clothes I've grown out of, and old school reports and pictures and, right at the back, Adam's things: baby clothes, school exercise books, and the paperwork for the gravestone.

By the time I've finished my list, I've worked myself back into bed and under the covers and the stereo is hissing and whirring to life. I will myself into the words, forming them with my lips, echoing them in my head. Keeping the voices out.

'She got six of them out right away. With this special little tool. It came all wrapped up in its own little bag thing. Like it was just for me. I wonder if they reuse them or what they do with them afterwards. But it had blue handles. It was just like pliers. Very small pliers. And she pushed it under the staples and they just sort of came out. But not the last two. One end came up and then the other end just wouldn't somehow.'

Something like a flinch passes over Ms Winters's face. Barely a ripple. 'Did it hurt?' she prompts, knowing it did. Getting me to admit it.

'A bit. Sort of. Well . . . Sort of. Mostly it just felt odd. Strange. Anyway, she kept twisting and twisting the one end round and round but the rest just wouldn't come out. So eventually she got up and she said, "I'll just go and get the pliers . . . I mean the forceps." But of course she really meant pliers. And they weren't small at all.'

This time Ms Winters lets herself show sympathy, drawing her lips back and sucking air through her teeth. But I can tell this is intended to encourage me to keep talking, not to indicate she'd rather not hear any more, because then she asks, 'And did she get it out with the . . . pliers?'

'Eventually. It took a while. She kept twisting it one way and then the other and then it sort of levered out eventually. And that did sort of hurt. A bit,' I say. And it did. But not as much as I'd expected. Really it was just a little bit gross-weird. Mostly it wasn't hurt, just that tingly sick feeling you get when you know something is *wrong* and your body doesn't like it. 'Anyway, they're out now and I can breathe and I can move and I can take a shower by myself. And Dr Barstow says I can go back to school in a few weeks.'

'Are you looking forward to that now that you know you won't be behind?'

'Mostly.' I shrug. It won't be the same, starting three

weeks late. Lynne and Phee said they'd saved me a desk, but it won't be the same as being there to pick together. They came over last weekend to visit, but everything we tried to talk about ended up taking us on to things I hadn't done and hadn't seen and couldn't understand. All the new things I wasn't part of. All the new ways I'd be different.

Ms Winters lets the silence sit between us. You'd think she'd know better by now. I finger the pot that holds the dragon and don't bite: I know exactly what she's up to.

Amy and Paul have wanted me to see a counsellor for ages now, but I'm not trying that again. I went to two different people and they were both awful. And stupid. But mostly awful. I had four hour-long sessions with each of them and I spent the whole time staring at the wall, reciting poetry in my head so I didn't have to hear any of the things they were saying. Because they shouldn't have been saying those things. No one should ever say those sorts of things.

And, as I told Amy and Paul when they begged me to give it another try, why would I want to talk to people who don't know the first thing about what to say? Because they didn't just get it wrong. They got it as wrong as people can get it.

So Amy and Paul let it go in the sense that they didn't make me go back, but they keep bringing it up... Only they haven't since the operation. And now I think I know why: they know I like Ms Winters and they know Ms Winters works with a victim support charity because she ran last year's school charity fair to raise money for it. So they've asked Ms Winters to work on getting me to *talk* in between helping me with my schoolwork. I wasn't sure before, but I am now. The question about the staples was just too ... focused somehow.

'Amy mentioned earlier that it's the anniversary of your ... of Fiona's death soon,' Ms Winters says then.

I heave a sigh and slump back into the cushions, turning my gaze to the window.

'Would it be so terrible to talk to me a little?' Ms Winters asks gently. 'It would make Amy and Paul feel better if they knew you were talking to someone, even if it's just the odd ten minutes between the two of us.'

I roll my head to look at her and see a little knowing smile on her face ... And I realise that she hasn't been trying to be subtle at all: she knew she wasn't going to fool me, and maybe she didn't want to. I reach up to twist a strand of hair about my finger and then shove it in my mouth to chew on as I consider this. She just sits there, giving me that warm little smile. Not saying anything. Not saying how I can trust her and it'll all be our little secret, or how I 'need to get things out' ... And I find myself taking the hair back out of my mouth and saying, somewhat grudgingly, 'Amy wants me to go to the cemetery.'

'Yes, she told me,' Ms Winters says. 'She said you've decided not to go.'

'I said I'd think about it,' I snap: if she wants to *talk* then she'll just have to deal with it if it makes me angry. 'I never said I wanted to go. I didn't even remember, you know. Amy and Paul are the ones who are worked up about it. When Amy first told me that Fiona had died, she made this whole fuss: you know, getting me to sit down first . . . all that stupid sort of thing.' Ms Winters just waits for me to go on, but I don't want to talk about the way Amy flinched when I said I was glad.

'Do you think you might want to go next year?' Ms Winters suggests.

This time I just shrug: a slow backward roll of my left shoulder. Free of the staples, there is just a dull burn creeping across my side and up under my arm. An ache rather than pain: something to remind me to be careful a while yet. But it's not that feeling of underlying wrongness I lived with for so long: there's no echo of broken bones grating and shifting, rough edges sliding over and under. It's strange to be free of it.

'It might be a good idea. And, you know, you don't have to go on the anniversary if you don't want to. Perhaps it would be better to just see if the mood catches you one day. It's only a few miles, after all.'

I let my gaze drift to the window and hum noncommittally.

'Are you worried about running into your . . . into Fiona's parents?'

'No.'

Ms Winters is back to pulling on that loose thread just under the arm of her chair: tugging at it fitfully, winding it around her finger, smoothing it up against the fabric as if it will melt back into the weave.

'I just don't see why I should. *I* don't owe *her* anything.'

'That's not the only reason to visit a grave, Evie,' Ms Winters says softly. 'None of us are suggesting that you go for her sake. I'm just saying that it might be . . . helpful. For you.' She is about to go on, but then she starts, draws her hand away from the arm of the chair, staring at the broken blue thread. Her fingers part. The thread drifts to the floor.

'How's seeing a bit of rock and some grass going to help?'

'Maybe it won't. It's just worth giving some thought to.'

But I don't want to think about it. I don't want to find out what the stone says. Whether they *dared* to use *those* words – the usual epitaph, the standard inscription. She wasn't beloved. Not beloved at all. For a second, I feel my fingers scrabble in the grooves of the letters, catching in the plinth of the 'M', in the belly-curve of the 'O', in the bar of the 'T'. My nails tear into splinters as I claw at smooth stone.

I snap my eyes closed, toss my head to the side and the image vanishes. But still my thumbs pincer to meet my middle fingers, nail sliding under nail. But there is no dirt, no blood, no fragments of marble dust to dislodge. My fingers are clean and whole. I curl them into my palm and watch my knuckles whiten.

'Amy and I went on a walk the other day, to celebrate the staples coming out,' I say cheerfully.

Ms Winters lets me: allows me to change the subject, change the mood. Even though she knows that I know she's not fooled, she's smart enough not to call me on it.

'We went down the towpath and fed the swans. There's a black one there, you know, with red eyes. And this houseboat came along and the swan swam after it making this noise just like the dinosaurs in *Jurassic Park*. There were two little girls on the boat and they went running up to the front, screaming. When it came over to us, Amy threw all the bread in the water in one go, then we went up to the lock and sat there for a while and looked at the clouds.'

Ms Winters rocks her left foot over on to its side, rubs her toes against the foot of the armchair without seeming to realise she's doing it.

'I used to watch the clouds when I climbed outside to sit on the roof at Fiona's parents' house when . . . And I made up stories about them. But my favourite one was about Roger, and he was a fish who swam in the sky. But he was my friend and he would always stop over the house and talk to me on the way to visit his Auntie Mabel, who was a bird who lived in the water. And he used to tell me all sorts of things, because he was a very nice, polite fish . . .'

'Did he ever ask why you were up on the roof?'

I shake my head – not letting her win that easily – and smile. 'Of course not! I told you: he was a very polite fish. He wouldn't have asked me something like that. And, besides, I was busy listening to his stories about his Auntie Mabel.' My words get faster: too fast for her to interrupt me without being rude. 'One time he invited me to go with him to meet her and have tea at her house in the water...'

And I stop because I didn't mean to tell her that. It's too close to things I'll never tell anyone.

'And did you go?'

'Of course not!' I say, as indignant as I can manage, to cover the sudden flatness in my voice. 'I didn't know how to swim in the sky!' But I thought about it. Wondered whether it would be worth trying, just to see if I could. Because the alternative was to stay on the roof until I couldn't stay any longer and I had to go back inside.

But I did stay. And eventually I did go back inside. And I never quite forgave myself for that.

The scales clothe all four legs now and cover the dragon's back with its ridge of little spikes. I've scraped and scraped the tool across the dragon's tiny feet to make clawed fingers, and scooped around the crest of the skull for the ears: small but long, they lie along the dragon's neck, tapering to a point. The jaw is square, sharp-angled at the corners and back towards its cheeks. The nostrils curve up into little points in the snout, while the muzzle flares back towards the eyes, set down on to the sides of the face like a cat. That is what the shape of the eyes reminds me of: a cat's eyes. Like a teardrop with two points, only one tilts downward towards the nose and the other points up towards the ears. If you crossed a cat with a lizard, this is what you would get: every line a study in power and arrogance, beautiful to the point of cruelty.

The dragon sits on my hand, bluish in the moonlight, while the stereo whirrs softly in the background and the wizard Howl surrenders his heart to a falling star to give it new life as a fire demon. I would give my heart to the dragon to bring it to life. I'd give it gladly to be tied so tight to something so wonderful.

My throat closes with longing and, as I swallow, the scar across my side and the bone-ends beneath ache anew with the sense that something is missing: some part of me is gone there, just a few inches below my heart.

Sometimes in the night I rear up from the bed, curling over that gap, trying to protect the place where I'm most vulnerable: more vulnerable than ever now with that hole in the armour of my ribcage where there isn't even broken bone any more.

I don't remember the nightmare that jerks me so roughly off my pillows: I never do. In the instant when the pain hits and I jolt awake, my attention goes to bracing my ribs, to registering the pain and the need to be still.

Moonlight is falling on the foot of the bed. The coverlet glows and darkens, glows and darkens. Slowly, so slowly, I shift to my knees, edge forwards until I can see out of the window. The clouds are ragged flecks of darkness fleeing across the sky, but as they pass the moon they blush suddenly with colour – dim blues and greens and yellows – until they almost dissolve into the light. Just for an instant.

From my palm, the dragon watches with me, unblinking.

Then there are no more tatters of clouds. Just the moon, heavy in the hollow sky amid the sharp, cruel points of the stars.

The stereo has hissed to a stop and in the silence the echo of a song surprises me: 'When you wish upon a star'. For an instant I remember the blue-white fairy moving brilliant across the screen in front of the dim interior of Geppetto's shop. And Fiona is in the seat on my left and she smiles in the darkness of the cinema as she turns to say something. Her hand is warm and soft around mine. And I know that we went in the middle of the day. Just the two of us. And she laughed and bought me an ice cream and neither of us wanted to go home. The light when we stepped out on to the street was a blow, ripping away the warm safety of the darkness.

I like the idea that it makes no difference who you are when you're wishing on star. It matters in prayers: it matters who you are and what you are and all sorts of things. If God listens, he listens differently to different people and so it matters. But it doesn't matter with wishes.

And even though I'm old enough to understand that neither wishes nor prayers really come true – things just happen or they don't – it's still nice to think that all that matters is me. All that matters is that I wish what I wish.

And so I wish. Even though I know it's stupid and childish and it won't make the slightest bit of difference. I wish until my heart aches with fierceness because it's night-time and it's dark and no one can see me. So I can wish if I want. There's nothing at all to stop me. No reason not to because, even if it is just silliness, I want to.

I wish for the dragon to come to life.

I wish until the clouds return, more and more and darker and darker. Until the moon is gone and so are the stars.

Then I click the stereo back on and put the dragon back in its pot on the table by the bed. As I slip towards sleep, I stumble between low stools and workbenches in Geppetto's shop as things unseen stir the darkness and the dust in the corners.

Then suddenly my body twitches reflexively, starting at a noise by my bed. My eyelids start to lift. My head starts to turn towards the bedside table . . . But the warmth of the quilt drags my eyes closed before they've truly opened and I'm back in the workshop, watching a mouse dart among the discarded tools on the old wooden table. As I turn to look out of the diagonal leadlight window panes at the cobbled street beyond, I know the mouse is watching.

I feel his eyes on me.

Mrs Poole stares down at my work, horror morphing into exasperation into something like sympathy. 'It's a little ambitious again, Evie. A good idea, but perhaps a little ambitious since you do only have a few weeks.'

I stare down at the pencil case too. It's nothing like what I imagined. The things I make for Mrs Poole's textiles projects never are. This is black and plasticky and the little bits of elastic made into loops to hold the pencils and pens in place are all different sizes and heights and most of them are lopsided. I pick up one side and the whole thing flops alarmingly. I can't imagine what it will look like full of pencils. And I forgot to think about ends – something to stop everything tipping out when I roll it up.

'Well, one thing we can do to make life easier is get you a better needle. I've got a nice, thick one that will go through that . . . er . . . fabric much more easily. Just be careful not to hurt yourself with it.'

The needle she hands me is short and squat with a vaguely rounded end: made more for piercing rubber than fabric. Not that the pencil-case material is fabric. I'm not sure what it is. It seemed like a good idea when I was in the shop.

'But can we really make spaghetti over a camp stove? What would we use for a sauce?' Phee is asking Lynne.

Her own pencil case – a nice, plain sort of thing – is all but finished. Glitter and glue are drying on it while she doodles absently on her folder.

'Do you really want to get one of those canned meat meals?' Lynne says, eyes fixed on her sewing as she coaxes gold thread into a chain stitch.

'How about SpaghettiOs? SpaghettiOs are OK.'

Lynne sighs. 'Do you know how many calories . . . ?'

Phee groans. 'So we're going to try to make a gourmet meal over a camp stove? Why don't we just take crisps and you can take some revolting low-fat bit of nastiness?'

'We'll be cold by the time we stop to camp. We'll need something hot,' she says, biting the words off to clamp the tip of her tongue between her teeth as the thread catches in the fabric.

'Are you sure this is a good idea, all this D of E stuff? I don't really like walking. And you're going to hate camping. And we still need two more people since Evie can't come.'

They both look up at me then with apologetic grimaces. They've been trying (and failing) not to talk about starting their Bronze Duke of Edinburgh Award all day. The first meeting did have to be this morning, didn't it? They keep taking out their little record booklets and thumbing through the pages, sighing and rolling their eyes about how they're going to fulfil the different requirements. The expedition bit is only a month away so I can't go. And of course it makes sense that they haven't invited me to their planning meeting: they'd think it was rubbing it in. And of course they need to invite the people they pick to team up with … But then they'll all go off together and when they come back they'll have two new friends to spend their time with, gossiping about their adventures.

Or perhaps they'll both hate it so much that they'll end up coming home early. It's probably mean of me to think that would serve them right, but I can't help it after my less than triumphant return to school this morning.

The bell rings then and, figuring I might as well have something to do while everyone else is running around having fun on the netball court during PE, I stab the needle into the rubber pencil case and put it in my bag. I doubt anyone else in the whole school is stupid enough to be making a rubber pencil case, so Mrs Poole isn't likely to miss it.

Out in the corridor, Sonny Rawlins sees me and whispers something to Fred, though his eyes remain on me all the while, flicking down to my feet before lifting slowly up my body. A sneer twists his lips as his eyes lock with mine. I turn away, pulling my bag across my chest with one hand and tugging at the hem of my skirt with the other. Sonny Rawlins starts to laugh.

Phee rolls her eyes, while Lynne snorts. 'It's such a pity. If he wasn't such a prat, he'd be really cute. What a waste.'

The wind is up tonight. Blowing hard across the fens, wailing through my dreams. I feel the moonlight dim then brighten on my face. And I can feel that someone is watching me.

I freeze, but I can't hear the other person breathing. When I slit my eyes open, there's no sign of light from the hall, so it's not Amy or Paul, peeking in to check on me. And I know the window is shut because the curtains are not snapping in the wind. There's no movement from anywhere in the room, just that feeling that someone is watching me, still and silent.

I look instinctively to the bedside table. And there is the dragon, crouched low over its front feet, like a cat hunkering down in the cold. Its eyes shine like haematite: silver over the darkest blue. It doesn't blink as we stare at each other, but after a moment the tiniest wisp of smoke curls from its nostrils.

I want to ask if it is real or if I'm dreaming. I open my mouth . . . then shut it again.

Very wise, says the Dragon.

Except that it doesn't speak. At least, its mouth doesn't move. But I know that that's what it means to say. And, after all, anything's possible in a dream. The odd thing is that I've always imagined that dragons would like basking in the sun like lizards. And it's one thing not to be able to control every aspect of a dream, but I have a tingly, uncomfortable feeling that I'm dreaming *against* myself somehow. As if I'm not dreaming at all because I'd never, ever imagine a dragon that liked the darkness. I just wouldn't.

I stare at the Dragon and then, without thinking, I blink. But the Dragon is still there: still there, watching me.

Do people blink in dreams? I wonder and am about to squeeze my eyes shut to see if the Dragon is still there when I open them once more only . . . even if it isn't at all what I thought a Dragon-dream would be there *is* still a Dragon. And it has sort of talked to me.

Then I blink again without meaning to. And again the Dragon doesn't disappear, though I sense its impatience growing.

Slowly, slowly, I roll over on to my side so that our eyes are level. And then, finally, I squeeze my eyes closed, until blue and green explode behind my eyelids. When I open them, the Dragon's expression speaks of disdain.

'Are you nocturnal?' I whisper, and my heart clenches with joy when I don't jolt myself awake by speaking.

After a fashion, the Dragon says. *Let us simply say that many things are easier at night.*

Then it slowly pushes up from its crouch, its shoulders rolling languorously backwards as it juts its breast out proudly. When it is sitting bolt upright, tail curled neatly over its feet, it opens its mouth and yawns hugely, just like a cat, showing long, razor-point teeth like stubby needles. Its tongue curls back and then arches out, flicking at the air as if tasting it.

We should go if we are to venture out tonight.

'Go where?'

The Dragon gives a tiny shake, like a shiver, and somehow I understand that this is a dragon's way of shrugging. *You do not have your strength back yet so tonight we will not go far. Other things will have to wait.*

I half expect to wake myself by sitting up, but all that happens is that the Dragon tilts its head back to follow my movements.

'Won't we wake Amy and Paul going downstairs?' I ask as I pull off my pyjamas, exchanging them for jeans, T-shirt and a hoodie.

We shall leave via the window, of course, the Dragon says.

I pause in rummaging at the bottom of my closet for trainers. 'Amy says that the garage roof isn't very strong. She says I should only try to cross it if there's a fire and I need to get out.'

The Dragon's expression grows disdainful. *You are not heavy. It will serve.*

I'm about to object when I realise that, since it's a dream, it doesn't matter anyway. A dream with a Dragon in it can certainly boast a sturdy roof. In fact, I could just dream myself creeping downstairs and not waking Paul and Amy ... only a Dragon-dream has to be more fun than that: if I can't even climb down the garden wall, the rest is bound to be pretty disappointing.

I tug on socks and then my trainers. 'Will you fly?' I ask.

The Dragon yawns again. *For now I shall journey on your shoulder.*

Stepping back towards the bedside table, I extend my hand, palm up, terrified suddenly that the Dragon will vanish: that our touching will be like a bolt of electricity, jolting me awake. But there is a sharp, firm pressure on my fingertip as the Dragon steps on to my hand. It fits neatly on my palm, somewhat bigger than the carving, as if the bare bone has literally fleshed out with skin and muscle. I lift my hand to my shoulder and the Dragon climbs gracefully from my palm to my collarbone, curling against my neck.

Its tail twitches against my shoulder blade as I open the window slowly, slowly, trying not to make a sound because it's more fun to pretend it's all real: that I really am creeping out into the night with a dragon.

There is a flash of irritation that my ribs hurt even in dreams as I inch my hip on to the window ledge, bracing a hand against the pull of the wound so I can swivel, drawing my legs up and over the sill.

But then the night air rushes clean and cold into my mouth and my throat, swelling my chest with pain and delight.

The world is silver and blue, shifting and changing as the moon surfaces from the clouds then dives down into darkness again. The garage roof holds firm as I walk to the edge and then step down on to the garden wall, following it along the edge of the house until, stretching down, I can place my foot safely on the top of the wrought-iron garden table. From there I step down to a chair and then to the ground. I want to race across the grass, run out into the maelstrom of cloud shadows, the rushing patches of dark and light, but I know my ribs will not allow it.

I keep to the garden path as I walk silently to the woods at the bottom of the garden and into the darkness under the trees, emerging on to the unpaved towpath beyond.

I can't help it. Even with my heart full of the joy of the Dragon, I find myself turning to stare down the towpath to my left. Seven miles. Only seven miles to the village where Fiona's parents live. By car, it takes ages – long enough to feel safe – but by river or on a bike, riding along the canal . . .

'To the right?' I ask, despite the fact that I'm leaning, leaning forwards as if drawn, as if the house and the people in it are pulling me. I don't know if the feeling this gives me is want or rage or fear or power that I could go there in the dark, ride up the towpath, and no one would ever know . . . But what sort of a victory would that be? To go and stand outside the house and hate.

I rock back on my heels, as if the thing that was drawing me forwards has suddenly released. I shiver, willing away the sense that my Dragon-dream is about to descend into nightmare.

When you are strong, we can do anything you wish, the

Dragon says softly: an answer to what is in my heart, not my question.

'To the right,' I say, stating it this time: resolving upon it.

The Dragon tightens its grip on my shoulder and I feel the steel-strength of its talons graze my skin.

Brackish water glints in the dyke between the fields as the world opens out around me. The Dragon's breath comes in little drifts of warmth against the side of my neck.

Here, the Dragon commands, and I turn off the path into the low scrub wood edging the fields.

The grass is long, but even the odd snatch and pull of a bramble cannot hold me back. Ahead, I can make out the outline of a wall and the ruin of a little building. Beyond it, catching the light in brief flashes between the clouds, there is a pool, still and dark. A single late-flowering evening primrose stem spears up from the reeds, bell-shaped flowers glowing a ghostly pale green.

I sink on to the moss-covered trunk of a fallen tree and watch the water, my eyes prickling with the threat of tears and that strange feeling that could be absolute happiness … or grief that you can never hold anything perfect still and safe.

The air is heavy with the sweet, viscous scent of fallen leaves mulching down into mud. The sharp smell of burning and the richness of charcoal. The acid tang of rotting reeds. And the thick copper and iron smell of slow water.

Something stirs in the pool. Ripples billow across the surface, fragmenting into waltzing shadows in the water. Above me, the bare tree branches spike upwards like long black thorns and the clouds rip and tear themselves ragged, raw edges weeping away into the light like blood fraying in water as they force themselves on: rank upon rank of tattered monsters, hunting each other across the sky. But as they cross in front of the moon they glow suddenly cream and gold, passing into greens and purples, making rainbows at the edge of darkness.

The Dragon and I don't speak there in the clearing, or on the walk home, or as I climb carefully back up to my window and into my bedroom. I settle the Dragon back on the bedside table, then undress, tucking my damp trainers away in the back of the wardrobe before pulling on my pyjamas and climbing into bed. I curl on to my side despite the pull across my chest.

'What should I call you?' I ask, as I lie watching the intermittent drift of smoke from the Dragon's nostrils.

Do I need a name? the Dragon asks. *Is there another like me?*

I smile, the question echoing after me as I drift into sleep.

When I wake, the Dragon is bare bone once more, solid and lifeless. I can't bear to check whether the trainers in the back of my wardrobe are still damp.

'You look like you slept well!' Amy says when I pad into the kitchen.

'No nightmares,' I say, putting some toast on.

'That's wonderful, darling. Maybe with your ribs getting better you'll start sleeping soundly more often.'

'Maybe.'

Amy doesn't tell me to think positively, but she smiles hopefully. 'Well, I'll keep my fingers crossed,' she says.

I think about night after night of uninterrupted sleep. Of Dragon-dreams, vivid and strange. Of waking and feeling calm and rested rather than as if I have been trapped, struggling desperately in the darkness all night long.

I should be glad that we're studying *Hamlet* for our English GCSE, but I'm not. It's like sand under my skin. Something about it bothers me.

'You look puzzled, Evie,' Ms Winters says.

'Hm?' I say stupidly, then realise I must have been pulling faces as I itch at the prickly feeling the play gives me. 'Oh. No. Just thinking.'

Someone – Sonny Rawlins probably – makes a rude noise at the back of the class.

Ms Winters ignores it. 'Anything good?' she asks. She's not being mean: she thinks it's as weird as I do that I just can't seem to get my head around the play. We've even stopped working on it in our little after-school sessions and swapped to *The Tempest* instead.

We're still doing our 'extra classes' even though I'm back at school and up to date with everything. When Ms Winters suggested we keep going, she phrased it in terms of it not being right for me to be bored in English when I love to read so much. But we both know *that* part of things is just a reward for my putting up with the not-counselling aspect of her visits.

'It's ... I'm just ... I'm really fed up about how much Hamlet whines about everything,' I say, and am both surprised and pleased when a whole bunch of the class laugh. 'I mean, I get that he's ... he's frustrated and angry and that he feels helpless. But why does he have to whinge about it so much? I mean, either he's willing to make sacrifices to get revenge for his father or he isn't, right? Why doesn't he just make a decision instead of mucking around so much?'

Ms Winters smiles. 'What does everyone else think?' she asks.

Everyone else is busy looking elsewhere, thinking nothing at all, at least about Hamlet. I prop my chin on my hand and let my gaze drift towards the windows.

For once, English drags by. When the bell goes, Lynne and Phee are out of their seats before I've even raised my head. I trail after them as they chatter on about some TV series I don't like, lamenting the lack of boys worth snogging in real life apart from sixth-formers, who aren't interested in Year 10s. Lynne laughs as Phee gesticulates energetically, her face alive with intent. They link arms: a careless, automatic gesture.

I slow, watching them laugh and jostle their way down the corridor, ploughing through the ranks.

Phee and Lynne were best friends for over a year before I started here and our form teacher asked them to look after me. Sometimes I wonder if that's all our friendship is: my tagging along after them and them feeling a bit sorry for me. I mean, I know they like me – it's not like I have any weird idea that they hate me and just pretend not to – but sometimes I think they'd be at least as happy without me always turning their pair into a trio. They're not the sort of people who'd tell me to push off and leave them alone just because they felt they could take or leave my company, but who wants to be tolerated, however nicely?

Most of the time, I try not to worry about it too much but recently, with all that's happened, I can't help feeling that gaps are opening up and showing how it was all along: that I'm not really wanted. That I don't really fit. That there's Phee and Lynne, and me somewhere on the outside, following along after them.

They're already queuing outside the science labs when I finally get there. They've got their heads pressed together, making plans for the evening.

'Can I come too?' I ask.

They both blink at me in surprise. I watch their eyes.

'But we're going to do a season one marathon,' Lynne says.

'We didn't think you'd want to,' adds Phee. 'But you're welcome if you fancy it.' She looks to Lynne and I try to translate what passes between them.

Lynne shrugs, then grins. 'So, does this mean you're finally ready to be inducted into the fan club?'

'Are we going to find out you've been sneakily watching by yourself? Will you know all the trivia in the special features?' Phee adds, laughing.

And I know that they're doing their best to make sure I don't think they're trying to exclude me, but perhaps that's just because their parents have told them to be extra nice to me ... But even if it's not, the united front, minds-in-concert thing they're doing is making all the unease that welled up in me during English a thousand times worse. As we're called into class, I trail after them wretchedly, wishing I could just go home and hide under my bed.

Instead, I reach into my bag and take out the pot with the Dragon in it and squeeze and squeeze and squeeze until I'm afraid the plastic will shatter as I will myself to believe that last night's Dragon-dream is just the first of many: that when I 'wake' tonight, the Dragon will be there watching me, waiting to greet me.

'Amy says you're still adamant that you don't want to visit Fiona's grave,' Ms Winters says out of the blue, as we pore over Waterhouse's painting of Miranda and the Tempest.

Pressing down on the book's spine to flatten the pages, I lean closer to the picture, refusing to look up.

Amy thinks that because she needs to visit Adam's gravestone, and Aunt Minnie's and Grandad Peter's and Nanna Florrie's, that it's the same for me and Fiona. But it's not. It's not the same thing at all.

'She's dead,' I say. 'She's buried. There's a grave. End of story.'

'Closure isn't that simple, Evie.'

I think of all sorts of things to say to that but manage to keep my mouth shut.

'Is there anything you *do* want to talk about?' Ms Winters asks when she sees that I'm not prepared to cooperate on the subject of visits to gravestones.

I shrug again. Talking about my frustrations over all the things I've missed at school – all the in-jokes I don't understand, all the memories I can't share – isn't going to make me feel any better about it. Besides, what can Ms Winters say? I'll get better. I'll catch up and there will be newer things that I am part of. It's just a matter of waiting. In the meantime I'm going to watch lots of TV that bores me to tears so that I'm no more out of the loop than I can help.

But before I can direct her attention back to the book, Ms Winters is asking, 'Do you have any good memories of Fiona you could tell me about?'

I hold very still while I think about how to deal with this. Only for a few seconds of course: any longer and I know Ms Winters will never let it drop. Oh, she might for today, but she'll come back to it. She'll keep coming back to it. I fix her with my most unpleasant stare and heave a grumpy, petulant sigh as if the whole thing is just an irritation.

But Ms Winters meets my stare and returns it.

I slump back into the armchair and look away. I want to ask how anyone could possibly think I associate anything good with Fiona ... but there is a picture of our old garden path in my mind, of the crooked concrete slabs leading to the blue back door and the dandelion by the mat.

'My old school had a half day once. I don't remember why,' I find myself saying. 'I thought for a while that no one was home, so I let myself in with the key they probably still keep under the petunia pot by the back door ... And Fiona was standing there in the kitchen, with an apron on, making a cake. *They* were both out. I don't know why. But it was just us, in the kitchen, making cake. We ate the whole thing, sitting at the kitchen table and playing games. It was sunny. I remember the kitchen all lit up with sunlight and Mum's ... Fiona's hair glowing like copper and gold.'

Outside our window, the day is grey and drizzly.

'That was before I knew she was sick. Before ... before,' I say firmly, closing down that avenue of discussion. 'I think we hadn't lived there very long yet,' I offer instead.

'Was it like that with Fiona and your dad, before you went to live with your ... her parents?' Ms Winters prompts, though she has the sense not to look at me as she says it, fixing her eyes on Miranda instead.

I shrug, going for nonchalant. 'I don't remember,' I lie. 'I just remember that I was really happy that day in the kitchen. And I hadn't been. Neither of us had been. That day in the kitchen, when we heard the front door open, Fiona started to cry. Then she started washing up. Things from the draining board. Clean things.'

For a moment, hope rises that I've said enough, but Ms Winters has her next question all lined up: 'Why do you think Fiona took you to live with her parents after your father died?'

I sigh inwardly. I know the only way to escape the topic is to go with it just enough for her to think I'm not afraid to talk about it. 'They probably told her to come home. Without Dad there to stop her, she probably didn't even argue. Just went,' I say shortly, hoping (against hope) that Ms Winters will decide not to push if I merely show annoyance. I turn my attention to a catch in my nail.

'I know you don't like thinking about it, Evie, but it's important that you understand that they probably did the same things to Fiona when she was young.'

Clearly Ms Winters, like Amy and Paul, thinks I'll feel sympathy for Fiona if I believe this. They don't seem to understand that, if it's true, then what Fiona did was even worse: if it's true, then Fiona *knew*. Didn't just close her eyes and ears so she could pretend nothing was happening. She knew. And she still just went into the kitchen, every time, and washed up the clean things from the draining board so she could pretend she wasn't meant to be doing anything else – anything else in the world – but that.

'Maybe Fiona was too frightened of her parents – had been frightened of them for far too long – to be able to stand up to them. I am not trying to excuse what she did,' Ms Winters adds quickly, 'but maybe it'll help to understand it.'

I dig the nail of my index finger into the catch in my left thumb nail. I want to say that I understand everything I care to. Fiona was a coward. She went back and took me with her. Because with me there she was safe.

'Do you think that perhaps Fiona let them persuade her to go back home when she found out about the cancer: when she knew she was going to keep getting sicker?'

The snag in my nail is proving stubborn. I work at it with my teeth to no avail, trying to ignore the fact that Amy has clearly told Ms Winters more about Fiona than I'd realised. Ms Winters just sits there, waiting patiently for me to answer.

'What difference would that have made?' I say eventually.

'Maybe she was hoping...'

'She knew what would happen,' I snap then, before

Ms Winters can continue. 'She didn't go so that there would be someone to look after me.'

'But you do recognise that she was grieving for your father. People do strange things when they're desperate, especially if they're also ill.'

'They told her to go and she went. That was it. She just did what they said. She always just did what they said.' I shove my nail back into my mouth to stop myself saying any more. The rough edge catches on my tongue. I swallow away the ferrous bite of blood.

'But she did marry your father, Evie,' Ms Winters is saying. 'Reading between the lines of what you've told me, that must have been very much against her parents' wishes.'

'It was Dad's idea,' I say as I return to digging my right thumb nail under the catch in the left. 'He joked about it once, though I didn't really understand it. How they ran away to get married, like she was a princess and he was a commoner. How Fiona looked over her shoulder the whole way to the registry office as if they were about to be chased down.'

'Perhaps, by that point, she couldn't believe that she would ever be able to escape her parents.'

'She didn't, did she? *He* rescued her.' The blood on my tongue tastes like acid as I swallow it away, swallow it away.

'Do you think your father knew about Fiona's parents?' Ms Winters asks, and I can tell that she's got her teeth into this: there's no hope now that she'll let go till she's said what she wants to say, asked what she wants to ask. It's just like in class when there's some really interesting thing she wants us to work out for ourselves and she just keeps pushing and dragging at us until we inch our way there.

'I expect he just thought that they were over-protective. A bit controlling. He hated my . . . Fiona's mother.' I feel my lips twist into a smile like a sneer. 'Why wouldn't he? But he just thought she was horrid. Just ordinary horrid.'

I want to ask Ms Winters if she thinks my father knew what would happen to us if anything ever happened to him, but I can't bear to. Even if he didn't know about Fiona's parents, he had to have known how spineless she was. And still he went racing through the fenland lanes on his motorcycle until he killed himself in a drainage ditch.

Fiona hadn't stopped him. Maybe she didn't even try. Sometimes I wonder if she ever asked him not to go, told him not to go so fast. Begged him not to risk leaving us. Even though *she* knew exactly what would happen without him around to make sure she stayed rescued.

Suddenly my right thumb nail slides deep into the catch in the left, opening it up, tearing the nail away down to the quick. I put my thumb in my mouth. Suck away the blood with spit already sweet and thick with it. The taste explodes on my tongue.

When I wake in the darkness to the feeling of being watched, I smile as I roll on to my side.

The Dragon is stretching its wings as if it is stiff after a long day in the pot.

'Should I leave you here, in my room, during the day?' I ask, as I scramble out of bed to put on my clothes, impatient to get out into the night.

The Dragon continues stretching, pushing its chest down and then arching its haunches up, spreading its wings wide and flicking its tail. *As you wish.*

As carved bone, the Dragon is pinkish but, when fleshed out, becomes the blue-white of moonlight.

'Where are we going tonight?' I ask, as I scoop the Dragon on to my shoulder and push open the window. Tonight, I remember to pull it slightly to so that Amy and Paul won't feel a chill in the corridor if they wake in the night. Maybe it's silly but I can't shake the feeling that if they catch me Dragon-dreaming that will be the end of it. And I won't let it be over. Not yet, when we've only just begun. So, even though it's all a dream and even though I know they won't come in to check on me anyway because they know how lightly I sleep, I've made my bed so that it looks like I'm still there.

I manoeuvre down the garden wall then hurry across the grass and through the woods to the river. For a moment I stop, staring up the towpath to the left. Seven miles . . .

We go to the right, the Dragon commands.

By the river's edge the reeds writhe as one creature attacks another with a piping scream. Heavy cloud blocks the moonlight and in the darkness the rising mist isn't white, but grey and green and blue. It is gathering over the fens now, coming at me in drifts, now faster, now slower: rushing at me, diving around me. Chilling my face. Caressing my hair. It pulls away and for a moment the air is clear, then it is thick once more, twisting about me in gossamer strands as if I'm being wrapped in cobwebs.

It seethes about my waist as I wade out into the fields, fixing my eyes on the rising and falling boundary between the blanketing, swirling greyness and the wet, dark night. Anything could lie below the mist and still it teases at all the normal things of a night on the fens, tempting them down into a stranger place, where things aren't quite what they seem: ceaselessly shifting, changing, defying all the rules.

And somehow there is so much to feel and smell and see and hear and taste that I forget to hurt. There's too much here and now for pain. Suddenly I am empty.

And it's like breathing in light.

I am gone from myself.

Unravelling into the mist, I become nothing. And there is respite. Finally, there is respite. As if the world has stopped turning and at last there is a space out of time where it's not pain on pain, hurt on hurt with each breath.

The Dragon is making a soft, breathy noise of

contentment, like purring. We wander on.

By the time we turn back to the canal, the mist is thick and heavy, boiling over from the fields, foaming down to swirl and roil above the dark, slow water. I laugh, raising my arms as I spin round and around until the wind drops and the mist dissolves, the last remnants flowing, snakelike, away to the river. Dizzy and stumbling, I watch as the wind whips up a little spiral of grey-green vapour, like an arm raised briefly in farewell.

In the morning I wake, expecting to be tired. But I feel light, refreshed. This time, though, I can't stop myself from opening the wardrobe to check. My trainers, hidden at the back, are damp and pungent.

'And finally a toast. To my beautiful, brilliant niece. One of a kind. Quite possibly the only girl in the world who, when she becomes a household name and some idiot interviewer complains that bone jewellery is cruelty to animals, can righteously retort, "It's my bone, so I can do what I like with it!"'

'Ben!' Amy complains, her mouth turning down in a disgusted pout.

Paul pats Uncle Ben on the shoulder, laughing. 'Our one of a kind,' he echoes, raising his glass. 'Happy adoption birthday.'

I grin and steal Amy's glass to clink to his. It's not

actually my official adoption birthday, but we decided that the important date wasn't when the paperwork came through: that didn't happen for more than another year 'cos there's so much rubbish that has to be done to make these things legal. The date that matters is when I came to live with Amy and Paul. All of my time with them counts.

'Evie dear,' Amy says awkwardly, 'I don't think you should . . .'

'A few sips won't hurt,' I say. 'Here, I'll toast with water for you.'

She shakes her head, smiling, as I pass her glass back. 'I'm so proud of you, Evie. You've been so brave,' she says, because it's the kind of thing Amy does say semi-regularly, not just once in a lifetime, and without ever blushing. It might just be my favourite thing about her. I can never quite decide between that and the fact that Amy really would do anything for me. I'm sure of it. If a car tried to mow me down, she'd jump in front of it. She and Paul would sell the house and everything they own if I were sick and the money could make me well.

When I first came to live with them, while the adoption was still in its probationary period, I thought I knew what the deal was: I'd live with them, become theirs after a fashion, but it wouldn't be like they were really my parents. I knew it just didn't work like that.

Only it did. With Amy and Paul, it really did. It didn't even take a full year for me to realise that when I made them angry, they didn't even think about the fact that they didn't have to put up with it: that they could take me back and be rid of me. They just didn't think it. I could tell. And that's when I realised I could tell them about all the things that hadn't mended right in my ribs: about the way they moved funny, and about the pain.

Of course I didn't tell them then: it took me months and months – so many months they became years – to work out *how* to tell them. I knew that the first time I mentioned having an ache in my ribs Amy wouldn't think anything of it. The plan was to mention it again about a week later and then perhaps a few days after that. I'd let myself brace my hand across my ribs occasionally, then more regularly. Eventually, I'd say something more about it *really* hurting and then . . .

But the very first time I mentioned the pain – just a passing comment about an ache – Amy whipped around from making dinner, wiping her hands down her clothes, and hurried over to me.

For a minute, I'd been sure she would just lift my shirt and, though I knew Amy wouldn't do anything more, it went all cold. But even though I hadn't told her anything then – anything at all – she knew better than that. She just always knew what not to do, right from the very start when we'd met by chance at the local Social Services office. Sometimes I wonder if she sort of knew everything I eventually told her all along. I think she might have. Not what happened exactly, of course. But somehow she knew *enough*, right from the first day I came home with them.

So she didn't touch me, just crouched down by my chair. 'Can you show me, Evie darling? Do you mind?' she asked.

And so I was the one who lifted my shirt and showed her. 'Here. It moves here,' I said. 'Feel,' I said, making the invitation to touch.

Five minutes later, the GP was on his way out for a home visit. Just like that. And then I knew that I could tell Amy things, little things, and she would understand: she would know all the things I couldn't say.

And she did.

And, really, that's my favourite thing about Amy: she understands without my having to say any of those things that can't be said without pain welling up as dull and dirty and deep as a freshly re-broken bone.

Some things should never be said. Not out loud in clear, simple words. You talk around them. You leave gaps and blanks. You use other words and talk in curves and arcs for the worst things because you need to keep them like mist. Words are dangerous. Like a spell, if you name the mist, call out all of the words that describe it sharp and clear, you turn it solid, into something that no one should ever hold in their hands. Better that it stays like water, slipping between your fingers.

'Ben, do you *really* have to persist with this horrible idea of making the dragon into a necklace?' Amy is saying. 'I know you and Evie think it'll be rather a good joke, but other people might think it's morbid.'

'Ninnies like you might think it's morbid,' Uncle Ben retorts. 'Other people, even if they don't get the joke, will just look at the beautiful carving your talented daughter has accomplished – with the help of yours truly, of course – and think it's a work of art.'

'A rather unusual work of art,' Paul concedes, as Amy looks beseechingly at him.

A waiter comes up then, so of course Amy, Paul and Uncle Ben launch into an argument about who will be paying . . . until it turns out that Uncle Ben left his credit card at the front desk when we came in. I'm busy weighing the fortune cookies that came on the little tray with the bill, trying to sense which one feels luckiest.

'Got a good feeling, that one?' Paul asks, turning away from the waiter and leaving Amy to carry on the argument with Uncle Ben. They'll probably be at it all the way out to the car.

I grin and shove the rest of the little foil-wrapped parcels in his direction, ripping into mine and crunching the cookie open.

'O, Highest Oracle! Great Oracle! Tell us, O Mightiest of Mighty Oracles, what hath the future in store!' Uncle Ben cries.

'"Dreams are the fire that warms the soul. Let them guide you,"' I read.

Uncle Ben nods sagely. 'Works for me. Here, Great Oracle! Reveal to me my fortune.'

I grin and tear open his cookie. '"When opportunity presents, seize it."'

Amy groans. 'As if my brother needed any encouragement.' But she smiles as she passes her cookie to me.

'"A friend is a present you give yourself,"' I read.

'Oh, I like that,' Amy says, looking relieved. But then Amy is always doing things like not walking under ladders and, whenever we see a single magpie, it's always 'Hello, sir, and how is your lady?' It always makes me laugh: sometimes I wonder if that's the real reason she says it.

Paul puts his arm over my shoulders, bending his head close to mine as we contemplate his fortune. '"You are almost there,"' I read.

'Oh, good,' Paul says. 'Saves me the humiliation of having to ask directions.'

'Hey ho, we've got a spare. Think that has to go as payment to the oracle,' Uncle Ben says, tossing the last cookie across the table to me.

'Well, that's one way to save her the effort of breaking it open,' Paul says as I tear into the foil package and the cookie crumbles out in pieces. 'What's the final word?'

'"Determination is all you need now."'

Paul stiffens beside me, but it is Uncle Ben who gives a heavy sigh and says, 'Well, in that case, you're set for life, Evie.' But instead of grinning and quirking an eyebrow as he says it, he sounds tired. Weary. As if having determination is a heavy sentence and not a compliment.

As if there's something sad about it and he wishes something different for me.

I frown, turning to look up at Paul. He pulls me closer and presses a kiss to my forehead. 'You could teach the world about determination, Evie,' he says. 'Amazing girl.'

It makes my throat hurt, so I look down again at the fortune and close my hand about the Dragon. The bone warms in my palm.

'Well, that was a lovely, lovely meal, Ben. Even though you really must stop being so impossible about paying,' Amy says brightly. 'But I, for one, need to take my bursting tummy off home to bed.'

'Can't argue with that,' Paul agrees, rubbing his belly as he pushes back from the table.

As Amy and Paul collect our coats from the waiter, I lean against Uncle Ben, yawning. He ruffles my hair, reaching over me to take a mint from what looks like a goldfish bowl on the counter.

'Want one?' he offers.

I shake my head, watching as he takes a second, tosses it into the air and catches it in his mouth.

'Ben!' scolds Amy, rolling her eyes. 'Could you stop teaching Evie bad habits for just a couple of minutes?'

Uncle Ben pulls a face. 'I suppose. Maybe. Actually, I'm not sure. It might be too painful. Perhaps even dangerous . . .'

Amy throws his coat at him.

'Or I could just get you teaching Evie even worse

habits,' he says cheerfully. 'Clearly I can do that.'

'Yes, clearly,' Amy says, but she is smiling, flushed from the wine they had with the meal.

I yawn again, slumping against the counter. There's a little tray next to the goldfish bowl filled with business cards and matchbooks. I pick one of the little booklets out, opening the flap and running my finger across the red-tipped matches.

'Evie, darling, do you really want matches?' Amy asks anxiously.

'Just as a memento,' I say, closing the little booklet and slipping it into my pocket.

'I don't think that's necessarily the best keepsake, darling. And you've got your fortune-cookie messages . . .'

Uncle Ben rolls his eyes at me and moves to put his arm about Amy's shoulders. 'Sister dearest, please stop pestering my niece. Those sorts of matches are always useless. They won't do her any harm.'

'But what if . . .'

'Matches, especially rubbish ones like those, don't light themselves, Amy.'

Amy looks to Paul, who grins. 'Worrywart,' he says and Amy relaxes, taking my coat from him and helping me into it.

'Don't worry,' I say. 'I promise not to burn our house down.'

Uncle Ben's mobile goes as I turn to follow Amy upstairs. I hear him say, 'Speaking,' though I also hear the unspoken 'Who is this? What's going on?' But it's the 'What do you mean, "damage"?' that stops Amy too.

'Is everything OK, Ben?' she calls, starting back down the stairs.

He turns at her voice, but I can see the response is automatic: his eyes look past us both and there is a dark scowl on his face. Then he blinks and focuses. 'Oh,' he says and blinks some more. 'Yes. Yes, everything's fine,' he tells us. 'Hang on one moment,' he says into the phone, then presses it against his chest. 'No worries,' he tells Amy, smiling. 'Off you go to bed.'

But then he turns away again – 'Sorry, didn't catch that. Just talking to my sister' – and there's an odd tone in his voice, something wrong about the way he's standing: big and angry. Looming somehow. Almost intimidating. I shiver and hurry up the rest of the stairs ahead of Amy – 'Evie, don't trip, darling. Please go slowly.' By the time Amy is putting my drink on the bedside table, it's clear she's forgotten all about the strange phone call and Uncle Ben's even stranger reaction as she cautions me about accidents and trying to run about too soon after the operation.

I take my time in the bathroom, washing my face, doing my teeth. Listening out. A few minutes later, someone comes running upstairs, two at a time by the sound of it, and I quickly shut off the water.

'Amy darling, I'm just popping out with Ben for a bit,' I hear Paul say. 'Won't be long.'

'What . . . ?'

'Nothing to worry about. Just some kids having one of those parties advertised on the internet and causing a bit of bother. The police want . . .' He stumbles over the next word, mumbling so badly I don't have a clue what he intended to say.

'Or maybe it was the Neighbourhood Watch?' he offers and I can practically hear his mind whirring. 'Anyway, I'm not sure who exactly it was that Ben spoke to, but they want everyone to come and check that there's no damage or anything.'

'But surely it can wait until the morning. I don't like the idea of the two of you running into . . .'

'Amy sweetheart,' Paul says firmly, in his most soothing voice, 'there will be a whole group of people and I'm sure the police must be in there too somewhere, even if they weren't the ones who called. In any case, all those horrible kids will have trogged off to cause mayhem elsewhere by now. We're just going to check that there aren't any broken windows that need to be boarded up.'

'No. No, of course. How awful if they came back later to rob people . . .'

'Well, we'll make sure that doesn't happen. And I promise we'll stick with a nice big gang of other blokes and we'll fetch the police sharpish if we think there're any troublemakers still loitering. Now, don't get your knickers in a twist over nothing. I probably won't be more than an hour, but try not to stay up, love.'

When Amy comes to tuck me in, I can tell she is distracted. After she's kissed me goodnight and closed the door behind her, I stare up at the ceiling, wondering if we're both lying awake in the dark. If so, Amy will be thinking up terrible worst-case scenarios whereas I'm curious: curious and maybe even a little excited. Paul didn't tell the truth about why they were going out. Amy was too busy being worried to realise, but I know that there is something more to all of this.

I roll over to face the Dragon and find that I am being watched.

We wait, says the Dragon before I have time to ask if we're still going out.

'You mean in case Paul and Uncle Ben come back? The driveway's the other side of the house. They'd never see. Though I suppose if they got back and went into the kitchen for a drink just when we were going down the garden it's possible . . . You don't think they might want to come and get me up?' I ask, suddenly worried.

The Dragon's mercury-dark eyes aren't catching the light, but I sense intensity in its gaze. *There are things we may learn tonight. We may need to alter our plans.*

'You mean alter *your* plans,' I scoff. 'You never tell me *what* you're planning for us.'

That is not part of our contract.

'What contract?' I protest. 'I didn't agree to any contract.'

The Dragon looks at me disdainfully, then turns its back, hunkering down into a crouch. I close my mouth on further denials.

It is safer to wait. Rest, says the Dragon. *Rest now, while you can.*

I come awake suddenly, without any sense of what has jolted me out of sleep. Sitting up, I see the Dragon watching me from the bedside table, but I know I didn't hear my name called. As I slide slowly, quietly out of bed, gathering the Dragon up in my palm, I realise I am not the least bit groggy, as if I haven't been asleep at all, just hovering below wakefulness, waiting.

I press myself against the window frame, turning back just the very corner of the curtain.

'Why are we out here in the garden?' I hear someone whisper so loudly I can't think why they've bothered. 'Can't we go in the kitchen where it's warm?'

'Don't want to wake Amy,' someone else whispers back just as loudly.

'You honestly think my sister's asleep?' Uncle Ben. Uncle Ben and Paul.

'Well, I don't want her overhearing,' Paul admits.

I can imagine Uncle Ben is sighing, but this I can't hear through the window I don't dare open. 'How about Evie?'

I press myself flat to the wall beside the window, though there's no way they can possibly see me from where I know they're standing.

'Thankfully Evie's not taking after Amy as the most accomplished worrier of the century,' Paul says. 'Besides, her window's closed: we won't wake her talking out here.'

'I'm just amazed Amy hasn't come creeping down to find out whether we've returned mortally wounded . . .'

'Which is precisely why we parked two houses over and came round the back instead of going in through the front door,' Paul interrupts, abandoning the whisper. 'Besides, maybe she really did fret herself to sleep. There's always hope I'll avoid the third degree until morning.'

'What will you tell her, though?'

'Just what I told her earlier. Plus that you're joining the Neighbourhood Watch and I'll be going with you on your rounds for safety in numbers. She'll be too happy about that to think anything of the rest.'

'I still think you should talk to Evie.'

There is a pause.

'She'd understand, Paul. She's old enough now. And it might help her, you know, in a funny, roundabout sort of way. It would certainly help you.'

'Are you honestly suggesting that there is the slightest good to be had from dragging her into all this with us?'

The snort is audible even through the window. 'As if Amy would ever agree to that in a million, trillion years.' Another pause. 'You know I'm not talking about bringing Evie with us. And I agree we can't tell Amy. I just think Evie's another matter.'

'Evie does not need to hear about my troubles. She's got enough – far more than enough – of her own.'

They don't speak again for a while after that. Finally, Uncle Ben says he'd better be going and I hear him turn down the side of the house while Paul works the lock on the back door.

I let the corner of the curtain fall closed and creep back to bed, settling against the headboard and placing the Dragon on my knee.

'Do you think Paul will listen to Uncle Ben and tell me what's going on if I ask? Or maybe not ask-ask: not outright. But maybe if I just give him plenty of opportunities without Amy there . . .'

We must be very careful, the Dragon says.

I wait, but the Dragon doesn't speak again.

I fall asleep watching its tail twitching back and forth, forking at the air, while I wonder if this is a sign of worry or frustration, excitement or concentration.

The Dragon is purring against my neck as I cycle slowly along the towpath.

I wish I knew how to describe the smell of the fens. Think of dark, slow waters lying heavy between rushes and grasses: see them in your mind's eye. Now try to imagine that image is a smell. Earth and water and decay and growing things, all combined with something secret: something you just can't put your finger on, can't pin down. Not a thing you see or smell or touch exactly. If you swapped all your senses around and tasted what you heard, smelt what you saw . . . then you might finally grasp the scent of that secret thing.

I don't say any of this to the Dragon, but feel its amusement anyway.

We turn off the towpath and bump along a farm track. To one side, a shallow wash of icy water glints across a flooded field. On the other, summer-golden grasses are crumpled, browning. I let the bike stutter to a stop. Leaning it against a fence post, I climb on to the top rail. In the bracken, dew has traced the lines of a pair of cobwebs.

'Do you think they share?' I ask the Dragon. 'The kills, I mean. Do you think one of them gives the other food if his web is unlucky?'

The Dragon communicates the fact that spiders do not hunt together and so they do not share: at least not willingly.

'Do dragons?' I ask.

Dragons are protectors, I am told, as if I should have known this without asking.

I watch a bead of dew run down a length of cobweb and drip on to a soggy, hunched frond of bracken. 'Are we going to go out every night now?'

When it does not rain, the Dragon says, as if such things matter even in dreams.

'So what are we going to do every night?' I press.

Tomorrow we will go to the mere and look at the birch trees in the moonlight. The stars will be very bright. And the night after.

'Ten days till the new moon.'

The next dark moon, the Dragon corrects me.

'The dark moon,' I say, testing out the words, feeling the weight of the power and portent in them.

The dark moon is a time of waking visions, the Dragon tells me. *Visions that show our deepest longings come to life. It is also a time for change: for beginnings. The dark moon marks the birth of the new moon, like a phoenix rising from the ashes.*

'Is there really such a thing as a phoenix?'

You may answer that for yourself, the Dragon says shortly. *Do not ask me about unicorns.*

'I don't want to,' I say. 'They only go to the pure. Those who are chaste.'

You have no need of a unicorn, the Dragon tells me firmly. *It would be of no use to you. It is well that you wished for a dragon. You have need of* me.

And with that the Dragon rises, moving with sinuous grace, winding down my arm and settling on the back of my hand, tail curled around my little finger, possessive and warm.

'I'm freezing. If you're so much more useful than a unicorn, you could help me build a fire.'

I will help, the Dragon says, *when my help is needed.*

'But what's the point of all this roaming about on the fens at night?' I burst out, despite myself. 'Am I meant to learn something? In books, when people have adventures with mystical creatures they have to learn something.'

And then the adventure is over, the Dragon says. *So although you are afraid to fail, you are also afraid to succeed. But you may learn what you will: that is your own affair. It is not my purpose, nor a part of our contract. I will only leave you if you wish me to.*

'Then what am I meant to do?' I plead.

The Dragon regards me steadily. *You are meant to heal. There is beauty and wild magic in the night. Enough to make you ache with joy and grow strong. There is no lesson in that. There is just reward, waiting for you, that asks nothing and demands no payment. Look!* the Dragon orders. *Look and tell me what more is needed.*

So I look out at the night-time fields and the yellow glow of storm clouds to the east.

Taste the stars and listen to the darkness, the Dragon commands and then we are silent.

Is this not enough? asks the Dragon.

'"To be or not to be: that is the question". Possibly the most famous line from any play in the English language,' Ms Winters is saying. 'Comic book *away*, Fred. Evie, could you read the next few lines for us?' she asks, smiling at me as if we're conspirators.

In a way we are: I know now that it's not just that Ms Winters is my favourite teacher, but I'm her favourite pupil too. Even now that she knows about Fiona and her parents.

Somehow I can't help thinking that maybe, after our sessions together, she even likes me a bit more than she did before and that makes me feel . . . warm. And strange. Because I'd never imagined anyone could possibly like me *more* for knowing. I always thought it would be 'in spite of'. But not with Ms Winters. It's not like that at all.

'Whether 'tis nobler in the mind to suffer
The slings and arrows of outrageous fortune,'

I recite.

'Or to take arms against a sea of troubles,
And by opposing end them . . .'

'Let's stop there for a moment,' Ms Winters interrupts.

'Who can tell me what this is all about? What is Hamlet asking when he delivers that famous question?'

No one puts up their hand. I sigh but I don't want to raise mine. Not after just reading aloud.

Some of the class are funny about me liking English so much. Not just Fred and Sonny Rawlins: I wouldn't really care if it was just them. But the last thing I want right now is to stick out even more than I do anyway after the operation, even if it *is* in a good way, like being clever enough to know what Shakespeare means.

'Jenny, what do you think?'

Jenny stares wall-eyed at Ms Winters. 'He's not sure that war is a good thing?'

Ms Winters smiles. 'Actually, that's not such a bad way to put it. But it's a little bit metaphorical . . . What sort of war is he talking about? Lynne, what do you think?'

Lynne elbows me as if I can somehow whisper the answer without Ms Winters hearing. 'Um . . .' she dithers. 'Well, I guess . . .' She nudges her notebook in my direction.

Revenge 4 dad, I scribble, pretending to stretch my other arm to hide the movements of my pen.

'He's . . .' Lynne's eyes flick down to the page. 'It's about getting revenge for his father. Because his uncle killed his father and that's who the ghost is, right?'

'Partly,' says Ms Winters, shooting me a look that plainly says 'Very subtle, Evie' before she turns to the blackboard. 'That *is* part of it . . . But what's the point of this particular section? Anyone?'

I raise my hand in the silence, speaking before Ms Winters has even given me the nod. 'But *isn't* it about revenge?' I insist, both confused and upset to have given Lynne the wrong answer. 'Only he's torn between what it'll cost him: he's afraid of losing even more than he already has. Isn't that what it's about? Whether he should hold on to what he's got – Ophelia and his friends and his place in the kingdom – or go after what the ghost is demanding? Isn't the problem that he doesn't know whether justice is worth all that?'

Ms Winters smiles. 'Well, you're not wrong about that being one of the questions that torments Hamlet throughout the play, as he struggles to decide what to do ... But I don't think that's what this bit is really about. Have another look.'

I slump back in my chair with a frustrated sigh. Lynne nudges my foot with hers.

'Sorry,' I whisper.

She shrugs, grinning to show there are no hard feelings.

'Why "To be or not to be"?' Ms Winters is asking. 'Why not "To do or not to do" if it's revenge he's talking about?'

''Cos it sounds better?' Jenny suggests. Tucking her chin in towards her chest, she pulls a suspicious face at her book as if it requires careful watching.

Several people, Ms Winters included, laugh. 'That may have played a role ... But the way this soliloquy is generally understood is that Hamlet is talking about suicide.'

I lose what she says next as I frown down at my book. I still don't get why my idea wasn't just as valid.

'Now who can give me another line from this soliloquy – remember that word from last week? – that's part of the same theme about escaping from troubles through death?'

'"The oppressor's wrong"?' Phee whispers to me. I nod quickly, but before Phee has even put up her hand, Sonny Rawlins is calling the words out.

All three of us turn to glare at him. He grins back and gives us the finger under the cover of his desk.

'Yes,' says Ms Winters, though her voice isn't as encouraging as normal: as I know all too well, Ms Winters doesn't miss much. 'Can you extend that phrase and give me the whole of the bit that you think is important?'

Sonny Rawlins shoots a glare at me as if this is my fault. '"The . . . the proud man's . . . con . . . contumely?"'

He pronounces it wrong and I grin.

'Contumely,' Ms Winters corrects. 'Well, that's part of the picture, but I was thinking more about the lead into the line you gave me, rather than the bit that follows on. "For who would bear the whips and scorns of time," then, on the next line, "The oppressor's wrong". And by this he means "*or* the oppressor's wrong" because he's listing these with a whole raft of other things – including that bit about "the proud man's contumely",' she adds, nodding in Sonny Rawlins's direction. He glowers and slouches

77

lower in his seat, turning his gaze to the window. 'In other words, who would just sit there if someone's doing you wrong: being mean to you? And how about the end of the next line: "the law's delay"? What is Hamlet referring to here?'

Something wet splats across my cheek, and I miss what Ms Winters says next as I turn to glare at Sonny Rawlins and Fred just in time to see Fred launch the spit-ball that hits Lynne. She shrieks.

'Are you all right, Lynne?' Ms Winters asks. I see her eyes flick in Sonny Rawlins's direction. They've tucked their 'weapons' away for now and are trying to smile innocently, pretending that they're both enthralled by the lesson. Ms Winters gives them an arch look. 'Perhaps it's the draught. Sonny, why don't you go and sit in that empty desk by the window. You're a big, tough lad: I expect you won't mind blocking some of that nasty breeze for the girls.'

Sonny kicks Phee's chair as he passes.

'Watch your feet with all those bags around,' Ms Winters orders. 'We don't want you falling on anyone, do we? Now, as we were saying, the answer is in the last bit of that speech. Phee, why don't you read that for us? From "And thus the native hue . . ."'

'"Of resolution is . . . is sickled"?' she hazards, turning it into a question and glancing over at me.

'Sicklied,' I whisper.

'". . . Sicklied o'er with the pale cast of thought". What

does sicklied mean?' she asks Ms Winters.

Something about the line nags me. I read it over, then over again, not even hearing Phee stumble through the rest of the speech until her voice goes up on, "'. . . turn awry".'

"'And lose the name of action,'" she finishes triumphantly.

Something about the words has them echoing in my head, tugging my thoughts and attention away from the lesson. I read on, hoping to recognise what it is that is making these words feel so familiar. I'm pretty sure I haven't read this scene yet, but I did flick through the play at one point, reading odd little bits.

I'd been whining about how much I hated *Hamlet* and how I couldn't bear to do the essay Ms Winters had set on it, GCSE or no GCSE, so Amy showed me a painting to try to get me interested: it was of Ophelia in an ornate silver gown, hands just lifting up out of the water of a narrow, weed-choked stream. The idea worked to the extent that I was curious enough to trawl through the rest of the play trying to figure out how she had ended up in the river. But Amy and I still had a huge argument over the essay.

I decided that, instead of writing about *Hamlet*, I'd just come up with my own essay question about *The Tempest*, then Amy could write me a note explaining. Only Amy refused to write the note or, indeed, to condone the alternative essay at all. First we argued about the fact that

Amy was sure I couldn't *really* be upset over an essay so there must be something else bothering me that we needed to talk about. By the time I convinced her that *Hamlet* really was the problem, we were both so fed up that we had one of our rare almost-shouting matches. Amy even threatened to withhold my allowance. And then Paul had to come weighing in, backing her up . . .

I did the essay: got it over with in one go between glaring at the book, at the table, at Paul when he interrupted to bring me a drink, which I would have fetched for myself if I'd wanted one since I was in the kitchen . . .

Amy insisted on checking the essay when I finished, though she *never* does that unless I ask her to: the fact that I wasn't talking to her by then meant we avoided another row over it, and somehow it had all blown over by bedtime. I mean, I understand that 'GCSEs aren't something to muck about with' (as Paul put it), but I really hate *Hamlet* – even more so after the argument. And now I've got this nasty déjà-vu feeling about it too, though I just can't quite put my finger on what it is exactly that seems so familiar.

But then I find the answer. It's on the next page, in a conversation between Hamlet and Ophelia. I remember reading this passage and having to ask Amy why Hamlet wanted Ophelia to go to a nunnery. But it's not the nunnery bit that's the problem. In any case, I think I read the line wrong the first time. It doesn't sound right when

I mouth the words 'more offences at my beck than I have thoughts to put them, imagination to give them shape or time to act them in' to myself. But I know that's the line, even though the 'or time' bit just doesn't sound right.

I flick back to the page the rest of the class is working on, but I can't concentrate.

Ms Winters comes over while I'm packing away my books at the end of the lesson. 'Are you feeling all right, Evie?' she asks. 'Are you in pain?'

I blink at her. 'I don't think so . . .' I consider it for a moment. There's a dull ache in my side, but nothing worse than usual. 'It's fine.'

'You just seem a little distracted.' She says it with a smile so I know she's not trying to tell me off.

'I was just thinking about the play,' I say.

Ms Winters's smile deepens and I can tell she's both relieved and pleased. 'In that case, I'll let you get on to your next class. But do remember to tell your teachers if you're not feeling well, Evie. It's quite all right to go to the nurse's office and lie down for a bit if you need to rest.'

'OK,' I say, though I don't have any intention of taking her up on her offer.

I spend the rest of the day distracted and irritable. Something about the lesson keeps nagging at me: some prickly feeling that's half frustration and half melancholy, blossoming suddenly into little stutters of rage.

I don't know why but something about the play makes me feel wrong inside. Like I've made some terrible mistake, or I've done something dreadful, or failed to do something, or . . . Sometimes it seems like misery, but then I think it must be guilt or even fear. I can't pin it down and so the feeling that something's wrong just keeps prickling and itching away along the inside of my skin.

It all centres on Hamlet. Every time I read his name, hear the sound of it in my mind, my teeth flood bitter with hatred. Why can't he make a decision and just stick to it? And why, if he is going to try to be cunning with that stupid little play within the play, can't he figure out a way to keep Ophelia and his friends safe? Why does he have to mess about until it all ends in disaster for everyone? What is the point in any of it if no one wins?

If I were Ophelia, I'd strip his skin off for such cowardice.

I think up alternative endings, torturous fates for Hamlet, all through lunch, ignoring Lynne and snapping at Phee when she demands my attention. None of it helps.

The wrongness prickles away along the inside of my skin until I'm so tired that my head hollows out and every thought sends such a cacophony of echoes through my brain that I let it go empty with the ringing silence of exhaustion.

Finally, finally, it's the end of the day and Phee and Lynne are kicking their way through the gravel to the back gate while I go trailing after them.

'Come on, Evie,' Phee says.

I look up to see that she and Lynne have linked arms.

Phee is pointing her elbow in my direction, inviting me to join them. I start forward with a weary smile, then stop with a sigh. 'Can't,' I say.

They pull to a halt, making the people streaming out behind them curse.

I shift the shoulder strap of my bag higher. 'Can't with my left arm.'

'Well come on my side then,' says Lynne, rolling her eyes.

'Can't carry my bag on my left.'

Lynne's mouth turns down and all the animation goes out of her face. She always gets upset when she feels that she's being insensitive about my ribs.

Phee just sighs. 'Here. Gimme,' she says, pulling my bag off my right shoulder and putting it on her own.

Lynne is smiling again as she darts forward, dragging Phee off balance. She swoops in and links her arm through mine. 'There!' she crows.

I laugh, but it turns into a gasp. We all stumble sideways as I lurch into Lynne, who falls into Phee. I tumble to my knees, my arm wrenching out of Lynne's as she thumps down heavily against my side.

'Evie! Are you OK?' Phee says, crawling over Lynne to check. 'Are you all right?'

'Fine,' I gasp, though I'm splinting my ribs with my left hand. Pressing against the tug of the still-healing skin. 'Are *you* all right?'

'What happened?' Lynne asks as they both look me up

and down. 'You jumped like you'd been electrocuted.'

'I . . .' I start and then feel myself flush as I realise what happened. 'Someone pinched me,' I whisper, and I can tell from their faces that they realise exactly *where* I got pinched.

Phee's round face is dark with anger as she pushes herself to her feet, dusting her knees off. She offers me her hand. 'Sonny stinking Rawlins,' she says, pulling me up and then doing the same for Lynne. 'You sure you're OK?'

I nod, glad not to have to meet her eyes as I turn to follow Phee's glare. And there he is, straddling a fancy mountain bike, clearly brand new, that must have cost his dad a small fortune. It's completely the wrong thing for tricks – even I know that – but he's trying to do them anyway. And sort of succeeding. Fred looks on appreciatively from his scratched old bike, begging for a turn.

Sonny Rawlins throws out a leg, spinning the bike to a sudden stop that hurls gravel in a thigh-high wave over a group of Year 7s. They squeal, huddling together, then streak off towards the gate. Sonny Rawlins stops to watch them run. A curl of disgust distorts his upper lip, but his eyes are avid. He seems to sense my gaze and glances over at us. Something else enters his expression: some emotion or thought I can't begin to decipher. An uneasy fit with whatever he was feeling before. His tongue darts out, sweeping over his bottom lip. Then he turns away and cycles on, throwing out a hand to shove a girl out of his way.

Sometimes I wonder what Ms Winters's story is: whether she understands because she's helped a dozen people like me at her victim support charity, or whether she understands because she *is* like me. Or maybe it's both. She's never tried to get us involved in any disaster relief efforts like the other teachers – which is fair enough – but it proves she only feels fiercely about one particular charity, not charity stuff in general. So there must be a reason behind her picking that specific cause.

She's sad sometimes, but that's about all I know for sure: that she understands deep, dull, constant pain. Sometimes there's that weariness in her: the knowledge that misery can just go on and on and on, getting worse and worse, and somehow you keep bending under it until you're all bowed over but you never splinter and break quite enough to escape the weight.

'Sometimes I wonder if I made it all up,' I find myself saying to the ugly rug in the middle of the floor. 'Sometimes I wonder if any of it really happened at all.' Sometimes I feel quite sick with guilt and horror that, really, it's all just lies. Even though I know it's not. Sometimes I have to remind myself of my ribs and the other scars before I end up dashing downstairs and crying to Amy that I'm just a liar.

When I look up, Ms Winters is smiling at me. It's a soft,

gentle smile. 'Everyone in your shoes wonders that, Evie. It's one of the reasons I know you're not making it up. Only the liars never wonder.'

My smile wavers on my lips. 'But why do I think like that?'

Ms Winters's smile gets even softer. 'Because some things are so awful they really are unbelievable. Sometimes, when life is better and things are OK, it seems impossible that any happiness is possible after that type of misery.'

This is why I talk to Ms Winters. She's not like the stupid counsellors. She knows. She really knows about people like me. And when I reach up to push away the not-there, not-now things, she just catches my hand, still smiling, and I can see in her eyes that she doesn't think I'm going mad. She knows, without my having to explain, that even though I'm starting to see things that aren't really there, I know they're not real. They're just echoes of things that were real once. But sometimes I can still see them, all out-of-time.

It starts like cobwebs at the edges of my vision: like the shadow of a fleck of dust floating across my eye. But one that can't be wiped away, though I always try. Just as, when that fails, I can't stop myself from trying to push the shadows back. First, I brush at my hair. *It must be that. It must just be my hair, billowing in some unseen, unfelt breeze . . .*

Only it never is and then I am reaching frantically into the air. *There must be a cobweb. There must be.*

But of course there isn't.

And the things in the corners of my vision are creeping forwards. They're no longer greyish and uncertain, but beginning to flush with colour, growing solid, taking shape.

And I know they're not really there because I can still see whatever place I'm in ... But I see those other things too – I *feel* them.

And it's no use telling myself that none of it is real, because that's not true: the past was once as real as now is. It's time that's the trouble and that's so much harder to pin down: how *do* you tell the difference between *then* and *now* when feelings and smells and sounds are creeping in too? When *then* is suddenly flaring into your senses again, no longer dim and distant but clear and sharp and *present*.

It's why I *hate* the story of Alice in Wonderland. Amy tried to read it to me once but I had to make her stop because it made me think about falling down into all the not-now, not-real things. In the book, all the characters are mad but funny: they all seem happy enough. But if I ever fell into my rabbit hole, it would swallow me down, down, down until I didn't know what to believe any more. Then it would all become real again. All those grey, wispy visions of the rooms of Fiona's parents' house ... the shiver of the floor against my bare skin. The way my bed was so old, with so much give, I could never get any leverage to push against to get away.

'Evie,' Ms Winters says, her voice commanding. 'Evie, take a deep breath.'

I'm panting, I realise. I gulp in a breath that makes me cough.

'OK,' Ms Winters says, leaning forwards to rub my back as I double over my knees and cough and whoop and cough and whoop. 'Slow, deep breaths.'

When I'm just hissing breath slowly through my teeth, pressing my burning forehead against my knees, Ms Winters pats my shoulder. 'I'll get you a glass of water.'

By the time she comes back, the Dragon is warming in my palm and I'm sitting up again, staring out of the window.

'Evie darling,' says Amy, and I pause in pulling the duvet out of its cover at the strange note in her voice. She's staring down at the under-sheet and I realise that there are smears of mud across it. 'What on earth have you been up to, darling?' she asks, pushing the duvet back to look more closely.

'It will come out, won't it?'

'I think so,' says Amy, 'but how did it get here? And look,' she adds, going over to the chair where I dump clothes that have been worn but aren't yet ready for the wash. 'It's all over your jeans ... and they're wet through.' I'm treated to a worried head-to-foot survey. 'You weren't walking about in wet clothes, were you, darling? It would be awful for you to get a cold so soon after the operation ...'

'I'm *fine*,' I interrupt, bundling the rest of the dirty clothes up with the sheets. 'I'll put it all on with some of that stain-remover powder.'

But Amy is still holding the jeans, pressing the fabric. 'How is this still so wet? I remember you getting changed into your pyjamas just after dinner. There isn't a draught in here, is there?' she asks, crossing to the window and feeling around the frame, then checking the radiator. 'You're not cold at night, are you?'

'Of course not. It's boiling in here.'

Amy's frown only deepens as she turns to glare at the bundle of washing in my arms. 'But then how on earth did . . .'

'I nipped out,' I say quickly. 'Last night.'

'Last night?' Amy asks. 'I didn't hear you come down the hall.'

'I didn't,' I say, then hurry on, 'I mean, I've just been checking something in the evening, sometimes early in the morning too. Out the bottom of the garden. Mushrooms,' I add. 'There are these really cool mushrooms. Or there were. There are all sorts of wonderful things out there. It all looks so different, so magical, at night. And there are blackberries too.'

'Yes, I can see that,' Amy says, quirking an eyebrow as she picks up a trailing sleeve and shows me a big purple stain near the cuff. 'You don't go beyond the garden though, do you, Evie? I know there's that nice spot of brambles just out on the towpath, but you know you mustn't go beyond the trees.'

I shrug then wriggle awkwardly on the spot.

'Darling,' Amy says, reaching out to touch my arm, 'I don't mind you getting a bit muddy, so long as you don't get chilled and catch a cold, but I don't think you should be wandering around beyond the garden. Especially at night. I don't want to make you scared because we *do* live in a nice, safe place but it's still important to be careful. I mean, you never know who or . . .'

I tuck myself under Amy's arm so she can hug me to her, putting my own arm about her waist to lead her to the door, anxious to get downstairs so I can put the incriminating laundry on and have the whole subject over and done with. 'I'll be safe and careful, I promise,' I say. 'I promise I won't get into trouble.'

Amy sighs. 'You got changed and went out while I was in the bath after dinner, didn't you? Because it wasn't *before* dinner and it wasn't this morning. Darling, why . . . ?' She trails off with another sigh and squeezes my shoulder. 'I'm a terrible busybody, aren't I, my love? You *do* know I can't help it, don't you? That I only do it because I love you?'

'I know,' I say, smiling up at her. I set my head on her shoulder for a moment before moving away so she can go ahead down the stairs: she always prefers to go first if I'm carrying so much as a handkerchief on the basis that if I fall I can fall on her.

While Amy measures out the washing powder, I shove

the laundry into the machine. 'Amy,' I say, putting just a hint of wheedling into my voice so she knows I'm about to ask for something I really want, 'I was thinking . . . I'm going to be fifteen soon – well, soonish – and . . . and I want to be a bit more independent now that I'm getting well again.'

'OK,' Amy says, looking puzzled.

'I want to do my own laundry. I mean, do it by myself.'

Amy frowns. 'But I like doing things for you, darling. If you want to walk – or even cycle – over to Phee's house and then go on from there to school together by yourselves, I don't mind that, so long as it's not raining, of course, but why . . .'

I shove the door to the washing machine shut with a little too much gusto and see Amy's eyes go first to the machine and then to me, trying to figure out why I care so much.

'I want to do it for myself,' I say, a hint of grumpiness in my tone. 'Now that I can stretch a bit because the ribs don't hurt, I just want to do it.'

Amy's eyebrows go up and she blinks at me for a moment, but then she smiles and shrugs. 'If that's really what you want, darling. But you mustn't feel as though I'll be cross if you change your mind again. It's not that exciting, doing laundry.' Then the frown is back. 'But I hope that's not some way of trying to get away with roaming about in the dark out on the towpath,' she says.

'Oh, you know how it is,' I say airily. 'Teenagers have to

be careful about making promises of that sort. Some of us need to be free to go out in the middle of the night to . . . to exercise our hidden mystical powers or . . . or become a righter of wrongs, a rescuer of . . . er . . . abandoned, uneaten blackberries.'

'Try to keep the blackberry rescuing to the daylight hours, darling,' Amy says, 'or at least let one of us know you're creeping out to stain yourself black and purple in future, won't you?'

I pull a face. 'So you can come and steal some of the kudos, you mean, for all that hard rescuing?' I heave a heavy sigh. 'I suppose it might just be possible for me to bring a few of the poor souls I save from the clutches of certain moulding to stand witness to my greatness.'

This leads on to a discussion of whether we should make marmalade this year when the Seville oranges are in season, so the subject drops. But when Amy goes out into the garden to pick the black-spotted leaves off the rose bushes, I sneak an empty bottle from the recycling bin, fill it with water, then hide it in my wardrobe. The last thing I need is a repeat of this near debacle if Amy realises how muddy and wet I keep getting my trainers. Trying to wash them off each night in the bathroom is just asking to get caught, as is hiding them somewhere in the garden: everything is far too well kept. But if I rinse them out of the window, no one need be any the wiser.

Today is Uncle Ben and Aunt Minnie's anniversary. Or what would have been their anniversary. I wish that Uncle Ben would tell stories about Aunt Minnie but, like Amy and Paul with Adam, he can't seem to bear to think about her, let alone allow her name or her memory to pass his lips.

This year is like every other since Amy and Paul got me. Uncle Ben arrives the night before, his usual cheerful self, though he fills his wine glass again and again at dinner. I do my best, while Amy is busy cooking, to hint that I'm old enough to talk about serious things: that it wouldn't burden me, that I'm willing to listen. That I'm even willing to share the subject of my rage since theirs is beyond reach, but neither Paul nor Uncle Ben takes the hint. Our conversation stays stubbornly fixed on brighter, lighter things, then, when Amy and I have gone to bed, it's Paul and Uncle Ben who stay up late talking. But I don't dare eavesdrop from the stairs: not tonight, when Amy may well be periodically checking on them.

When I get up the next morning, Uncle Ben is already sitting at the kitchen table, turning a mug of coffee around and around in his hands while Amy cooks pancakes.

This is the first time since Amy and Paul got me that the anniversary has fallen on a weekend. So, instead of Amy packing me off to school and Paul off to work while Uncle Ben takes the day off, we all eat breakfast together.

Slowly. And quietly. Amy and Paul have obviously discussed how the day will go because once everything is cleaned away – for once, Uncle Ben makes no move to help and simply sits staring into his coffee, turning and turning the cup around on the table as if he'll be able to see visions in it if he gets the liquid spinning just right – Amy collects her hat, scarf and coat and bullies Uncle Ben into his. Then they set off down the garden path.

I stare after them out of the kitchen window until Paul comes over and puts his hand on my shoulder. 'We could go for our own walk if you'd like,' he offers.

I shake my head. It's dank and drizzly outside with none of the charm of a nursery-rhyme 'misty, moisty morning'. The fens smell of rotting reeds and stagnant pools on days like this when the air is heavy with damp. The fog gets into your clothes, soaking through until everything down to your skin is warm and moist as fever-sweat. I wriggle uncomfortably at the thought. 'Too wet,' I say.

'I was thinking we could go out and get a few movies. Something to cheer Uncle Ben up.'

'And take his mind off things?' I ask.

Paul smiles. 'Go wrap up warm.'

As we drive, I think that Paul looks almost as much in need of cheering up as Uncle Ben. But somehow, now that I've finally got the perfect moment to ask what they've been up to together on their night-time excursions, I find I can't. Or won't. As if I suddenly don't know what I want the answer to be.

'Do you think we should try to find someone for Uncle Ben to date?' I ask instead.

Paul flicks a grin at me that makes me cross as well as relieved that the moment for other questions is gone. 'Amy's been watching *Fiddler on the Roof* again, hasn't she? That "Matchmaker, Matchmaker" song.'

I roll my eyes, itching against the unease of knowing that I've missed my chance and the simultaneous relief of having evaded something troubling. Something dangerous. 'Uncle Ben's so nice. He deserves to have someone to appreciate him. I mean, someone just for him.'

The smile fades slowly from Paul's face, from his mouth first, then it bleeds away from his eyes. 'Your Uncle Ben's a wonderful man, Evie. But a lot of people . . . Well, they wouldn't necessarily . . . I mean . . .'

'You mean that Uncle Ben's not very good-looking.'

The car drifts a little to the right as Paul jerks round to look at me. He mutters something under his breath and fixes his eyes on the road again, huffing with what should have been a laugh. 'That's exactly what I mean.'

'But he's not *bad*-looking,' I protest. 'I mean, he's not fat or bald or anything. He's just . . . a bit ordinary sometimes. But if he got his hair cut more often and remembered to iron his clothes and not wear colours that don't go . . . I think it's just when he frowns and stuff or goes all distracted. He's always laughing around me and being funny. I never think about what he looks like, so . . .'

Paul is smiling again. 'But you've hit the nail on the head, Evie. He's always happy around *you*.'

I twist in my seat to look at Paul, then wince and flop back in frustration at all the stupid little things the ribs won't let me do. It's nothing that really matters in the scheme of things, only it does sort of matter when I can only sit and sleep and do things in such specific ways. I sigh, reminding myself that maybe when the ribs finish healing that won't be true any more, then turn my thoughts back to Uncle Ben.

'He'd smile around someone he really liked. Someone who made him happy. You and Amy must know some nice women who are single. You could invite one of them over for dinner when Uncle Ben's there too . . . and maybe you could even invite some other people too so it's not so obvious.'

'It's a good idea, Evie,' Paul says, though I can tell he doesn't really mean it, 'but I don't think Uncle Ben is ready to think about dating.'

'So?' I press. 'If he met someone really nice . . .'

Paul sighs. 'I know it can't seem like it, because Uncle Ben's always so happy with you, Evie, but he's not like that all the time. Not with other adults. I don't think he'd mean to put anyone off exactly, but people can tell when someone isn't really interested in dating.'

I purse my mouth mutinously.

Paul catches sight of my expression and grins. 'Here's what we can do, though. The moment Uncle Ben says the least little thing about women or dating or anything like that, Amy and I will throw a party and invite all the eligible ladies we know. Will that suit, M'mselle?'

I scrunch my face up at him. 'Maybe someone needs to make Uncle Ben think about dating first.'

Paul is pulling into a parking spot and doesn't reply. As I stand by the boot, fumbling with my gloves, he comes around the car and puts his arm across my shoulders. 'I'm not saying you're wrong, Evie, but ... Well, how about we get some romantic comedies. Will that do in terms of dropping a hint?'

I shrug and lean into his side as he starts us towards the shops. In the DVD store, we usually have a pretty lively debate about what to rent, but my heart's not in it. My thoughts have turned to Paul and Amy and the fact that all of Adam's things are packed away at the top of the upstairs cupboard. Looking about the house, you'd never know that Amy and Paul had had a son.

There aren't any photos even, except the one in Paul's wallet that I saw one day when he asked me to fetch his credit card. Amy's one picture of Adam is in the locket she always wears: Adam is on one side, her parents on the other.

I've only seen inside the locket twice. The first time was just after I'd come to live with Amy and Paul, even though I'd known them for more than a year by then and stayed over several times on trial visits. I was sitting at one end of the kitchen table, fluffing some maths homework, while

Paul did tax stuff at the other and Amy pottered about cooking and fiddling with the radio. I wanted to slam my book shut then throw it at the wall, and everything else on the table with it. But while I knew that, at the worst, Amy would tell me off – and it was tempting to test the theory just to be sure – my stomach lurched the second I gripped the book in preparation to hurl it. I hadn't gone about throwing things in Fiona's parents' house. I wasn't going to start with Amy and Paul, who'd only ever been good and kind to me.

So I let go of the book, crossed my arms over it and put my head down on them, heaving a sigh. A moment later, Amy was sitting down next to me, wiping her hands on a tea-towel.

'Can I?' she asked, smiling encouragingly as she gestured at the book.

I sat up and pushed it towards her. 'I just don't *get* it.'

'Must run in the family. Adam always hated fractions, too,' she said.

I could tell that she hadn't meant to – that it had just come out – because she went very still and Paul took his feet off the spare chair.

'What did Adam look like?' I asked because it was the first time the subject had come up since they had brought me to live with them. They didn't hide it, of course: I knew right from the start that they'd had a little boy who'd died. And I knew too that they didn't like to talk about him, so I'd never asked, but I'd been waiting and waiting for one of them to mention him.

Paul and Amy exchanged a look over my head. Emotions bled so quickly across Amy's face that, for a moment, it twitched and twisted as if she were trying to be funny. Then she took a deep breath, smoothing her hands down her arms, all the way from her shoulders to her elbows.

Because there's still water on them, I thought, then wondered if maybe it wasn't more than that: an attempt to push the pain away from her chest. Push it down and away, out of her fingers.

And I opened my mouth to apologise, to tell her I didn't really need to know, that it wasn't any of my business . . . But Amy was already getting up.

I thought she was going to walk away, but she just turned her chair to the side and sat down again so that we were neatly at right angles to each other: every movement precise and careful, as if it was important to get the actions just right. Then she drew the locket out from under her jumper, peering down at it as she flicked open the tiny catch with her nail. I twisted, turning in my chair so I could peer close as she held it out to me.

'Who're they?' I asked, pointing at the second photo.

'My parents.'

I reached out to tug Amy's hands closer because the light was reflecting off the glass over the pictures, obscuring the tiny faces. Her fingers were cold and rigid as if they'd frozen.

Little by little, Amy leaned forwards, further and further forwards, until our heads touched. Then she jumped, jerking back into her chair, hand reflexively shielding the locket against her chest.

For a moment, there was nothing in her face or her eyes, then she started.

'Goodness,' she said in this strange voice, the words too light for the heaviness in her tone. 'I really let myself get swept away for a minute there. Let's have a look at this maths, then.'

When I turned back to my book, I realised that Paul was gone.

That was one of the only times either of them has mentioned Adam in front of me while the other was there. Separately, they've added a few facts over the years. Hints at happy memories. Fragments. Tatters of a different life. They've never refused to answer the few questions I've dared to ask – only when I'm with just one of them, of course – but they've always cut those conversations short. Uncle Ben's the one I go to when there's something I've just *got* to know about Adam, just like it's Amy or Paul I ask when I want to know something about Aunt Minnie.

But while Amy and Paul adopted me only two years after the deaths, I'm pretty sure Uncle Ben hasn't gone on a single date. Lately, I've been thinking more and more about how Uncle Ben seems like he needs some help to start moving on a bit. But this is the first time it's struck me that the only way Uncle Ben is different from Paul and Amy is that they've found themselves a new child to love while he hasn't found a new wife. I never really thought about it before but in some ways Amy and Paul haven't moved on with life any more than Uncle Ben has: they've just tried to start a new one, as if they've pushed all their memories of Adam into a room and closed the door on the wreckage and then papered over that door to pretend it's not even there any more: that there never was another door to another room. Maybe they think they can eventually open the door and all those broken things will have mouldered away, or been dissolved by time, so that all the wood splinters and the glass shards will be rounded at the edges, safe to pick up again. Soft as ashes.

I tried that. With my memories of Fiona and her parents. But it never worked. Not properly. The pain in my ribs made it impossible to pretend that none of it had happened: to pretend that I had always been Amy and Paul's daughter. There were all sorts of stories I tried to pretend. But then my ribs would shift and grate, the ends of the bones rubbing together – or I'd twist and there would be sharp, long needles of pain through my chest – and it would all still be here and now instead of there and then. And here and now can't be pretended away.

As I drift from one aisle of the shop to another, for the first time it strikes me that maybe it's worse to be able to do that thing with the room and the locked door all papered over. Even though it seems easier to lock misery away, perhaps it's just as much work to pretend you can't ever hear things shifting and sliding behind the door behind the wallpaper when a wind creeps in through some unstoppered gap. Perhaps it hurts less, but there's something infinitely sad about that store of discarded, broken things that used to be part of happiness.

Paul asks me a question and I hum in reply. This seems to satisfy him, and he turns away towards the till. I trail behind.

When I first saw the pictures in the locket, oh how I longed to have mine added. But I'm not jealous any more. Amy keeps Adam's picture close, but locked away. And I have everything else.

'Is this because of what Paul and Uncle Ben are up to?' I huff to the Dragon as I stump along the furrow between two rows of cabbages or cauliflowers or whatever the low-growing crop is: the lines of plants are merely darker stripes of near-black across the fenland fields. It is so dark I could easily be walking between little bushes with squirls of pasta hanging off them. 'Couldn't we stay out of their way somewhere nicer?' The Dragon does not deign to reply. With a sigh, I give in to the silence.

The world is purple and velvet blue, the darkness like black mist. One minute I think my eyes are starting to adjust to the night and I can see. The next, the image of the landscape around me fades away and reforms into something different. The horizon, usually a faint grey-orange cast by the distant lights of Cambridge, is rust and brown tonight, like long-dried blood.

But with the Dragon on my shoulder I am not afraid. Rather I am slowly growing dizzy with disorientation. Down keeps shifting, just slightly, as I step on the bank of the crop-row to my right then stumble into the rise on the left.

'Where are we going?' I hiss in exasperation as I stagger to a stop, panting with the effort of wading through the darkness. 'I thought we were going to do something special tonight.'

This dark moon is not the one for action, the Dragon says.

I snort. 'Sounds like a big, fat excuse to me.'

The Dragon tightens its grip on my shoulder until I feel the pinch of its claws even through my coat.

'OK, then tell me what wonderful plans we're going to be working on in the middle of this field in the pitch black!'

That is not the way to persuade me to share anything of value, the Dragon returns sniffily, managing to convey the fact that dragons require a certain level of respect whether one is standing ankle-deep in mud or not. *A wish must always have a purpose*, the Dragon finally deigns to tell me. *And a purpose is the seed of a plan.*

'Well, I wished you were a real dragon and you are, so

that was the purpose of the wish, but I don't see where the plans come in unless they're the same as the purpose ...'

The Dragon efficiently communicates the message that I am being immensely stupid.

'OK, so ... So if I wished you, then your purpose is to grow plans?' I venture. 'At least with seed packets you know what you're growing,' I say grumpily.

A part of my purpose – and the keystone of our contract – is that you should only understand as much as is to your benefit. You must trust. You wished me and I am here.

I roll my eyes but continue along the furrow. 'Don't I even get a hint instead of all this cryptic ...' – the word 'rubbish' comes into my head: the Dragon seems to read it from my thoughts and its disdain magnifies – '... stuff?' I amend, trying to make my tone as polite and conciliatory as it's possible to be while sliding about in a field on a moonless night.

Reach out your hand, the Dragon commands.

I touch tree bark.

Move ahead carefully.

Long grasses tug at my legs, treacherous with rotting leaves. Roots distort the ground. There are branches in my hair, thin and cold, as if I have plunged underwater in the blackness and the long, long reeds of the fenland waterways are reaching out to caress my face.

We may stop here.

I stand in the embrace of the trees, the branches grounding me in the darkness. 'What are we waiting for?'

I whisper. 'I can't see a thing!'

No, says the Dragon, *you cannot.*

'So what do you expect me to look at?'

I do not expect you to see anything.

'Then . . .' I start, but understanding comes rushing in before I have formed the question. I feel the Dragon settle itself in contentment.

Somewhere off to my right, I can hear and smell water. A rustle to the left. A hiss. A shriek. A skirmish in the grasses.

Something passes overhead. I can hear the strength of feathers, tightly woven, as they catch so gently at the air, cupping it, tugging on it like gossamer-thin silk but never pulling a single thread. The twigs against my cheek stir faintly, oh so faintly, with its passing, and settle.

I open my mouth and taste the air. There is a rich, deep scent from the field of autumn crops behind me. I savour iron and deep, verdant green. The gold of grasses grown long in the summer and softening now. A sultry, damp taste is creeping in: the taste of moisture stealing the brittle, dry strength of the stalks, turning them rubbery and fibrous. I smell the tang of brambles and the sweetness of fruit, taste the scent of quince, complex and mysterious. Branches crack and shift, snap and splinter, and things move in the darkness around me, breathing in the colours in the air.

And I grow light with joy, free and wild as the night around me. In the darkness I have no limits, no boundaries: I bleed into the hugeness of the night, reaching out and growing strong, filling up with power.

The dark moon is not always a time for action, the Dragon says softly. *Sometimes it is a time for laying preparations and gathering strength. Sometimes it is a time for making plans, not for carrying them out. And we have many plans to make. But after, when the days are longer and the nights are light, then we shall watch the nymphs become dragonflies,* the Dragon pledges. *I will take you to taste the sourness of daffodils growing in the moonlight, let you stand in chaos of honeysuckle in still midnight air. I will show you where to gather primrose and violets from the banks. Where to walk over mint and wild thyme so that each step raises a spell of scents into the air. We shall see fox cubs and the black balls of new-hatched moorhens. When the dawn comes early, we shall watch the sun rise in the water.*

'Here you go,' Uncle Ben says, thrusting a large bag into my hands before I've even got the door fully open.

I leave him to hang up his coat and take the present into the kitchen. It's a book about Dalí: a glorious, glossy-paged book full of prints of paintings and photos of statues and glasswork. I laugh, throwing my arms about Uncle Ben's neck. 'Thank you!' I try to say, though it comes out as a squeal because the book is great but the really wonderful thing is having an uncle who'll get me something like this just because we watched the Hitchcock movie *Spellbound* last weekend and I loved the dream sequence by Dalí at the end of it.

Uncle Ben bends to kiss my cheek as I flop into a chair to pore over the glossy pages. Then he moves to lean over my shoulder to look with me.

But I've barely had time to freeze at the feeling that someone is standing Right Behind Me, where I can't see them and can't know what they're about to do . . . when he pulls out the chair next to mine and sits down instead. As if he meant to do that all along. I lean into him in apology, fumbling for the words to explain that it's not *him*, but he just drapes his arm over my shoulders and squeezes and says, 'I figure I might get away without Amy telling me off for spoiling you since it *is* an art book,' in a perfectly normal voice, without the faintest hint of offence, as if nothing out of the ordinary has happened.

I summon a slightly watery grin. 'Fat chance,' I retort, and my tone is only a hair's breadth from cheerful.

Uncle Ben rolls his eyes, only overdoing it very slightly, and grins back as he reaches out to stop me turning the page. 'Alice in Wonderland,' he reads.

I glare at the caption but, canting my head to the side, I'm relieved to find I don't get why the statue in the photo is Alice at all. It's a lovely thing but I'd have to hate it even so if I saw Alice in it.

It's of a girl. She's just flung a skipping rope up above

her head. Somehow the odd bit isn't that her hands and hair are dissolving into flowers, or that the top of her dress has faded away, leaving her naked to the waist. The really strange bit is that she doesn't look like she's jumping at all. She's leaning, tilting, as if there is a strong wind blowing. And although her face has no features, there's something intent about the angle of her head, the way it's turned, as if everything is deliberate. As if she has planned it all, this strange, frozen moment: she hasn't been caught unaware in a moment of play by the sculptor. No, she's picked this. And I like that: that she's the one who's decided how she'll be seen.

It's spoilt by the stick jutting up to her right. I'm pretty sure it's meant to be a crutch and I hate it. I wish I could reach into the picture, tear it out and throw it away. I don't know whether it's there to show she doesn't need it – that she's in control – or whether it's there because really she's falling, tilting sideways and falling, and help is just out of reach.

We both start when the doorbell chimes. I'd forgotten that it's Ms Winters's day to come over. Uncle Ben trails after me as I hurry to let her in.

'Uncle Ben bought me the best present,' I tell her by way of introduction as I take her coat.

'Don't mind me,' he says, smiling as he lounges in the doorway. 'I've been promising Amy I'd look at that computer of hers, so I'll stay out of your hair.'

Ms Winters turns to greet him, putting out her hand

politely … Only something funny happens then. She stops, with her hand not quite outstretched, just a few inches too far away for a comfortable handshake. There's something like surprise on her face, a sudden intensity in her eyes. Uncle Ben's usual easy grin is gone. He has that look you get when you reach the bottom of a staircase only somehow you don't see the last step and end up not quite falling when the ground isn't where you expect it to be. For a minute I think they know each other, but it's not that. It's something like recognition but … not. Then it's gone, and they both step forwards to close the distance so they can shake hands.

And it should be perfectly normal, only there's something odd in Ms Winters's voice – just a hint of something I can't put my finger on – though all she says is 'Nice to finally meet you.'

'Yes. Right. Well, I should leave you to it,' Uncle Ben says, and there's something almost sheepish in his tone.

'I'll get you some tea first,' I say. 'Come on.' And I lead the way into the kitchen, watching over my shoulder as Ms Winters steps back to let Uncle Ben go first, just as he does the same. They both laugh awkwardly as Uncle Ben puts out his hand, gesturing for her to go ahead.

'So why the present?' Ms Winters asks. 'I thought your birthday was in March, Evie.'

'It is,' I say, fetching down a third mug and clicking the kettle on. 'But Uncle Ben spoils me all year round.'

Uncle Ben smiles, rocking back then forwards on his

heels. 'Well, it's not *spoiling* exactly when it's a book. An art book.'

'He's working on his excuse for Amy,' I tell Ms Winters.

'My sister has a *lot* of rules,' Uncle Ben tells her in a stage whisper.

Ms Winters's smile is warm, her eyes almost tender as she says, 'I can't imagine they apply when you've found something so wonderful. I mean,' she adds quickly, 'it's always so valuable to encourage an interest in art.'

'Well, I'll leave you ladies to your tea and studies,' he says, tousling my hair. 'See you in a bit.'

But when I glance up from drawing my chair in close to the table, it's to find that Uncle Ben is still standing in the doorway with a faintly puzzled look on his face and his head slightly cocked to one side. And suddenly I wonder if they have met before. After all, I suppose Uncle Ben – and Paul and Amy – are victims of a sort . . . Could Uncle Ben have gone to Ms Winters's charity for advice? It's not impossible, I realise. It's not impossible at all, though I'd never thought about it like that before.

Then Uncle Ben seems to shake himself. He tosses me a grin and whistles his way nonchalantly upstairs.

'He seems very fond of you,' Ms Winters says. 'It's obviously been a good day, but how about your week as a whole?'

And my good mood is gone just like that. 'I hate Sonny Rawlins,' I say, practically spitting out the name. I know I shouldn't really talk to Ms Winters about Sonny Rawlins since she teaches him too, and I don't want to be a tattle-tale, but ... 'He's been throwing eggs at our front door. Putting leaves and stuff through the letter-box. I know it's him. I saw him riding off on that stupid, fancy new mountain bike of his last week, and a few days ago too. Next time I catch him, I'm going to chuck something back. Like a brick.'

Ms Winters frowns. 'No bricks, Evie. It's not a good idea. You don't want to end up in trouble.'

I slump forwards with a sigh, resting my chin on the book and staring at the wall. 'I'm not telling you so you'll sort him out, you know. Just ... You know how horrid he is, so you understand. So we can talk about it, can't we? Just between the two of us?' I ask, turning to look at her.

Ms Winters smiles down at me. 'Just between us, Evie,' she promises. 'And I appreciate that, you know.'

I wrinkle my nose and turn back to glaring at the wall, but I don't do a very good job of the glare because I'm smiling too much, gathering the pride and fondness in her voice to me.

'Have you told Amy and Paul it was Sonny?'

I shrug, sighing. 'They say I can't be sure it's him just from his back and his bike. But I know it is. He hates me even more than I hate him.'

Ms Winters settles back into her chair. I wonder if she knows that she always wriggles a bit when she does that. 'Why do you think Sonny has singled you out?'

'He hates me,' I correct. 'He really does. Why else would he do something like that?'

Ms Winters shrugs. 'Boys your age can be very funny, you know. They do all sorts of nasty things for no apparent reason whatsoever. Have your neighbours been having the same problems?'

'No.'

Ms Winters's mouth flattens into a line and I can see she's persuaded that the eggs and leaves thing is personal.

'Why do you think Sonny has singled you out?' she asks.

'He's nasty to all of us – to Lynne and Phee as well – but mostly to me. And it's not just in my head: Phee and Lynne say so too. Lynne says that one of her brothers was a bit like that with a girl he liked, but none of us thinks that Sonny Rawlins could possibly like me like that.' I pull a face. 'Besides, I'd rather he hated me. He's just horrible. Yuck. Wouldn't want him liking me.' I don't have to force the shudder of disgust that ripples through me.

Ms Winters is smiling. Just a little, but knowingly. And I wonder if maybe she's trying to demonstrate a normal response to Sonny Rawlins's awfulness: a condescending amusement for how stupid he is. If so, it's not helping. I still want to rip his throat out.

From my first day at school – midway through the Autumn Term – he'd stared at me. That look – part speculation, part appraisal, and just a little greed – followed me silently down corridors, prickled between my shoulder blades in the classroom, refused to leave me when I glared in return. We hardly spoke those first few weeks, or after the Christmas holidays, until Valentine's Day revealed Sonny Rawlins behind the door of my locker, holding out a bunch of flowers. I took them automatically. Stupidly.

'Do you know what they're called?' he asked, smirking.

My gaze dropped to the flowers in my hand and suddenly I remembered the one positive thing I knew about Sonny Rawlins: that his mother was a garden designer. And, just for a moment, I thought about the fact that he had been brought up by a woman who loves flowers. And so, just for a moment, I wondered if I had been misreading those looks.

His self-satisfied words rang in my ears: *Do you know what they're called?*

'Yes,' I told the flowers. 'Yes, I know what they're called.'

I looked up with a smile. And threw the flowers in his smug, expectant face. 'You can have your deadly nightshade back, thank you *very* much.'

'Wait! No . . .'

But I spoke over him, raising my voice so that the whole corridor could hear. 'You'll have to try harder than that,' I sneered, 'if you want to make me look even half as stupid as you are. As if I'd want flowers from *you* anyway!'

Sonny Rawlins's face grew red with rage and humiliation, and for a moment I was stunned to see his eyes full of hurt. Full of tears. *He must have been planning this for weeks, for months perhaps*, I realised: the perfect trick to play on the clever new girl. Step One: give her flowers on Valentine's Day. Make her think that she is admired. Step Two, watch her bashful pleasure.

Then Step Three: shout to the whole school that the flowers are poisonous, just like she is, making a fool of her in front of everybody. He must have dreamt of the moment, rehearsing his triumph over and over . . .

And then I beat him at his own game, in the one area where he might be expected to know more than I did.

Half the school saw it: Sonny Rawlins fighting back tears of fury, utterly routed by the quiet, clever new girl. And I smiled as I watched all his planning go to waste, all his delicious anticipation turning to shame. After all, I thought, why shouldn't I enjoy turning his own malice back on him, making him his own victim? Why shouldn't I revel in my little moment of triumph? Because I hadn't escaped Fiona and her parents to become Sonny Rawlins's plaything.

'Well, I wouldn't be surprised if Lynne turns out to be right,' Ms Winters says, jolting me out of the memory. I stare blankly into her face, retrospectively processing her words.

I wonder for a moment if she's going to say something more. But she looks away and doesn't. I can't imagine Sonny Rawlins ever said anything nice about me, let alone about fancying me, to her – or to anyone else for that matter – so she can't have overheard anything … but Ms Winters doesn't miss much. And she knows how to understand what you mean, rather than what you say or do. That's the heart of the reason I talk to her: I don't have to say things for her to hear them.

I sigh. 'It still doesn't change the fact that he really does hate me, and I hate him back. I wish he'd just die. People have all sorts of horrible accidents all the time. Why can't Sonny Rawlins be one of them?'

Ms Winters clearly takes this as a joke since the next thing she says is 'Perhaps Amy and Paul should have a little talk with his parents since he's bothering you at home. Do you want me to suggest it to them for you?'

'No,' I say sulkily. 'He lives two streets away. He'll just be even worse than before.'

'Not necessarily,' Ms Winters says. 'I've met his family a few times and they seem like nice enough people.'

I shrug, thinking about sports days and parents' evenings. 'I guess,' I say unenthusiastically. 'He doesn't make a prat of himself when they're around.' But then I think back to the school fair Ms Winters organised for her charity the summer before last. When the parents had retreated to the tea-tent, Lynne, Phee and I had gone to find Jenny, who'd won the 'Guess the number of Smarties in a jar' competition; instead, we found Sonny Rawlins and Fred, and ended up running squealing from them as they threw handfuls of gravel at us.

And yet Sonny Rawlins has a mother who loves flowers

and cares about growing beautiful things, like Amy. Who knows the names of all the plants and when they bloom, like Paul. Who can point to all the special little things about each that you only notice if you look really close, like I can after nearly four years with Amy and Paul. But what did Sonny Rawlins learn from his mother? How to try to hurt people with flowers: how to see the poison in them.

'Well, why don't you have a little talk about it with Amy and Paul, then we can discuss it again next week,' Ms Winters says. 'For now, how about we focus on what you can do to stop Sonny upsetting you so much?'

'Uncle Ben had some wonderful suggestions. He said we could make a trap. Like a snare for a rabbit,' I say, sitting up so that I can gesture. 'You know, one of those things that hoik people up in the air so they end up upside down. Or something that launches rotten eggs back if something hits the front door. Like a catapult.'

'Your postman might not like that too much if he set it off by accident,' Ms Winters says, looking as if she wants to laugh.

'I know. Uncle Ben said that too. But he said we could have it so that we only set it after the post comes and then we can unset it at night. Anyway, he said the best option would be something like a crossbow that fired a water balloon filled with washing-up liquid. Because washing-up liquid's so slimy and if you get lots of it on you it takes ages to wash off because you just foam. Can you imagine Sonny Rawlins foaming all the way through school and going to the loo to try to wash it off and just foaming even more?' I ask, giggling. 'Even without the catapult, I'm thinking that could be a good idea. Only it might be difficult to carry a balloon with enough washing-up liquid around in my pocket. And if I put it in my bag it might burst. Uncle Ben says he'll see if he can come up with a good solution so I can go armed if necessary.'

'Your Uncle Ben seems like a wonderful man,' Ms Winters says with a warm smile.

As soon as she says it, we both realise how unexpected the words are: oddly tender, wistful, as if she is lonely for kindness.

'You must be very glad to have him to cheer you up and bring you such lovely books,' Ms Winters says quickly, her tone firm and encouraging, all of that soft yearning gone out of her voice. Her eyes go to the book.

I nod vaguely.

'But, you know, while I think it's a good idea about the washing-up liquid, you might want to save it for the summer. And perhaps for a time when Sonny comes over to your house. I'm afraid I can't condone it as a good tactic for school.'

I shrug. 'Even Mrs Henderson can't do much more than give me detention though, can she? I mean, it *is* only soap after all.'

Ms Winters smiles. 'All I will say on that subject,' she

says firmly, 'is that, on balance, especially knowing teenage boys, a little soap might just do Sonny Rawlins a world of good.'

I grin.

Phee, Lynne and I kick our way through the leaves between the science block and the Portakabins, arms linked. We spent the weekend watching what felt like thousands of episodes of a whole set of different soap operas, and Lynne and Phee are still gushing over which of the boy actors is the cutest overall, who has the best butt and who is most snoggable. I can't honestly dredge up a clear memory of any of them, but it doesn't really matter: I just keep pretending to change sides on the debate about who should be in the Top Five to keep them arguing. What's important to me is that we've got something in common again to talk about.

Lynne jerks us to a stop as we round the corner by the gym. Jenny is standing with Sonny Rawlins and Fred. They're all holding cigarettes.

Before I can tug the other two away, Phee marches over. 'You said you were quitting, Jenny. What are you doing letting these two morons get you started again?'

'Hey, she's the one begging fags off us,' Fred retorts. 'Maybe she just likes it.'

'What would a stuck-up swot like you know who's

never even tried one?' Sonny Rawlins sneers. 'Come on, I dare you.'

'Like I care. Why would I want to try something that can give me cancer?' Phee asks. 'Come on, Jenny...'

'You scared you're gonna die from one little puff?' Fred taunts.

'Well, delicate little Evie might,' Sonny Rawlins adds with a snort. 'Poor baby.'

'OK,' I say. 'Give me one then.'

'Evie, don't be stupid,' Phee says, pulling at my arm. 'Why would you let him talk you into anything this dumb?'

I shrug. 'One isn't going to do me any harm and then I can sneer at him all I like and what'll he be able to say to that?' When we went to live with her parents, Fiona soon picked up her mother's pack-a-day habit. I stole one once, on one of those days when my hands were shaking, just like Fiona's sometimes did, and I couldn't stop crying. It didn't help then, but I am pretty sure that I can at least take a few puffs now without puking, perhaps without even coughing, and won't that just show Sonny Rawlins.

Jenny shuffles awkwardly on the spot, taking a last drag of her cigarette, then she grinds the butt into the mud, mumbles something under her breath and hurries away.

Phee turns her glare from me to Lynne. 'Thanks for the help,' she says.

Lynne raises her hands with a shrug. 'So I want to see Evie get one over on the little git. So sue me.'

'Well?' I say, raising an eyebrow as I hold out a hand.

Sonny Rawlins glares at me while Fred fumbles in his pocket for the packet and reluctantly holds it out to me.

'Yeah, you can give me one too,' Lynne says staunchly.

'Jesus,' Fred says. 'Why don't you just take the whole pack while you're at it?'

It is Sonny Rawlins who takes out a lighter. He flicks it on, twisting it so that the flame catches my thumb instead of the cigarette.

I jerk my hand away, dropping the unlit cigarette.

'God, you're such a jerk,' Lynne says, snatching the lighter away from him.

Phee gives him a solid shove to the shoulder that pushes him back a pace before he lunges forwards, shouting in her face. 'You want to try that again, bitch?'

'What on earth is going on here?' someone asks.

Already crouched over the fallen cigarette, I snatch it from the mud and palm it, then stuff my hands in my pockets as I stand. I needn't have bothered with the subterfuge: Mrs Poole's attention is fixed on the boys, her hand outstretched as Fred slouches forward to hand her the cigarette packet.

'We were trying to explain to the boys about how it's probably the smoking that's stunted their physical and mental development,' I say, 'and how they shouldn't be encouraging other people to end up the same way.'

'A perfectly reasonable concern for your classmates' health,' Mrs Poole says tartly. 'One that, however tactlessly worded,' here she turns her glare briefly on me, 'does not merit violence or swearing in return.' She looks pointedly down at the butt Sonny Rawlins tried to grind into the mud when she came round the corner. Mumbling under his breath, he picks it up and pushes it into the cigarette packet proffered to receive it.

'Well, you know how it is. Boys our age, with their hormones running wild, trying to show off to impress the girls,' Lynne says airily. 'I don't suppose they can help it, poor dears.'

'Though it's a shame they didn't think about how *un*impressive the smoking's made their growth. I mean, the three of us are nearly taller than Sonny Rawlins now,' I add, smiling sweetly.

Mrs Poole, who has said as much about the results of smoking before, gives me a hard look.

Lynne, Phee and I assume bland expressions.

'Mockery is rarely effective in encouraging people to address their difficulties. And taunting people never makes for attractive behaviour, whatever the provocation,' Mrs Poole says, looking pointedly at me.

Then suddenly her expression softens, and I can see that's the end of it: whatever else she was going to say – would have said if it were anyone else – has been washed away by pity. Irritation sparks for a moment, then fades; I may not like being pitied but if it's actually going to do me some good by getting me – and, by extension, Phee and Lynne – out of trouble, it's worth putting up with.

'Now,' Mrs Poole says, her voice matter-of-fact once more, 'I'd better not see you girls near any cigarettes again or I'll start to think it wasn't just the boys here smoking. As it is, I think you'd better go and spend the rest of your break elsewhere.'

'Sorry, Mrs Poole,' we mumble, trying our best to look humble and repentant.

She rolls her eyes, but turns her attention back to the boys. 'And now we shall have a few words about appropriate language,' she tells them, 'before we go and see Mrs Henderson. Which we will be doing,' she adds, raising her voice over their protests of unfair treatment, 'since this is far from the first time the two of *you* have been caught smoking.'

Phee, Lynne and I exchange grins as we hurry away to the girls' loos, though we make sure to get out of earshot before breaking into giggles.

'They're so going to get you for that, Evie!' Lynne gasps.

'Me? Why me?'

'I just backed you up. You're the one they're going to want to get even with.'

'Great.'

Phee grins and tucks her arm through mine. 'But it was *so* worth it.'

'Depends how they get even,' I say ruefully.

Lynne links arms with me on the other side and, for now, the ribs allow it. 'Still worth it.'

The garden table is slick underfoot and treacherous. Even the rough flagstones of the patio feel smooth. I keep to the path because the grass is so thickly frosted, every blade sharp-coated with ice, that there is no hope my tracks would vanish by morning.

The berberis is an armoury of silver-green weapons. The acer a marvel of white over red, stepped limbs dripping tiny crystals. The skeleton of the tree glows in the frozen night air as if displaying its soul to the heavens. Beneath, a plant with wide, awkward leaves – probably a weed – looks like folds of lace over silk.

The hoar frost is so thick that the world glows, though the moon is only a thin crescent. Just as deep snowfalls draw in the light and cast it back out tenfold, the frost brings even the deep shadows into half-light. But unlike the snow the frost has robbed everything of colour. No late-falling orange pyracantha berries peek out of the fur of ice. The winter pansies are ghostly, hinting only faintly of mauve where, earlier today, they were imperial purple: a wine-dark colour thick and heavy enough to drown in. Now everything is shaded in grey and silver and white. But with it the world sparkles. As I walk, diamond-flashes catch off the newly strange plants in the beds, curled over in furious rigour from the cold. The nude tree branches glimmer with the sharp sheen of sheet metal.

The cold prickles and scratches at my face, catches in my throat and chest. My ribs have been aching since the afternoon, the way they always do when the temperature is falling and there is water in the air. Rain, snow or frost: it makes no difference. The damaged bones herald it earlier and surer than any forecast.

But the frosted fens are too beautiful for me to dwell on the pain. The river is dark and free between the banks. The orange glow of a distant streetlight bleeds poison into the night.

And then we are in the fields and the whole world is alight, shimmering. Everything solid has turned to crystal. Even the mud of the path and the black late-autumn mulch of leaves is purified, rarefied. I crouch to look at the delicate filigree of a crystallised fern.

The last tall-standing grasses are planted sword blades. I lift my finger to trace a knife-sharp edge. The ice stings my fingertip and then suddenly there is a little circle of gold in the midst of the grey and silver as a tiny droplet of water rolls downwards.

The Dragon and I don't speak as we examine ice-furred bramble-leaves cloaking barbed-wire vines. Tiny mirrors of ice crack, splintering into wicked shards beneath my feet.

In all the nights we have walked, this is the one that the Dragon belongs to. Or which belongs to the Dragon. This enchantment of ice and crystal. Of glowing things and strangeness. As if time has frozen, and all the magic beneath the everyday world of mud and slow water is finally revealed, uncloaked beneath the cold light of the stars.

The Dragon is suddenly rigid: muscles locked with intent. It takes me longer to see it: something ghostly approaching across the fields. The Dragon tracks its progress, turning its head in so smooth and controlled a motion that it seems half-fixed into carved bone once more. But then its tail starts to twitch back and forth and, for a moment, I wonder if it is going to leap into the air and fell the approaching creature.

This is not the type of prey I hunt, the Dragon tells me.

I realise what it is just as it swoops into a dive, thick legs extended, claws outstretched. The owl draws the mouse in and sails away. In my palm, the Dragon purrs with the thrill of power and the delight of dominion over this wide, strange world of ice. And I thrill with it for in my palm I hold all the power that anyone could ever need: power that is bound to me not by blood, but by bone.

My eyes ache with the cold, but I try not to blink as I stare around, trying to fix the vision of the hoar-frosted fens in my mind and, with it, this terrifying and wonderful feeling that I will never be helpless again.

I shall make sure of it, the Dragon says. And then we are silent.

We go back the long way tonight, pressing footsteps like bruises into the frost-brittle grass of the golf course until finally we turn on to the blackly glittering footpath by the graveyard wall.

A sudden raucous laugh sends me darting into the shadow of the dry-stone wall. The moss prickles sharply against my fingers as I fumble for purchase to hold myself tight into the lee of the darkness. More laughter. Shouts. A beam of torchlight spears into the branches of the yew tree above me, then dances away.

Someone starts singing in the graveyard. Other voices join in. But it's not a song to the beauty of the ice. It's barely a song at all. More like a roar of anger. Of mindless defiance and ready cruelty. A song for drunken men to yell to the streetlights as they stagger home.

I feel a rush of anger, cold and sharp as the ice. Adam is buried somewhere beyond this wall. Adam and Aunt Minnie and Grandad Peter and Nanna Florrie. And there are drunken men shouting and laughing in that place of sadness. I peer over the wall, see dim shapes moving and staggering over the uneven ground.

And then the Dragon is in front of me and saying, *No. This is not for us.*

And I want to say 'But' and invoke the names of Amy and Paul's family like a spell, but the Dragon breathes warm, moist smoke in my face and I turn away, creeping along, bent over, until I can't stand the pain the position calls up in my ribs. And then I am running. Running, running, running. Trading hurt for hurt as the air and ice bite sharp and bitter in my chest as if I'm breathing fir needles. I stumble to a halt, bent over the stile to the canal path, and gasp as pain blinds my thoughts.

The Dragon settles on the back of my hand, splayed shaking over the top of the fence post.

Ms Winters is studying me, waiting to see if I'll decide to fill the silence if she doesn't speak. I'm not biting today, so I just study her back. But I've got no clue what she's thinking. I don't recognise the expression on her face at all and wonder what to make of that. Is it a good or a bad thing, this look that I've not seen before?

Then Ms Winters's expression shifts: she's come to some sort of decision and, sure enough, a moment later she says, 'You seem happier today, Evie.'

I take a minute to answer, not quite sure what to make of this statement: not sure what sort of response she's looking for. 'My ribs don't hurt all the time and I get to sleep every night,' I offer. 'Proper, deep sleep, not just little catnaps where I wake up every time I move. Before, I had maybe one day a month when I really slept, rather than just dozed all night. And now I *sleep*,' I say, drawing the word out reverently, 'and it's *lovely*. Why wouldn't I be happy?'

'And school?' Ms Winters asks, and I still can't tell if the questions are as simple as they seem or if they're leading somewhere.

'It's good,' I say cautiously. 'I'm getting back into things. I mean, I'm still sitting and watching during PE, working on that stinking pencil case,' I say, wrinkling my nose as I think about the number of times I've let my concentration wander for a moment and ended up clumsily sticking the blunt needle under a nail. 'Lynne's always running by sticking her tongue out at me.'

'Does it upset you that she's jealous?'

'No.'

Ms Winters sighs. She thinks I'm being difficult and maybe I am, but I wish she'd just come clean with what this is all about.

'What I *meant*,' Ms Winters continues, 'was that it might bother you that Lynne is thinking about not wanting to do sports and being jealous that you aren't, rather than thinking about the fact that you can't ... and why you can't.'

'Lynne thinks I broke my ribs in a car crash. Everyone at school thinks that, apart from you and Mrs Henderson, and she only knows because my stupid social worker insisted that my headmistress needed to be told,' I say, a hint of irritation creeping into my tone.

Not all of it is directed towards the stupid social worker: Ms Winters knows exactly what everyone else at school thinks, so why would she expect me to hold what Lynne doesn't know against her?

'Perhaps we should talk about whether you should confide a little in your friends,' Ms Winters says then, and my heart sinks. 'You've been best friends with Phee and Lynne for almost four years now.'

'And that means I shouldn't have any secrets from them?'

'It's not so much that you *shouldn't* have secrets, Evie, but perhaps you shouldn't let your close friends believe a lie.'

I roll my eyes, slouching down into my chair. 'So what if it's a lie? They don't need to know the truth. It's nothing to do with them. The only thing it'll do is make everything awkward. They'll be all sorry for me. Even more than they already are. They'll look at me and all they'll see is ...' I shut my eyes, trying to close out the images that flood across my mind. 'The first thing they'll think of every time they see me is all the things I don't want them to.'

'I know it might feel that way, Evie, but ...'

'What do you think of first when you think of me?' I snap.

Ms Winters's face goes blank. 'That's different, Evie,' she says, but I can see that the calm, even tone takes effort. 'Especially at the moment, when part of what I'm doing here, out of school, is talking with you about your problems. But it's not always the first thing I think of, you know. Sometimes I think about how nice it is to have a pupil who really loves books the way that I do: sometimes I think about how much I'm looking forward to sharing my favourite books with you, especially the ones you haven't read before. It almost makes me feel like I'm reading them for the first time all over again.'

I turn my gaze to the window. A robin darts into the pyracantha, tearing away a stem of berries, then flutters off again. 'Does it really count as a lie when you have to tell people something to explain things but you can't tell the truth?'

'Who says you can't tell the truth?' Ms Winters asks. My face must have done something peculiar then, because she hurries on, 'I'm not trying to criticise you, Evie, or call you a liar. I'm just suggesting that you might want to think about telling your closest friends about some of your problems.'

'It'll end up all over school.'

Ms Winters frowns. 'Do you really think Lynne and Phee are so untrustworthy?'

I shake my head, wondering why Ms Winters is being so thick today. 'They're fine. They're just *normal*. They tell people things. Even secrets. They tell one person and then that person tells one person ... And how could I blame them? No one wants to hear this stuff. They'll be upset.'

'You don't think it'll be enough that Phee and Lynne can talk to each other?'

'They're *normal*,' I say again, and can't stop it coming out sharp and impatient.

'What does that mean to you, Evie?'

I roll my eyes and slump lower in the armchair. Surely this is the sort of thing she should be explaining to me, not vice versa.

Today, Ms Winters is the one who fidgets. I outwait her. After a while she sighs, uncrosses her legs, then crosses them the other way. Finally, she sighs again and says, 'Let's go back to what we were talking about earlier. The fact that you're sleeping better, feeling happier, not being in pain. It's natural that you've been focused on those things, but since that's all in hand I think it would be good to start talking about what your goals are now.'

I frown, still stuck on why she's so keen on my blabbing my secrets all over the place.

'OK,' Ms Winters says, 'I can see that that's a pretty broad subject. How about we start by exploring what your general goals are? What do you want to accomplish? Do you have any plans for things you want to do?'

'At school, you mean?' I venture.

Ms Winters shrugs. 'At school, at home ... Do you ... want to get picked for a sports team? Or get a part in the school play? Or get invited to a particular party?'

I squirm around so that I can tuck my feet up underneath me. 'I want to catch up with everything that I've missed,' I say.

'Well, I think we're pretty much there on the schoolwork side. How about everything else?'

I tug a strand of hair loose from my ponytail and start twisting it around my finger, round and around. I'm trying to get out of the habit of chewing the ends when I'm thinking, but this alternative just isn't as effective.

'It's OK, I guess. Sometimes they still talk about things

I've missed, but not so much now. And I'm not really missing anything important any more. Jenny is having her birthday party at the pool, but I should be able to go in the water by then so . . . And there's the D of E thing, but it's not such a big deal any more. I think Lynne's going to give it up soon anyway.'

'And how about the things you're looking forward to after Jenny's party?'

'I don't know,' I have to admit, somewhat surprised at the realisation. 'I don't really know now that my ribs don't hurt and I can sleep without it being awful. I guess I'm just getting used to it all being different.'

'Well, it's not unreasonable that you need some time to adjust, Evie. Those were pretty big challenges – pretty all-consuming – and now those things are resolved, it's natural for you to feel a little unsettled: a little unsure what to focus on next. But we all need goals: things to aim for and work on. Maybe it's time to start figuring out what those might be.'

A wisp of thought crosses my mind but by the time I try to grasp it, it dances out of reach. It feels important and I know I am frowning as I try to catch hold of it. It's something to do with the Dragon. And lightness: a feeling of lightness. Of expansiveness. As if there were something made up of broken glass somewhere inside me that's been taken away with the broken bit of my rib.

I give up twisting the strand of hair and bite down on the ends instead.

'You don't have to figure it out right away, Evie,' Ms Winters says when I remain silent. 'But perhaps that would be good homework for the next few weeks: to have a think about what good things you want to accomplish now that so much bad stuff is out of the way. It doesn't have to have anything to do with studying, though it can if you like. But even if it's just saving up for a pair of jeans you really like, I want you to tell me about one new goal by the end of the month: about a goal and what exactly you're going to do to try to accomplish that goal.'

'So a goal and a plan,' I say thoughtfully, not fully paying attention. I am still trying to work out what exactly it is that got taken away, apart from the rib, and whether that bad thing got turned into a good thing when the rib turned into the Dragon, or whether it was the Dragon that took the bad thing away in the first place. I spit my hair out and brush the wet strand away from my cheek. 'I can do that.'

I have one leg over the window sill when I hear the winch-squeak of the back gate.

'Shhhhhh!' someone hisses.

I practically fall back into my room. Biting my lip over the pain exploding in my ribs, I wrench the window all but closed. My hands shake as I coax the curtain rings along the rod. Along, along ... Somehow, with all that's happened, I forgot what day it is: every Friday now, Paul and Uncle Ben go off together, late at night.

I crouch below the window, splinting my hand across my ribs as I listen to the scrape of the garden chairs on the flagstones.

'Look at all this mud,' Paul says. 'Next door's blasted cat's been on the table again.'

'Big feet for a cat,' Uncle Ben says and I freeze.

My shoes may be clean when I climb down on to the table every night, but they're not when I'm climbing back up to my room *after* an adventure with the Dragon.

'Disgusting beast,' Paul says dismissively. 'Has this huge, bushy tail matted with filth.'

Tomorrow, I tell myself, I will find an old dishcloth from the shed and keep it in my pocket whenever I go out so I can clean away enough mud that there won't be any more footprints on the table.

'Maybe this whole thing's been a waste of time, Ben,' Paul says, drawing my attention back to their conversation. 'Amy's going to be none too happy to find I've dipped my trouser cuffs an inch deep in mud again, and where's it getting us?'

'The opportunity will present itself eventually,' Uncle Ben says in a surprisingly bullish tone. 'But it only needs one of us: no need for you to keep coming along.'

Paul sighs. 'Not what I'm saying, Ben,' he replies softly. 'Just ... Friday night's clearly not the night. So what is?'

They're quiet for a while. 'Things like this . . . People go for darkness, right?'

'And it's not been dark at eleven o'clock at night every blessed time so far?' Paul says irritably. Then he sighs again. 'Cloudy nights?' he suggests.

'Nights where it doesn't matter. New moon nights.'

'Well, they do say the full moon brings out the crazies. Maybe it's similar with the new moon,' Paul says and I can hear he's trying to make peace.

My heart clenches at the thought of another dark moon stolen. *It's mine!* I want to shout. *It's* my *dark moon, not yours.*

Uncle Ben forces out a huff of laughter. 'Sounds about right for the two of us.'

'And it about fits what we've got in mind.'

'No, it doesn't,' Uncle Ben says, though his tone is friendly enough. 'Justice not trouble, we agreed.'

'I know what we agreed, Ben. I just don't like the thought of all the things that could go wrong.'

They're both silent for so long I start to wonder if I should just give up and go back to bed, but then Uncle Ben says, 'I still think you should talk to Evie.'

'And *I* keep telling you she doesn't need any other burdens,' Paul replies but, though the words are angry, his tone is merely weary.

Part of me wants to stand up, open the window and say *Tell me!* While another part whispers, *No. No, don't. Please don't. You'll ruin everything.*

'I really don't think she'd see it that way, Paul,' Uncle Ben says softly.

A sigh. 'Maybe,' Paul says. 'Maybe.'

Uncle Ben leaves soon after and I creep back to bed. Shedding clothes as I go, I toss my trainers to the back of the open wardrobe and then crawl into bed, pulling my dressing gown around me since my ribs are too sore to contemplate raising my arms to put on the big, floppy T-shirt I usually wear as a nightdress. Sinking into the softness of the bed, I curl on to my good side and set the Dragon down in the curve of my body.

'I guess they deserve to have one dark moon to themselves,' I whisper. Then sigh.

There are plenty of other nights to fit our purposes, the Dragon says. *And when the time comes, we will not waste it. It is only this next dark moon we must approach with caution. And perhaps it is as well.*

'What do you think they're up to? What do you think Uncle Ben thinks Paul should tell me?' I ask despite myself, because I think maybe I know . . . only I'm not sure that I want to.

The Dragon is silent.

I sigh and turn on to my back, staring up at the ceiling. 'Do you think . . .' But I don't dare put my suspicions into words, partly because then I would barely be able to breathe for worry and guilt over Uncle Ben and Paul if I'm right. But there's something else too: a strange feeling almost like anger.

I sigh again. Despite my best efforts, my thoughts keep going back to that night, listening through the banisters, the wound over my ribs still fresh and the Dragon only half carved in my hand. Memories of Paul and Uncle Ben talking tonight merge with memories of their voices, their words from before: Paul saying, 'I don't want to have to tell Evie that there isn't any fair for her.' And Uncle Ben's reply, 'If only I were a braver man . . .'

Phee, Lynne and I sit on the edge of the pool, kicking our feet in the water and watching Jenny shrieking with laughter as Fred chases her towards the deep end.

'Do you really think she likes him?' Phee asks, wonder warring with disgust in her tone. 'She looks like she likes him.'

'He looks like he likes her. Like actually *likes* her,' Lynne says as Jenny slows to let Fred catch her and push her under the water. 'Who'd've thought he could manage to not be a total jerk for ten whole minutes at a time?'

'Yeah, well let's see how that goes when Sonny Rawlins turns up,' I say.

Lynne sighs dramatically.

'People get hit by cars all the time,' Phee says thoughtfully. 'Maybe Sonny's been hit by a car . . .'

'Squished flat!' Lynne crows. 'Oooo, I like it.'

'No such luck,' I sigh, as Sonny Rawlins comes strutting

out of the changing rooms. We turn as one to glare at him.

'You finally growing some tits then?' he says, smirking as he fixes his gaze on my chest when he sees us watching.

'At least she's not stuffing her swimming costume like you're stuffing your trunks,' Phee sneers, her hand finding mine as I flinch instinctively away from his words, feeling my skin prickle with goosebumps.

'You afraid the lifeguard'll tell you you have to go to the kiddies' pool if you don't?' I snap, leaning into Phee's warmth and pushing the words out all mocking and hard so that my voice doesn't waver.

'Better watch that sock doesn't fall out. No cannonballs for you,' Lynne adds, putting her arm about my shoulders.

I take a deep breath, tilting my chin up defiantly as Sonny Rawlins's lips thin and his eyes go flat and nasty. 'Better hurry into the water before anyone notices what you *haven't* got,' I say, then turn purposefully away, refusing to hear what he calls me in reply.

Lynne laughs contemptuously at him. After a moment, I feel his shadow pass over us as he walks on to the shallow end.

'Maybe he and Fred will accidentally drown each other,' Lynne says loudly.

'There's always hope,' I agree, though it comes out rather weaker than I'd intended.

'Well,' Phee says purposefully, pushing herself to her feet. 'Are you guys coming, or are we just going to sit here all day?' She grins and offers me a hand. 'Come on, Evie.'

I grin back and let her pull me carefully to my feet. We look down at Lynne, who quirks an eyebrow. 'Voluntary exercise? You've *got* to be kidding me. I'll just recline here, looking gorgeous, and watch, thanks.'

'Well, it's always nice to have an admiring audience,' I say. Phee snorts, leading the way towards the shallow end. I turn to follow, take two steps . . .

Suddenly the floor rears up and the ceiling dives to roll under me.

Suddenly I am weightless and the world is white: so white my eyes burn as if a camera flash has been frozen in time.

Pressure and weight and force pummel me as I hit the surface of the water.

My neck snaps back. My mouth opens reflexively but my chest is so compressed with pain that I cannot scream.

Water floods into my open mouth.

My eyes open – when did they shut? – and the world around me is blue and distorted, curved and twisted. Sound echoes dully.

I am sinking down under the water, down, down . . . Tendrils of my own hair frame my vision. I see my hand, fingers lax, floating above me.

Then the pressure is gone. My chest expands without thought. Water floods down my throat.

The world twists and writhes as I curl over the pain, the wrongness of the water in my lungs. My hair whips red-gold around me, wild and furious.

Another breath of water. And pain. Wrongness and pain, and desperation and wild fury.

The water around me boils as I thrash. Then something is thrashing with me, forcing its way under my arm and across my chest. Another slow flash of purest white dissolves my vision. The world is torn away into darkness.

Hurts.

Hurts, hurts, *hurts*.

It hurts in my chest.

My throat is liquid with fire. I feel the flesh bubble with pain.

Wet. My hair is wet, tangled over my face, clinging to my neck.

My ribs hurt, hurt, *hurt* and a dog is barking above me. Harsh, wet, snarling barks. His voice breaks. He whines. Then barks again. Barks and barks.

And someone is sobbing, and people are shouting, angry and scared.

I'm on my left side and it hurts, hurts, hurts. My ribs hurt. I can't lie on this side. I twist, but something stops me from turning.

The dog growls. Barks and growls. I jerk but cannot turn.

The dog's bark breaks again and he whines.

'Evie,' someone says. A man. 'Evie, can you hear me?

Evie, squeeze my hand if you can hear me.' The calm, low, cautious tone makes no impact on the dog's barking.

'Evie, squeeze my hand. Come on, squeeze my hand.'

There's something warm around my fingers. Something warm holding my hand. But my ribs hurt, hurt, *hurt* and there's something stopping me from turning.

Have to turn. Hurts. Have to turn. I start pushing, flailing, thrashing against the thing stopping me from turning. The dog is whining, high and shrill, whining and then barking, whining then barking.

The thing that won't let me turn presses me down. I kick and scratch at it, twisting on the cold, wet ground. Suddenly there is give and I throw myself at it, wrench round on to my back and then curl on to my right side.

Relief. Oh, *relief.*

I shudder as the dirty, bloodstain pain vibrates through my bones, through the ribs still holding my chest together.

Something warm encompasses my fingers once again.

'Evie. Evie, if you can hear me, I really need you to squeeze my hand.'

I curl my fingers towards my palm.

'That's great, Evie. That's really good. Now squeeze my hand again, just like that. Good girl. That's really good.'

Something soft is draped over me. A hand strokes my hair off my face, then rests gently on the back of my head before moving to squeeze my shoulder.

'Evie, can you tell me if your head hurts?'

The pain in my ribs is fading, fading. I'm cold. I'm really cold. The dog is barking more quietly now. A little burst, then silence. Then another. A shiver drifts through me.

'Evie, did you hit your head when you fell? Can you nod your head yes or no for me?'

Did I hit my head?

The question echoes through my brain. *When did I fall?*

The world whirls around me as if I am weightless once more. The air and the floor wrench at me from every direction . . .

And then it's gone: everything is still and clear and normal.

And I am lying on my side in a thin layer of water over tile.

I'm lying by the edge of the pool. Somehow I fell in the pool. Somehow I fell in the pool and someone fished me out. They fished me out and put me on my bad side. They put me on my bad side and . . . I was coughing. Of course there wasn't a dog. It was just me, coughing. I breathed in the water . . .

'Evie? Evie, can you squeeze my hand if your head hurts?'

I roll my head so I can look up at the person bending over me. My vision wavers as my eyes water with the pain in my throat, in my chest.

'Hi,' I say. It comes out with a little hiccup-cough in the middle.

'Hey there, Evie,' the man says, smiling down at me. 'How's your head?'

Did I hit my head? I don't know. I don't remember. It hurts, but whether it hurts from choking up half the pool, from passing out with the pain, or from hitting the edge when I fell, I can't tell – and don't care. Next to the pain in my ribs . . .

'Evie?' the man – a lifeguard, I realise – prompts.

''S OK,' I get out, blinking away fresh tears at the pain in my throat as I hold down the need to cough. *Mustn't cough again. Mustn't. Mustn't ever cough like that again.* 'Co-*old*,' I say.

The lifeguard grins and pulls the towel tighter around me, rubbing my shoulder. 'You've been wriggling around quite a bit, so I think we can rule out spinal injury or anything like that. How do you feel about sitting up a bit so we can try to get you wrapped up a bit better?'

'Let-me-do-it!' I rush out. 'Don't touch.'

The lifeguard frowns.

'Had an . . . operation. Know how to move so . . . so it doesn't hurt,' I warn him around more of those nasty, barking hiccup-coughs.

The lifeguard's smile returns. He sits back on his heels, raising his hands, though he watches me closely.

I keep my breathing light and shallow, panting to lessen the pain as I press my hand across my ribs to brace the gap between the bones. I lever myself up on to my elbow, wriggling so I can twist my legs to the side and use their strength to help me push upwards. Then I draw my knees up to take the pressure off my chest, reducing the ache of the scar and the pull of the bone-ends against the skin. Dr Barstow said that they filed the ends of the bones down on either side of the broken bit so it's not exactly sharp, but there's just not meant to be an end there, blunt or not. Even rounded, it still pokes the skin awkwardly when I bend to the left.

I hunch over my knees, tucking my left arm to my side. The pain is stretched taut across my ribs, up over my shoulder, into my neck and down my arm. As if someone has poured acid on to my shoulder and let it trickle down my arm, under my elbow and along the side of my forearm, fizzing on to the side of my palm and the two smallest fingers. I wish I could double over the pain but I can't curl any further without the bone-ends in my ribcage stretching the healing skin around the scar.

The pain is different now: sharp and immediate, clean. But the dull, dirty pain of the damaged bones is there underneath, grinding: as if the broken ends are still grating against each other inside. The pain ebbs and flows from my ribs through my arm into my fingers. The muscles in my back and neck are locked tight, trying to contain the pain but only making it worse, adding the rope-burn sting of tired muscles. One type of pain layers over another. And my fingers burn with acid. I raise my hand to check that they're not dissolving with the pain.

Through the curtain of my hair, I see Lynne and Phee huddled together. Jenny's mum is standing next to them, white-faced, her arm around about Phee's heaving shoulders. Lynne's mascara has run. A line of snot glints, oozing down to the curve of her lip. Her tongue darts out to lick it away. She smears the rest across her face with her hand.

Behind them, most of our year are hovering, staring at me.

Jenny's mum keeps sniffing. Sniffing and apologising. Well, sometimes apologising. Mostly she just keeps going on and on about the fact that she 'wasn't to know Sonny Rawlins would do something as reckless' as pushing me in the pool, how 'he'd always seemed a bit troubled' but she'd 'never thought he'd take his bullying to a physical level with a girl' and how she *couldn't* have known that she shouldn't have let Jenny invite him . . .

I am almost grateful for the regular interruptions from the doctors and nurses who've bundled me into a hospital gown and wrapped me in blankets. X-rayed me and listened to my chest. Checked my blood pressure and my temperature. And asked me a full million questions about what hurts, and where, and how much.

Through it all, Jenny's mum has paced back and forth wringing her hands – literally wringing her hands – and saying that she doesn't know what she is going to tell Amy when she arrives.

I suppose I should be grateful that she is in such a state: she hasn't even noticed all the times I've ignored or deflected the curious questions of the nurses and doctors about how exactly I'd managed to injure my ribs that way. Paul and I agreed a while back that consultants have to know, but that doctors and nurses don't. They need to know what is wrong but satisfying their idle curiosity about how my ribcage ended up in pieces isn't necessary: it doesn't make a blind bit of difference to their ability to look after me.

I tap the oxygen monitor clipped over my index finger against the mattress and blow out a heavy sigh.

'Shall I get you something to eat, Evie? How about another cup of hot chocolate?'

The first cup was grey and grainy with sugar: they'd said the sugar would help the shock wear off and the heat would bring my temperature back up to normal. But they had all agreed that my lungs were clear, my ribs didn't seem to be injured any further, and that I wasn't hypothermic or anything else.

A woman in one of the other A & E beds sets up a steady groaning. My fingers twitch with the urge to go over and tell her to shut up. No one groans like that when they're in the throes of agony. Each of these groans is perfectly crafted: a row of fat little clichés.

'Oh dear,' says Jenny's mother, practising her

hand-wringing some more. 'Oh, oh, do you think I should go and find a nurse?'

I close my eyes and breathe rhythmically. Maybe Jenny is adopted too because I kind of always figured that women who'd had kids knew all about proper pain, but Jenny's mum is oblivious to the fact that the groaning woman needs to be reminded of the story of the boy who cried wolf.

I listen to the sounds of the ward, thankful that it's only lunchtime. When I fell off my bike a year ago, and Amy and Paul insisted we come to the hospital to check that my melon-sized ankle wasn't broken, it was evening, so my first experience of A & E was that it was full of drunk people yelling, screaming, sobbing. Not to mention all the drunk friends and relatives who were also yelling, screaming and sobbing. It's a relief that today the biggest problem is the fussers. I'm coming round to the conclusion that it's kind of nice to be taken to the hospital, even if I don't need to be here. A nice change from cleaning myself up in the bathroom and then making sure I didn't gasp or moan no matter how much my ribs hurt when I had to pick up my school backpack the next morning.

A nurse turns up to deal with the groaner. There are some hiccupy tears. Then someone comes fast-marching down the ward, the way Amy does when she's really stressed.

'It's just this one here. We closed the curtains to ...' someone says.

The rest is lost in the angry whoosh as the curtains are ripped open.

'Evie,' Amy says.

Just 'Evie'. She looks me up and down in the time it takes to step up to the edge of the bed. One hand cups my cheek and the other strokes my hair as she presses a fierce kiss to my forehead. 'What have they given you for the pain?'

'Codeine. I asked for . . .'

Amy kisses my forehead again, already turning to the nurse. 'My daughter needs a prescription for some Oramorph to take home with us. A hundred-millilitre bottle will do.'

The nurse makes a face that she clearly thinks is sympathetic and apologetic. 'Well, we do prefer to avoid giving morphine to adolescents unless there's a serious injury. You see . . .'

'My daughter is recovering from chest surgery. She's got a three-inch gap in her ribcage, fresh scarring and bones that haven't finished healing, so you'd better not think to tell me that getting shoved into a pool, having to be fished out by a lifeguard and coughing her lungs out to expel all the water she breathed in doesn't require some decent pain relief. I want to speak to the duty doctor as soon as she's available. In the meantime, you go and tell her that my daughter needs some pain relief that will actually *relieve* her pain.'

The nurse pulls a different face (this one is not in the

least apologetic) and stomps off.

'Oh Amy,' says Jenny's mum, showing off her freshly honed hand-wringing skills. 'Oh Amy, I'm so sorry about all this. I never dreamt . . .'

'Thanks for coming to the hospital with Evie, Janet,' Amy interrupts. 'But please could you be quiet and give me a few minutes to see how my daughter is.'

Jenny's mother's mouth actually falls open. I know how she feels. She mumbles something completely inarticulate and goes away. Amy has eased herself on to the edge of the bed on my right side even before Jenny's mum is gone. One hand is now gently massaging the knots around my left shoulder blade, while the other continues to stroke my hair.

'Have they said anything about the water you swallowed?' Amy asks.

'They keep fussing because they don't understand my ribs, but I'm fine. Just . . .' I cut myself off. I don't want to think about how humiliated I am, about what everyone will be saying back at the party, let alone what they'll all say at school on Monday.

Amy tilts my face up gently and looks into my eyes. She stops stroking my hair long enough to rummage in her handbag.

'I brought your dragon,' she says.

And just like that my eyes flood with tears and the pain in my chest is solid and heavy.

'Oh, Evie, I thought you might like . . .'

'*Want*,' I gasp, having to force so hard to get the word out around the pain that my voice goes all squashed. I am grabbing for the little pot with the yellow lid before Amy has even drawn it fully out of the bag. I let her adjust me so that I'm sitting back against her chest and her arms are around me and because it's Amy I don't have to remind her to keep her left arm high so it doesn't press against my rib.

I fumble the Dragon out of the pot and push it against my breastbone. It's a lovely clean pain, sharp and fresh as tea with lemon. I pant through the urge to cry: shallow little puffs against the pain in my ribs and the other pain in the middle of my chest, like terror and fury and hurt all fused together.

'Blue pill,' I grit out, knowing that Amy will have one with her: she always carries a little box with some of my painkillers and blue pills just in case.

'We need to ask the doctor, Evie.'

Without intending to, I make a sharp high noise in the back of my throat. That's what agony sounds like, I think, my head twitching in the direction of the groaner.

Amy kisses the side of my head as she gropes one-handed in her bag for the pillbox. She flicks the box's catch up and the moment she shakes the contents out on to my palm, I cram the little powder-blue oblong into my mouth. Dry-swallowing it makes me cough but Amy pats my back in just the right way, in just the right place to stop the cough without hurting my ribs. Once I've tipped the remaining pills back into the box and she's put it away again in her bag, she goes back to kneading the muscles in my shoulder without my needing to ask.

'There was a crooked man,' she whispers, breath warm against my hair.

'And he . . . he walked a crooked mile,' I gasp. 'He found a crooked sixpence . . . Upon a cr-crooked stile.'

The Dragon is safe in my hand and I fix an image of it in the front of my mind, painting the words of the nursery rhyme beneath, not letting the other things creep in from the sides.

The curtain rustles and my eyes open before I think to stop them, but it's just a draught.

'He had a crooked cat,' Amy says.

The room is all distorted in ways I can't put my finger on. And there are things at the edges of my vision. Like wisps of curtain or cobweb. And I know that there are pictures on them, like the web that the Lady of Shalott wove.

'He had a crooked cat,' Amy says again.

'And it . . . it caught . . . it caught a crooked, a crooked mouse.'

Amy kisses my hair.

The rhyme is like the Lady's weaving. If I stop, if I let myself look at those things in the corner, I'll call down the curse: the web will float wide and engulf me, dragging me down into those pictures. Because I know that they're pictures of Fiona, and her parents, and their house: real things that aren't real any more. They're just fragments now, hovering ghosts, making the room grow cold.

'And they all lived together in a little crooked house.'

'A little crooked house,' I echo, squeezing my eyes closed. 'A little crooked house.'

'There was a crooked man,' Amy whispers into my hair, soft and gentle and patient. 'And he walked a crooked mile.'

Over and over we go: the crooked man in his crooked world. And then slowly, slowly the room warms. It begins to bob very slightly, dipping gently from side to side, as if we're on water. In a boat on the water.

I sigh, feel Amy's hot breath in my hair as she does too.

The cold and fear and fury in my chest are being put to sleep. Their claws no longer dig into my heart and lungs. They have stopped snarling and writhing in my chest. It's all growing quiet and calm.

I open my eyes and watch the room rock me gently. There's nothing in the corners now. They're just blurred and misty: my field of vision is narrowed down, all the edges blunted. I blink around a yawn: my eyelids sink lazily, rise reluctantly, like Lynne chasing after a netball when it gets knocked out of bounds. Bounds? Is that the right word for netball? Out ... When it gets knocked out ...

I sigh and yawn again.

'How're your ribs feeling?' Amy asks.

Another yawn. ''S OK. Don't care any more.'

I love the blue pills. Dr Barstow suggested them. My GP wasn't sure but agreed to let me try them and they're the best thing ever. They're only for emergencies, so I don't take them very often. Just when I can't stand it. When everything slips sideways as if I've fallen into a nightmare without ever falling asleep and it's like being dragged down a rabbit hole by a rabbit that's all black and snarling, red eyes and sharp teeth and claws . . . The blue pills push the world away a few steps, let me float beyond it for a while.

I know my ribs hurt, but the pain is a few paces off to the side. It doesn't bother me there.

I should be huddled, shivering, on the edge of the playing field, with Lynne and Phee getting told off for ignoring the ball and coming over to chat to me. I should be splitting my attention between the desultory lacrosse game and my stupid pencil case, the shivering making me even clumsier with the big needle than usual until I end up accidentally shoving it halfway down under one of my fingernails and give up. But I'm not sitting there, biting my hair, wishing that Phee and Lynne would come over to distract me. Instead, I'm in the headmistress's office with Amy and Paul, waiting for Mrs Henderson to finish her business in the anteroom with her secretary, so that we can talk about Sonny Rawlins.

It's the perfect opportunity to focus on how much I hate him: it's probably the one time when no one would fault me for thinking of nothing else. But for some reason even *I* can't put my finger on, I am not cooperating with Amy's attempts to make his life as miserable as possible.

I try to concentrate on making out Mrs Henderson's voice from behind the office door, but there are too many other people talking out there and, in any case, I don't really care what she's got to say. Paul shifts with a sigh and rubs at the bridge of his nose. Amy glares at him, then sets about arranging her skirt over her knees in little pleats. Paul heaves in a deep breath as if he's going to sigh again, then makes a face and lets his breath out silently.

Amy, Paul and I are fed up with each other. Amy wants to show me that they're ready to stick up for me and not let anyone else get away with hurting me. I get it. I really do. And I appreciate it. I really, really do, but … But I'm not quite sure what. Just *but*. Maybe it has something to do with the fact that it's Amy who's baying for blood, while Paul seems oddly unwilling to rock the boat at school by bringing in the police or lawyers. So Amy's cross with Paul, while I'm openly cross with Amy for pushing and less openly cross with Paul because he's not.

I'm actually looking forward to talking it over tonight with Ms Winters: maybe she'll be able to help me figure it out, provided she's done apologising, that is. She came over the day after the thing at the pool, all distraught that she'd somehow ignored hints that something like this would happen ... But I was so matter-of-fact about how even I hadn't ever expected Sonny Rawlins to do more than pinch me in the corridor that the weird spots of colour in her cheeks faded away and she went all normal again. Then Amy made us each a huge mug of hot chocolate and she stayed to play Cluedo with us for an hour.

But I was being funny about the whole thing even then: when Ms Winters swore she would make sure Mrs Henderson understood that the thing at the pool wasn't a one-off, I told her not to. She thought it was because I didn't want her to say anything about what we talk about together, but that's not it. Or not really. It's all part of how upside-down I am – how upside-down we all are – about what happened.

I mean, I get that this thing about Sonny Rawlins is all mixed up in my mind with Fiona and her parents, not just for me but for Amy and Paul too. I get it, but I don't get quite why I don't want there to be a big fuss about what Sonny Rawlins did. Maybe it's partly because the whispering that follows me about school is bad enough already, let alone the fact that people from other years have started coming up to ask me whether Sonny Rawlins has been arrested and whether I'm going to testify at the trial. But that's not really it.

Amy said we should go to the police and press charges and everything. Not that Sonny Rawlins would go to prison or anything, but it still wouldn't be much fun for him. Only I hate talking to the police. I get all the stuff Uncle Ben told me about the fact that it's their job to explore whether what you say will hold up in court, but they're not very nice about it. The woman who took my statement about Fiona and her parents was awful. I hate her ten times more than I could ever hate Sonny Rawlins. She wouldn't let me talk around things. And then she wrote up everything I said with about seven billion spelling mistakes and no grammar. All those things she'd made me say that I'd never said out loud before ... that I never would have said out loud, not to anyone, ever ... and she wrote them all up with spelling mistakes.

The door clicks open and as Mrs Henderson comes in, crossing to sit behind her desk, I turn my thoughts gratefully from the memories.

Mrs Henderson leans casually back, propping her elbows on the arms of her chair and steepling her fingers together. 'Sorry about that,' she says, smiling, but her fingers collapse down into a white-knuckled grip. I miss what she says next in the hope that she'll turn her hands over and do 'and here's all the people', fingers waving like centipede legs when you accidentally tip one over lifting a garden stone to see what's lurking underneath.

'Evie?' Amy prompts, and I realise they're all waiting for a response to a question I didn't hear.

Mrs Henderson sighs, pushing her hands back into the steeple position, and I wonder if this is an unconscious attempt to pray for patience. 'What do you think we should do, Evie?'

What does she expect me to say? 'Please could you boil him in oil?' Perhaps they think they're giving me an opportunity to get it out of my system, but I don't want to get angry if all they're going to do is *listen*. And I'm not going to give them the chance to try to talk me round to whatever it is they've already decided to do.

'I think Sonny Rawlins is a rotten bully, but he probably did just mean to push me in, like you'd push anyone else. And he might have known it would hurt me a bit more, but I don't think he realised what would happen,' I say, though I don't understand why. I'd quite like Sonny Rawlins to drop dead in a ditch after all.

'Well, Evie, that's a very mature perspective on things,' Mrs Henderson says. The long, polished nails on her right hand slide under the long, polished nails on her left.

'We all know Evie's very mature,' Amy snaps. Paul leans over, as if to take one of her hands, but she shifts away from him, shoving them into her pockets.

'I'm very pleased to see that you understand Sonny's motivation, Evie,' Mrs Henderson says quickly, and slightly too loudly, 'but you didn't tell me what you thought about his punishment.'

I shrug, keeping my gaze fixed on her hands. Her fingers have been scratching reflexively at a mark on her folder. Now a little piece of polish flakes away. The muscles in her cheek work as she glares down at the ragged patch of yellow showing through the white polish painted on to the tip of the nail.

I feel my lip curve with the urge to sneer, but manage to keep my voice neutral. 'Amy and Paul said that because the thing at the pool didn't happen in school time, it's difficult for you to punish him for it directly so you have to treat it in terms of ongoing bullying at school that's spilled over. They said you *can* suspend him for two weeks for that at least.'

'And you think that's a good idea.' A statement, not a question.

Which is just as well, as I'm not at all sure what I think. It'll make everyone talk at school and of course some people are already saying that it's not Sonny Rawlins's fault that I'm such a wimp, while others think I was just making a fuss to get attention. The last thing I need is for Sonny Rawlins or his horrid little friends to take to shoving me in the school corridors every chance they get: the thing at the pool was humiliation enough for a couple of lifetimes. I don't need to do an encore performance of passing out in the hall with the whole school looking on.

When I see her later, Ms Winters will probably ask me if I'm afraid of Sonny Rawlins now. And I want to say no but it's not that simple. I'm not afraid of him in the sense that I know he can't get away with seriously hurting me – isn't getting away with it, at least not completely, even now – and he won't bother to try unless he thinks it won't come back on him. But he could still make my life miserable.

No, the thing I'm afraid of is something to do with wanting him to be at least as miserable as he's made me and, ideally, more. That's part of it. But it's also something to do with wanting him to be afraid of me: something to do with how unfair it is that the only payback I'm allowed is this stupid suspension or making myself miserable by going back to the police.

It's all bound up with how angry, angry, angry I am that I never get to hurt anyone half as much as they hurt me. Except just that once. The tang of the memory warms me from the inside out, like heat in my veins. It was nice to be powerful. About the nicest thing I've ever felt. How I'd love to show Sonny Rawlins just how powerful I can be.

'Will a suspension make any difference to him later on?' I ask. 'Like for applying to uni?'

'Well, these things never look good,' Mrs Henderson says, but her eyes move past me and she doesn't look at Amy at all.

'They most certainly wouldn't if we decided to pursue things via the police,' Amy says.

Mrs Henderson's lips thin into an apologetic line. 'Yes, I can see that might be an attractive option, but I doubt it will make any great difference in the end, juvenile records being treated in much the same way as school ones in these regards. I'm not sure the trauma of going down that route . . .'

'As opposed to the trauma of letting the boy who tried to drown my daughter come back to class with her?'

Usually Amy gets loud when she's angry, but today she's quiet. Quiet and cold.

'He didn't try to drown me,' I say. 'He's horrible, but he's just normal horrible, Amy.'

Amy's gaze is anguished. 'It's not right,' she says and there's a quiver in her voice.

'I'm sure that what your husband proposed the other evening about getting Sonny's parents to arrange some counselling involving anger management therapy would be a far more productive avenue to pursue.'

'And less messy,' Amy adds acidly.

'Yes,' Mrs Henderson says, suddenly sharp. 'It would be *much* less messy. For everyone. You won't get anywhere with the police. Which is not to say that I don't see where you're coming from,' she adds quickly, holding up a hand, though Amy hasn't made any move to interrupt, 'or that I won't push as much as I can with Sonny's parents. They will, I am sure, be *most* unhappy to realise that the agreement the four of us reach here is not open for debate. Not unless they want to test my willingness to consider something more serious than a short suspension. And that's not the sort of trouble they'll want to invite.' Mrs Henderson is looking at me, and I'm surprised by what I see in her gaze now. 'It's better than nothing,' she tells me. And this time the apology is sincere.

And so is my smile. I like the idea of Mrs Henderson blackmailing Sonny Rawlins and his parents because I know that making Sonny Rawlins pay – really pay – will ruin things, even though it's wrong that that's the way things are. It's wrong that some people get away with things and other people have to hold themselves in because they know they won't.

But even though I've got Amy and Paul and Uncle Ben now, and that's too much to risk losing, I'm afraid that one day all that unfairness will spill over, spill out and all I'll be able to think of is how the things I've got to lose stop me being free. Stop me being powerful. Stop me *making* things fair.

Usually Amy would tell me stuff about 'an eye for an eye making us all blind' and I know Gandhi said it and it was a smart thing to say if we want the world to be a good place. Only it doesn't feel like that. And the worst bit is that I know that if I *did* make Sonny Rawlins pay, he'd never dare to even *look* at me wrong again. It wouldn't be like the time with the flowers, or the cigarettes, or every other little thing since, when my pushing back against his attempts to hurt me have only made him try harder. It wouldn't just be a little victory in the moment, making sure his hatefulness backfires – *Yes, I know what these flowers are called*. No, if I ever really made him pay, that would be the end of it.

'Ms Winters has volunteered to keep a particularly close eye on things when Sonny comes back to school, so hopefully that will help Evie feel more secure,' Mrs Henderson is saying when I tune back into the conversation, 'and I have every confidence that that will do the trick to keep him in line. Now, was there anything else you wanted to discuss, Evie?'

Paul puts his hand on my shoulder and squeezes, but when I turn to Amy, her face is still full of anger and frustration.

'No,' I say. 'There's nothing else.' I don't listen to Mrs Henderson's parting words.

By then it's the end of the day so, after passing by the classroom to pick up my stuff, we head home. In the car, Amy glares into the window, while Paul's fingers jitter and drum against the wheel.

Amy is out of the car as soon as Paul parks. He pulls a face and sighs.

When we sidle into the kitchen together, Amy is slamming cupboards open, wrenching the drawers out so roughly that the cutlery jangles discordantly. A fork falls, hits the floor at a strange angle and ricochets back into the air, then clatters a drumroll against the tiles as if fighting to stay airborne. When it has stilled, I look up to find Amy standing braced over the sink.

'I'm sorry, Evie.' Her voice is hoarse.

'It's OK,' I whisper. I swallow and try again, louder. 'It's OK.'

Amy shakes her head, but doesn't turn.

Paul moves to touch her arm, but she steps away from him, hands raking through her hair. 'I know you think I'm not pushing,' Paul says, his voice tight, 'but Evie's got enough to deal with without a pointless battle.'

'It's not pointless, Paul,' Amy hisses, still not looking at either of us.

'Yes,' Paul says as I take a quiet step towards the door, 'it is.'

'It's not pointless just because we can't win,' Amy whispers. I take another step. 'Sometimes people need to fight, Paul. We can't always just give in.'

'And which battle should we fight?' Paul demands suddenly. 'The little one we can't win or the big one? Which unwinnable battle should we make Evie fight, given that she'll have to do most of the work? What type of losing is going to make her feel better?'

I turn and leave them to it, though they fall silent as I make my way upstairs.

'There are better things to spend our energies on,' I hear Paul say as I reach the top of the steps. 'There's more than one way to get where we need to be, Amy.'

I curl up in bed with a book, but I don't even manage to turn one page before Amy, eyes rather red, comes to fetch me for dinner an hour later. It's a quiet meal, though the tension that has haunted the week seems to have gone for now.

Amy goes to bed early, while Paul and I stay up to watch a movie. Only neither of us watches. Instead, I watch Paul as he stares blankly at the TV, wondering if we're both thinking about the same thing: other ways of getting even and those night-time adventures he keeps having with Uncle Ben.

And that's when I realise what my 'but' is: why I'm with Paul rather than Amy on the whole Sonny Rawlins thing. Although I'm glad they would if I asked them to, I don't want Paul and Amy fighting this battle for me because they don't understand how much I want Sonny Rawlins to pay. They'd never make him sorry enough. They just don't have it in them.

And I love them for it. I love that they don't know how wonderful, and terrible, it is to be powerful. I couldn't bear for them to lose that . . . that *innocence* because of me. It wouldn't be right. If it was going to happen, it should have been when Adam and Aunt Minnie and Nanna Florrie and Grandad Peter died. But it didn't.

And it mustn't happen now, over me. Because if it did, it would mean that Fiona and her parents had taken away some of what makes Paul and Amy and Uncle Ben so different from them: it would be like the worst people I know making the best just a little bit like them.

But Paul doesn't understand that. You can't really, until it's too late.

'What is *with* you this week?' Lynne hisses, kicking my ankle to draw my attention back to the board and the rubbish we're supposed to be copying into our notes. I let my pen drift across the page while I continue fretting over last Friday: the night of the second dark moon since

I wished the Dragon into being.

Even though the Dragon and I stayed in, I waited up, listening for Paul and Uncle Ben's triumphant return, hurrying to the window the moment I heard movement below in the garden, but Paul was alone. He walked straight to the back door and let himself into the kitchen and that was that.

The next morning, he was irritable over breakfast, slugging his coffee down and taking off early for work. Was he just tired or was he worried about the consequences of his dark moon adventure? Or was he disappointed because their plans had somehow fallen through or, worse yet, because something had gone wrong? I spent the whole weekend brooding over it and I'm still not done.

Lynne kicks me again and I look up to find Mrs Poole staring at me. I blink at her for a moment, receive another kick, and realise I've been asked a question.

'I don't know?' I say. It comes out sounding like a question and I have to resist the urge to flinch in case what Mrs Poole actually asked was something along the lines of 'Do you think pupils who ignore their teachers should get detention?' But Mrs Poole just sighs and turns to Jenny instead.

'Are you sick?' Lynne whispers. 'Do your ribs hurt?'

I shake my head, then sigh and shrug. 'Sort of. A little. Didn't sleep last night.'

'Shall I ask to take you to the nurse?' Lynne offers.

I sigh again. 'No. It's nearly break anyway.'

I try, I really do, but although there are only ten minutes left my thoughts immediately drift back to Paul and Uncle Ben. The only thing I know for certain is that Amy fussed at Paul, first for coming in so late, then for tossing and turning all night (plus he tracked mud into the house: a cardinal sin).

The day grinds past. Phee and Lynne stop bothering to kick my ankles to make me pay attention, realising that it's a lost cause, before we even get to lunchtime. I expect to spend the afternoon lurching from one telling-off to another. Instead the teachers just get this weird, sad look in their eyes and ignore my daydreaming or ask if I need to go and lie down. Even more strangely, no one picks on me about this preferential treatment: no one says anything about the fact that I should be in trouble left, right and centre today, and yet I'm not. Instead, six different classmates tell me they're glad I'm OK and don't have to go back to hospital, or some variation on that theme.

By the time the final bell goes, I'm so confused and baffled that my head hurts.

Usually Amy would be collecting me because Phee has tennis on Mondays so she can't cycle home with me. But, as Lynne is off to her grandmother's tonight and that's just a few streets over from us, Amy said we could walk back together.

We've only just turned the corner from school when Lynne says, 'See: people really *do* like you,' as if she's picking up a conversation that was interrupted earlier. 'You shouldn't always assume the worst.'

'I don't!' I protest, but Lynne loops her arm through mine and says, 'Yes, you do, Evie. Maybe you don't mean to, but you always think that if people are a bit funny it's because they don't like you. You never think that maybe they just don't know quite what to say.'

For a moment, I consider asking 'About what?' but end up not saying anything at all.

When we get to my gate, Lynne surprises me with a hug, throwing her arms tight around me and stroking her hand once down the back of my head. Then she's off down the path before I have the chance to hug back or even call 'See you tomorrow' after her. I stand, watching, waiting for her to turn the corner into her gran's street and wishing she would look back, knowing she won't. But she does, spinning with a grin and a wave. I wave back and then she's gone.

Amy is bustling about upstairs when I let myself in, though she calls down a hello and I call up an 'I'll make some tea.' But first I go to the TV and turn on the news, sitting on the very, very edge of the sofa, leaning forwards . . . But there's nothing. Nothing at all.

When the news cycles back to sport again, I stomp into the kitchen and viciously slap the kettle on, scowling at the fridge as I slump, arms crossed over my chest, against the counter.

Maybe there won't be anything until tomorrow, I tell

myself. All sorts of things can happen and not get found out right away. It might take days, a week . . .

I shiver and push away from the counter, busying myself with getting the mugs down, fetching the milk, spooning out sugar, arranging biscuits on a plate. Telling myself that I can't afford to go on thinking like this: that I can't keep on waiting and hoping and willing for days on end.

I shove the tea-tin lid back on so violently it dents.

Suddenly my eyes are flooded with tears and I'm gripping the counter, shoulders bowed, because I'd been sure, so sure that Paul and Uncle Ben were going to do *something* on their dark moon. Even though I'd tried to tell myself that there were all sorts of explanations for why they kept going out at night, why they have been keeping secrets that for some reason Uncle Ben thinks they should share with me but not Amy . . . All that guilt and worry, all those Friday nights we stayed in, the Dragon and I, all of it wasted.

I whirl away from the counter and go hammering upstairs, slamming the door to my room behind me and throwing myself down on to the bed, careless of the agony I awaken in my ribs.

'Evie? Evie darling, are you OK?' Amy calls.

'Be right there!' I garble out around the tears, cutting my nails into my palm to steady my voice.

I hear Amy's footsteps move away from my door and have to gulp down the sob that escapes before it becomes something louder. Catching up the Dragon, I roll over with my back to the door, face pressed into my pillow.

The Dragon winds itself around my thumb and presses its nose to mine. Through my tears, its outline seems to ripple like dispersing vapour. I don't even know why I feel so awful. Part of me is happy and relieved: it's good that Paul and Uncle Ben haven't done anything that will make them unhappy or get them in trouble. Another part is angry and disappointed and betrayed . . . And another part is breathless. Still full of anticipation, as if the numbness from earlier has somehow passed it by.

I jump as a needle-sharp claw sinks into my finger.

We must not assume anything, the Dragon says. *We must remain vigilant. We do not know what has happened or what is yet to come. We must wait.*

The Dragon's outline wavers once again and suddenly all my confusion over Paul and Uncle Ben – whether they have done something, whether that would be a good thing or a bad, bad, bad one – is gone in a rush of fear that the Dragon will dissolve away in front of me.

I am still here, the Dragon says.

I lie there shaking, staring and staring as if a blink will reveal that there never was any Dragon at all, just my little carved bit of rib.

I am still here, the Dragon repeats.

I draw in a breath and blink without intending to.

The Dragon regards me steadily.

I draw in another breath. And blink.

The Dragon's breath warms my palm.

I am still here, the Dragon says again. *Do you need anything more?*

Another breath. Another blink.

My eyes lock with the Dragon's.

'No,' I say.

The Dragon smiles.

'Evie darling, Lynne and Phee are here to see you,' Amy calls from the hall.

I toss my book aside and gallop downstairs. Paul looks up from the sofa with a smile. 'That keen to escape a Saturday morning with your Aged Ps?'

I grin as I tear around the corner of the sofa, completely ignoring Amy's warning to be careful. Lynne and Phee are standing in the hall, all muffled up, and grinning in deepest satisfaction.

'Look at those smiles,' Uncle Ben says to me. 'There's trouble if I ever saw it. Don't tell us. You've fed Sonny Rawlins cupcakes with rat poison and you want Evie's help to dig a really big hole?'

Lynne wrinkles up her nose.

'I wouldn't bother to bury Sonny Rawlins if I bumped him off,' Phee says.

'Exactly! Why would we want to get all muddy for him?' Lynne adds.

'You're going to lure him to your garage and dissolve him in acid?' Uncle Ben suggests.

'Eeeeew!' Lynne says. 'These are my favourite jeans. I'm not getting acid spatter on my favourite jeans.'

Amy sets about smoothing down my flyaway hair. I bat at her hands and she leaves off with a sigh, trying to summon a smile for my friends.

'We've got a much better idea than anything to do with Sonny Rawlins,' Phee says.

'Yes. Because we're *proactive*,' Lynne adds, savouring the word.

I wonder what she's been reading. Probably her mum's latest self-help bible.

'We're going to take charge of making ourselves happy, instead of letting him make us dwell on being miserable.'

Amy blinks in surprise. 'That's ... That's very sensible, Lynne,' she says.

Phee rolls her eyes. 'It's a lot of psychobabble is what my dad would say.' Lynne elbows her in the side. 'But fun is always a good thing. So we're here to take Evie out to have some. Because we're just the most stellar friends ever.'

'She can come, can't she?' Lynne asks, opening her big green eyes wide and looking soulfully at Amy. 'We promise to look after her, and not walk her off her feet, and to sit down and have a hot drink and something to eat ...'

'My mum's waiting outside to drive us into town *and* she said she'd pick us up when we've had enough, so you don't have to worry about Evie getting jostled about on the bus.'

'Yes, and we promise to bring her back before dinner, when the mov—'

'Shh!' Phee hisses. 'It's meant to be a surprise, you dork.'

'Oh,' says Lynne. 'Anyway, anyway, the thing . . . the thing we're planning to do. I mean, one of the things . . . Well, it'll be over . . .'

'We'll bring Evie back by six o'clock,' Phee interrupts. '*Please*, Amy.'

'Yes, *please*,' echoes Lynne.

'I'll go and get my stuff,' I say, stopping just long enough to kiss Amy's cheek as she rolls her eyes at me.

'Just don't . . . run . . . on the stairs . . .' I hear her call (to absolutely no avail) as I thunder back up to my room for my favourite jacket: the one I keep in my wardrobe to wear at night with the Dragon.

It's one of the best days ever. Uncle Ben slid two twenties – two! – into my pocket before we set off, then Amy gave me another in case we got the munchies. We end up treating ourselves to double burgers, fries *and* onion rings, followed by chocolate fudge cake, despite Lynne's wails of 'I'm going to be so fat tomorrow!' My hamburger is so huge that I wrap half of it up in a napkin and put it in my pocket for later. ('It's too good to leave, but I've *got* to have room for cake,' is my argument, while Phee grins and says, 'It would practically be a sin not to on a girls' day out. I shan't be your friend any more if you don't at least split a piece with me and you can't leave the *cake*.') Then off we go to the cinema (to see something I've been dying to go to for ages but haven't because it's not really Phee and Lynne's sort of thing). We're all high on Pepsi and sweet popcorn (with Lynne grumping 'I'm going to have to diet for a *year*!' at semi-regular intervals) when we leave the cinema and duck back into the shops for that dress that looked so good on Phee but that she really didn't need but . . .

It's all stuff we've done before, of course, just not for a while, because of the ribs. But it's more than that. It's not that I mind doing the things that Phee and Lynne like or that they never do anything I want when we go out together . . . But today is all about what I enjoy. It's all about me. And not for any special reason, like it's my birthday or something, but just because. Just because they want me to be happy.

Outside my house, they both hug me, seemingly without care, but I don't have to remind them not to press on my ribs.

It's a perfect day.

They both twist around in the back seat to wave as Phee's mum drives off, leaving me on the garden path. Amy already has the door open to welcome me home. I stand for a moment, taking in her smile. Right now I am happy and lucky and my ribs don't hurt and the world is wonderful. I walk up the path into a house full of people who love me.

Uncle Ben challenges me and Paul to Monopoly. We gang up on him, but it doesn't help. With defeat in sight, I abandon the game and go into the kitchen to help Amy with dinner. I find her opening what looks like a small cardboard tissue box and taking out something that looks like a plastic bag gone wrong.

'I was just going to call you,' she says. She laughs when she sees me staring dubiously at the things on the table. 'Disposable plastic gloves,' she explains, holding one up by the fingers. 'And no, they're not for dinner. Remember Dr Barstow gave us a prescription for an anaesthetic cream to help with the aches once your wound was healed up? Well, I picked it up this afternoon and the pharmacist said we'd need gloves because the effects are cumulative. I don't think either of us really wants to gradually numb our fingers along with your ribs.'

I pick up the leaflet Amy has spread out on the counter. *Capsaicin cream*, I read, wondering how it's pronounced, as I pull a glove out of the packet and wriggle my hand into it. 'It says it's made from chillies: actual chilli peppers.'

Amy squeezes a little dollop onto the tip of my finger. 'Now, don't get it on the scar itself,' she cautions and we both bite our lips as I rub the cream into my skin. It's disappointingly white for something made from chillies; we exchange a sceptical look as I pull my top back down and start to rinse the glove under the tap.

'Just throw it away, darling,' Amy says. 'There's a

hundred in the box so we might as well start afresh each time, just in case.'

'The leaflet says I need to "apply two or three times per day". I'll do it down here in the mornings, but is it OK if I take some of the gloves upstairs so I can put it on again at night?' I ask, gingerly stretching a fresh glove.

'So long as you're careful, darling,' Amy says.

By the time I return from taking the cream and extra gloves upstairs, the kitchen is glorious with the fragrance of ginger, garlic and spring onions.

'Bruise the lemongrass stalks,' Amy reads, squinting at the recipe book as she passes the packet absently to me.

I take the meat tenderiser to them and bash happily away, breathing in the clean citrus perfume with relish as I reduce the stems to mush (I'm nothing if not thorough when a recipe invites me to crush something).

'That's probably enough, darling,' Amy suggests as she peers down at the spatter on the chopping board.

Her tone heralds a tentative question about what's bothering me and usually this would make me roll my eyes but smile all the same. Today I know I am going to snap instead. I haven't finished obliterating the lemongrass and I don't have any intention of talking about what's really on my mind.

'Ms Winters wants me to think about goals,' I say before Amy can open her mouth.

As I hoped, she looks relieved, taking this to mean I'm just feeling a little pensive, and resumes her chopping, though her eyes flick over to me with every few beats of the knife against the board. 'And what do you think?'

I shrug and slouch against the counter, then sigh and move to start separating the coriander leaves from the stems. 'Today was brilliant. Can I have a goal that I always have really good friends that will do things like this for me?'

Amy smiles. 'That's a very wise goal, Evie.'

I wrinkle my nose, then stop myself from saying something snotty. 'I'm really happy now,' I say. 'I've got you and Paul and Uncle Ben ... and I've got Phee and Lynne. And I came top in history last week and the only thing I'm rubbish at is Mrs Poole's sewing projects and I don't care about that anyway since none of it counts towards my coursework portfolio. I don't really know what I want apart from keeping things the way they are and doing well in my GCSE modules ... until A-levels and university, I mean. But right now ... right now things are good, you know? I've got everything I really want.'

Amy has stopped chopping. I look at her hands, rather than her face, because I know what sort of expression she'll have and it'll just be embarrassing to see it.

'I love you so much, Evie,' Amy says, because Amy says stuff like that. Right out. No mucking about.

I stare at the mushrooms she's just finished slicing. 'I know,' I say because I know that Amy will get what I am really saying.

'Maybe I should develop a yearning for a sports car anyway,' I say. 'Just so I've got something to tell Ms Winters.'

Amy laughs and sets to work on the pak choi.

We have work to do, says the Dragon when I open my eyes in the dark.

The urgency tumbles me out of bed. I am hurrying so much I nearly fall as I rush down the garden wall. I stumble to one knee, locking my fingers into the channels between the bricks and swaying as I struggle not to topple off. The Dragon hisses, a little spitting sound of fear and anger. I kneel there, even when I know I won't fall, panting, letting my heart rate ease. Finally, I rise again, but slowly, wavering with the rush of expended adrenalin. I make my way cautiously down to the ground.

We're silent all the way through the woods, along the towpath and then out on to the street.

It's cloudy tonight, the air heavy with dew. Fallen leaves make the pavements treacherous and slimy.

'Where are we going?' I whisper. 'There's nothing pretty down this way. It's just houses.'

The Dragon does not reply.

We turn down an alley and emerge on to a track along the back of a street of terraced houses. When the Dragon starts to creep down my arm, I stop and stare into a carefully manicured garden with precisely cut flower-beds and neatly trimmed shrubs, and there, leaning carelessly up against the wall of the house, is Sonny Rawlins's shiny new top-of-the-range mountain bike.

It's padlocked to the drainpipe, but honestly – like that's going to stop anyone. I mean, I don't padlock my bike, but then no one can see into our garden because of the trees. And even if they could, I keep my bike hidden in the gap between the shed and the fence. But of course Sonny Rawlins would want *his* bike on display.

'What are we doing here?' I hiss at the Dragon, as it seats itself regally in my palm.

You have meat in your pocket, says the Dragon.

I stare stupidly into the smug, upturned face.

Take the meat out of your pocket, the Dragon insists.

I reach into the left pocket of my jacket, then the right, before realising what the Dragon is talking about: I'd completely forgotten about the half-eaten hamburger from yesterday.

I take it out wonderingly, nonplussed at the thought that dragons might like hamburger as much as humans. Somehow I'd never imagined that. Grimacing at the stale bread and the slightly grey cast to the meat, I fumble the napkin open one-handed so that I don't have to upset the Dragon's comfortable position, but the Dragon leaps from one palm to the other ... and starts to tear into the hamburger: squeezing the day-old meat between its talons, coating its feet and legs and tail with it.

You will help me to wash later, the Dragon tells me, conveying serious disgust.

I just stare.

Now put the rest away.

Then the Dragon gathers its haunches, wriggling like a cat does just before it pounces, and launches itself into the air. It alights neatly on the back tyre of Sonny Rawlins's bike.

I stand frozen by the garden gate. I daren't call the Dragon back, but neither do I dare to climb over the gate to join it.

The Dragon turns to regard me solemnly, chest pushed out proudly. Then it smiles a smile full of needle-sharp teeth . . . and sinks them into the tyre. And again. And again. Then the front tyre. Then it swarms up to the handlebars, needle-sharp claws clicking softly on the metal as it scratches through the paintwork. It sinks its teeth into the brake-line before climbing on to the gearbox and fishing about in one of the little openings, just like Phee's cat did the time it brought a mouse into the house then let it go and it ran under the piano.

'Quick, quick . . . Let's go. Let's go,' I whisper to myself, my blood thrumming so hard and fast that I have to hold on to the gate to keep my balance.

The Dragon extracts its claws from the gearbox, takes a moment to sink its teeth into a cable emerging from the box. Then, before I realise it's all over, the Dragon is sailing back towards me.

But suddenly it is changing direction, diving on to a black rubbish bag scrunched down beside one of those grey-green wheelie bins. I watch the Dragon tear into the bag, tear and tear until the ground is littered with little scraps of black plastic and rubbish.

Finally, the Dragon comes soaring towards me again. I reach out my hand. As soon as the Dragon's claws touch my fingertips, I am running, running back down the track to the alley and out on to the street. But I have to stop before I've gone more than a hundred paces. I turn into another little snicket and gasp for breath. The Dragon scrambles on to my shoulder while I press my fist against my chest and try to make my breaths shallow. Bile floods into my mouth and I have to cough, cough and spit on to the ground against the urge to throw up.

It is too soon to be running, the Dragon says solemnly. *In any case, there is no need. That also is part of our contract. I shall not put you in any true danger.*

I want to ask what contract the Dragon keeps talking about, because I don't remember agreeing to anything, but I am finally getting control of the nausea and don't want to risk setting it off again by speaking just yet.

We will go down to the river, the Dragon says. *Tonight's venture has been most successful. Now you must grow calm again so that you may sleep.*

There are bats out tonight: jagged little shadows darting through the air above the riverbank, diving around like swallows. We sit on the edge of the tumbledown wall along our section of the canal and stare at the sluggish water. Suddenly there is a flurry of movement and the bats dive away.

A fox emerges from the reeds on the far bank. He turns to regard me and I almost think he winks at me. Perhaps he would grin too if not for the sad little vole hanging from his mouth. The fox pads off into the brambles.

There, says the Dragon. *When you hunt wisely, there is no need to run afterwards.*

'The fox wouldn't need to run anyway,' I counter, rubbing grumpily at the ache in my chest. 'It's so much bigger and stronger than everything else on the riverbank.'

It would not matter against a mink, boiling black and frenzied, attacking from behind. Mink are not so large, but they are savage creatures. And they are also very cunning. They plan and follow and wait. They have all the determination in the world.

'You think I shouldn't have needed you to get back at Sonny Rawlins,' I sigh.

The Dragon sinks its claws into my thigh. *No!*

It's not an exclamation or a protest, not a shout, but there is something urgent and intense in the word.

I stare down into the Dragon's eyes, reflecting the night mist above the river so that the blackness of the huge pupils seems to swirl like oil on dark water.

I am your Protector, says the Dragon. *That is the heart of our contract. I have come to you so that you will be free.*

I rub at the bridge of my nose. In the wake of the running, I'm getting a horrible headache. 'I don't understand what you're talking about. What contract? Free from what?' I snap.

You wished *me*, the Dragon says. *You made a contract when you wished me just as I am: a small wish for such a powerful token. Neither more than you needed nor less.*

I suppose it's natural that dragons talk in riddles. Just like it's a relief to know that they don't actually like day-old hamburger: it wouldn't be very dragonly. But the whole 'riddle me this' thing is very annoying sometimes.

'I don't *understand*,' I say.

The Dragon regards me steadily. *That, too, is part of the contract.*

I roll my eyes skywards and blow out a sigh that turns into a cough that kicks my headache up to migraine proportions. 'I give up.'

The Dragon smiles – mysteriously, of course. *We will return now.*

Back in my room, I tuck my clothes and shoes into the back of the closet before creeping out to the bathroom. I help the Dragon to clean itself, then fumble around for paracetamol. There's a soft knock on the door.

'Evie darling, are you feeling all right?'

'Sorry I woke you,' I whisper, opening the door. 'It's just a headache. I can't find the paracetamol.'

Amy brushes my hair away from my eyes, then feels my forehead, frowning. 'You're like ice, Evie. Are you sure you're all right? There's nothing wrong with the radiator in your room, is there?'

I blink at her for a moment. 'I put my head out of the window for a while,' I say. 'I thought the cold would help with the headache.'

'Oh, Evie,' Amy sighs, handing me the paracetamol then ushering me back to my room. 'You'll give yourself pneumonia and that's *not* going to help.'

I let Amy fuss with the bedclothes as I swallow the pills.

'Shall I leave your stereo off if you've got such a bad headache, darling?'

'Hm? Oh. No, it's fine. I'd like it now,' I say.

Amy smiles, kisses my forehead and clicks the stereo to play.

I watch the angle of light from the door diminish then vanish, as she eases it to, before I roll over, taking the Dragon out of my pocket and setting it on my nightstand. From the corner of my eye, as I squirm to get comfy, I see the Dragon settle down, tail neatly curled over out-turned feet. Something about the pose says 'lesson time' and I sigh, but it quickly turns into a yawn.

You must clean your shoes, the Dragon commands.

'It can wait,' I mumble around a second yawn, closing my eyes.

No, says the Dragon.

I turn my face away and sink into the pillow.

No, says the Dragon again. *It cannot wait. Not tonight. Nor any night. You must always remember to clean your shoes when there is no frost. There must be no exceptions. It must be as automatic as breathing.*

I long to scoff at the ridiculousness of this statement. Nothing about our night-time adventures is even remotely automatic. How could it possibly be?

You must be able to do all these things, remember all these things, even in your sleep.

I manage a faint snort, but am too warm and sleepy to vocalise my disdain.

No, commands the Dragon. *You asked once what I am here to teach you.*

I sigh and sit up in bed, scrubbing wearily at my eyes. 'You're here to teach me to clean my shoes when I'm half asleep?' I mumble scornfully.

Yes, says the Dragon. *Yes, that is part of it.*

I stare down at the headstone as Amy puts her arm about my shoulders and hugs me close to her. I can feel her trembling. Paul is on Amy's other side, his arm about her waist. She has already laid the flowers on the grave, cleaned away the bird-muck and bits of dried cut grass, though there was surprisingly little this year. I suspect from the look Uncle Ben cast in Amy's direction as she set to work that he had something to do with this.

Now Paul and I have finished pulling out the weeds and deadheading the winter pansies and, like every year,

Amy is telling Adam about everything that has been happening in our lives since our last visit.

Uncle Ben is standing a few steps away, midway between Adam's grave and Aunt Minnie's. I helped weed that one too since Adam's was already so tidy. Besides, I'm worried about Uncle Ben. Usually he stays over on the night before the anniversary of the deaths, just like on his and Aunt Minnie's wedding anniversary, but last night he went home again once Amy had gone to bed. He didn't even come back for breakfast but met us here, at the graveyard. He seemed normal enough, greeting Amy with a smile and a big hug and lots of reassurances about inconvenient problems at work.

But he keeps cleaning his glasses. Amy hasn't noticed – not surprising, given what day it is – but she knows as well as I do that he only does that when he's told a fib. I just can't figure out what he might need to lie about. He doesn't look like he's been crying. And he doesn't smell like he's been drinking.

Amy fretted us half crazy this morning until she clapped eyes on him and could see he was OK. Paul was tense too, but thankfully he goes quiet and stiff when he's worried, so no one hurled any cereal about the kitchen. The really weird thing is that Paul relaxed as soon as we stepped into the graveyard, before we even saw Uncle Ben. I wonder for a moment, as Amy tells Adam about my getting top marks in history, if it was because he'd seen Uncle Ben's car in the car park and figured he must be all right. But that's not it: when Amy pointed the car out, Paul didn't relax at all. Just took out his phone as if checking for messages.

Now I study them each in turn, but the only interesting thing is that, once, Paul catches Uncle Ben's eye and inclines his head very slightly, smiling. Uncle Ben smiles back, then carries on pruning Aunt Minnie's ballerina rose. And that is it.

I don't get it. I mean, of course Uncle Ben's not going to be himself today – I don't expect any of them to be – but this is the third anniversary I've been around for and I don't see what's different about it. Or why Amy doesn't think it's different too. Because she doesn't. I can tell she doesn't. She is exactly the same this year as she's been every year so far.

Once Amy has finished talking to Adam, we set to work on Nanna Florrie and Grandad Peter's graves. Again, there's amazingly little to do. About the only thing I find as I pick a few stems of dry grass off the face of the stone is a few strange little flecks of bright blue stuff, like paint, in the curve of the 'P' and the plinth of the 'T'. I scratch it out with my nail, watch it drift down to join other tiny spots of green and blue and red in the mud underfoot.

Now that I'm looking, I realise that the grass for twenty paces all around is highlighted with points of colour. And the ground is damp, as if it's been raining just here. I crouch down to inspect a patch of grass mottled with red and yellow and blue as if someone has been scattering the shavings from freshly sharpened coloured pencils. I reach out to touch, but the flecks of colour melt away on my fingertips. It's like someone came and threw handfuls of tiny, tiny confetti on one of the graves, then someone else tried to wash it away because people aren't meant to celebrate a lost life in a graveyard: signs of festivity don't belong here, where everything is expected to be solemn. And of course no one expects people to want to celebrate a *death*.

But if I ever went to Fiona's grave, that's exactly what I'd want to do: celebrate. And I suppose I can't be the *only* person in the world who'd feel like that. I look about with renewed interest, wondering which grave holds a person someone hates as much as I hate Fiona. Wondering how that other person came to feel the same way I do about the dead.

Amy and Paul and Uncle Ben visit their graves. They care for them. Tend them. So it's oddly reassuring to discover that perhaps I'm not so unique in my horribleness for only wanting to visit Fiona's grave if I could dance and celebrate over it and chuck rubbish about. I mean, it may not be my fault that I feel that way – probably even Amy would feel that way in my shoes – but she's not and so she doesn't. Instead, anniversary days show how lovely and decent and *nice* Amy and Paul and Uncle Ben are. And how different I am. How even all the niceness and love they lavish on me can't change how I feel when I think about Fiona: cold and hard and nasty inside, just like Fiona's parents always said I was. I'm so lucky now, so very, very lucky, but I still can't stop myself from being just a little bit Fiona's daughter. Paul and Amy deserve so much better.

I sigh, turning away from the sight of Amy stroking her hand gently across the word 'mother' on Nanna Florrie's headstone. And suddenly I remember the night of the hoar frost and the people singing and shouting in the graveyard, and how I'd been horrified that anyone should be so happy in Amy and Paul and Uncle Ben's most sacred place . . . And I realise that perhaps it wasn't people being nasty and inconsiderate of the tragedy around them after all. Perhaps it was people celebrating: celebrating over a particular grave, with a particular person in it. A person just like Fiona.

Suddenly I'm not angry any more. I'm curious.

I wander absently away along the line of graves, peering down to see where the flecks of colour are densest in the grass, where the ground has been churned most violently to mud.

'Evie love, you OK?' Paul calls.

I jump. Swinging round, I realise I've drifted further than I'd intended and I hurry back to Paul's side. 'Sorry,' I say. 'Got caught up in thoughts.'

Paul puts his arm about me, though he doesn't take his eyes off his son's headstone. I look from Adam's to Aunt Minnie's, then back to Grandad Peter and Nanna Florrie's.

All four bear the same date.

Six years ago today they were all driving back from a big family party at Paul's parents' house. They had to take two cars, and that's just how it divided up: Grandad Peter driving Nanna Florrie, Aunt Minnie and Adam, and Uncle Ben driving Amy and Paul. Paul told me once that because Uncle Ben was driving, he saw the accident in the rear-view mirror. They were driving in convoy across a T-junction by a bridge when a drunk driver in one of those stupid, fancy 4 x 4s ran a red light at sixty-five in a thirty zone and smashed Grandad Peter's car through the barrier and down into the river. The drunk driver's car followed.

'Which was something,' Paul said the one time he talked about the accident. 'If I'd seen him coming up the bank after, I'd have had to go and beat his head in.'

Paul and Uncle Ben both went in the water, but because the drunk driver had smashed into the back of Grandad Peter's car, Nanna Florrie and Adam died in the back seat before Paul and Uncle Ben reached them. Paul told me that Aunt Minnie died on the riverbank. Grandad Peter made it to the hospital.

All Paul would say about the drunk driver was that he'd been dead when the police pulled him out of the car. I think he must have been killed on impact. There was guilt and bleakness in Paul's eyes when he told me, but nothing else. No stirrings of hunger. So the guilt's not for anything Paul and Uncle Ben did to him . . . or failed to do to help him. It's because Paul isn't sure what he *would* have chosen. If the driver had been pinned but alive, would Paul and Uncle Ben have helped him to get out or left him to drown? If he had been stuck and bleeding, would they have done what they could?

But it never came down to it, so Paul doesn't know. And he doesn't know how to feel about that: that mix of hope that he and Uncle Ben would have made sure the drunk driver died too, and the fear that he would have discovered that they couldn't. I wouldn't have found it hard at all.

I never met any of them, of course, but I love them anyway. They're the reason that Amy and Paul got me. Amy says that they'd always considered adopting because of the problems with getting pregnant that run in her family. I sometimes wonder if that was a little white lie as they never mentioned any difficulty with having Adam, but I don't mind either way. Amy and Paul did get me and that's what counts.

Now, Uncle Ben comes over to press Amy's shoulder, then Paul's. Amy stands staring at Adam's grave a moment longer, then we all turn away and set off for the car park. No one speaks as we walk, or on the drive home. I sit, staring out of the window, thinking about anniversaries past.

I came to live with Amy and Paul just over two years after the deaths. That's what Amy always calls what happened. I understand why, so that's what I say too.

When it came round to the third anniversary and I'd been with Amy and Paul for nearly a year, they sat me down and asked whether I wanted to 'join' them in visiting the graves. That's another word that stuck. Not 'come with them' but 'join': become part of. They didn't just want me for a new family, but as part of *all* their family: even the part of it I'd never get to know.

Amy and Paul had completely misunderstood why my eyes filled up with tears and hurried to reassure me that of course they wouldn't be insulted or anything if I preferred not to deal with that trauma. I didn't explain it to them. But I did go. Of course I did. Why wouldn't I want to be loved that much?

I think maybe the reason I nearly cried (the first time Amy and Paul had even seen me come close) was something to do with the fact that being asked to 'join' them made me really believe that they loved me. I'd been so happy I'd hurt.

But happy isn't the right word, and getting words right is important. And joy isn't exactly right either. It was more like relief. Though I hadn't even realised there was something I *needed* relief from. The something wasn't fear that Amy and Paul would never love me: I'd never expected they would, and that was fine with me. I'd agreed to it all, understanding that fully. I'd seen that they were nice, honestly nice, decent people and I knew that not only would they not do anything horrible to me, they would actively feel responsible for being good to me. And they were good to me of course, right from the start: affectionate and warm without being pushy, and that really was more than enough. But then the anniversary came around and ... I'd wondered a few times by then if they did love me after all since they were so much nicer to me than I'd ever imagined they could be, but I'd figured I'd never really know one way or the other ... and then I did. So of course I went: of course I go.

If the anniversary is a school day, I stay home. Like today. Every year, Phee and Lynne are agog with curiosity over the whole thing: they're fascinated afresh every time I tell them about it. Only some of it, of course. I wouldn't tell them about Amy talking to Adam, or the expression on her face when she does. Or the fact that when we get home the first thing Amy does is take out the stepladder. Some years she goes to the kitchen and cooks, or takes down all the curtains to wash, or attacks the rust on the garden furniture with sandpaper. But this year she takes out the stepladder.

I give Paul a worried look.

He shrugs, looking tired. He draws his lips inwards and sighs. 'I'll go make some tea, sweetheart,' he says, stopping to press a kiss – presses it just a little too hard – to my forehead. 'Why don't you go and hold the bottom of the ladder for Amy?'

So I do. Amy has a fixed, intense look on her face. She is up on the stepladder, fiddling with the smoke alarm in the living room. She presses something in the machine and it squeals. I slap my hands over my ears, putting my foot on the crossbar of the stepladder to keep it balanced. The noise stops, but Amy glares at the machine as if she is about to rip it from the ceiling.

'Is it all right?' I dare to ask.

'I don't know,' says Amy in a blunt, quick sort of way. 'It thinks it's fine, but I can't remember the last time I replaced that battery. I thought I heard it beep when we came in.'

'I don't think so. It only started beeping when you pressed the thingy.'

'Not that kind of beeping. It does this very slow beeping – just once every few minutes – when the battery is getting low, before it runs out altogether. I thought I heard it.'

'Maybe it was the one next to the cupboard at the top of the stairs?'

Amy slams the lid closed on the alarm and I hurry out of her way as she kicks the stepladder into flattened submission and marches up the stairs. The upstairs alarm is fine too. Next we go to the kitchen.

Doesn't that just say it all? Fiona's parents had one smoke alarm in their house. I can't remember anyone ever checking it. Amy and Paul have three and on the anniversary of the worst day of her life, Amy checks them all.

The one in the kitchen is fine too, only this time, when

she finishes checking, the stepladder decides to stand firm, refusing to close. There's a horrid shrieking of metal on metal and floor tiles.

'Amy,' says Paul, reaching out cautiously to her. 'Amy, darling, let me do that for you.'

Amy ignores him, wrenching even more violently at the stepladder. 'Why can't I find which one it is? One of them isn't working. One of these stinking, stupid alarms . . .'

'Amy . . .'

'Don't Amy me, Paul! One of the alarms isn't working. It's important. They're there to protect us.'

'Amy . . .'

'They're meant to protect our family, Paul. And I'm going to find which one it is . . .'

A hand comes down on my shoulder and I look up to find Uncle Ben standing next to me, holding out a cup of tea. 'Come on, Evie. Let's go in the garden for a bit. Clear up some of those leaves for your . . . for Amy and Paul.'

As we work, I think I hear snatches of shouting.

Soon we've gathered a most satisfactory heap of leaves. I stare down at it and then sigh and stump off to get the garden bin-bags from the shed. I don't dare chuck leaves at Uncle Ben today. It might cheer him up, but it also might make him feel that I don't understand. It seems better not to risk it: everyone's allowed one day a year when they're not all that much fun.

I get one of the bags opened up, and Uncle Ben bends

to draw up a huge armful to chuck in . . . and suddenly I'm in a hurricane of leaves. I'm laughing and spitting, then, even before the leaves have finished falling around me, I'm diving towards the pile for ammunition of my own.

Eventually we collapse together on the ground, spreadeagled, my head on Uncle Ben's stomach to indicate my victory. I stare up at the grey clouds as we both gasp for breath to laugh with and I pretend I don't notice when there's an extra sobbing rhythm to Uncle Ben's laughter. After a while, I reach out until I find his hand and tuck mine into it.

'I love you, Evie-girl,' Uncle Ben gasps, gritting the words out so that they sound furious, enraged.

I squeeze his hand. 'Me too.'

'Me too?' Uncle Ben asks, his voice going almost normal. 'Me too? You love you too, do you?' he asks, sitting up so he can lean over and tickle me as I shriek and curl into a ball in the curve of his body.

When Uncle Ben pauses, I wriggle around until I can hug him about the middle. 'Love you too.'

Uncle Ben kisses my hair.

Somehow I don't hear the front door open, even though I've been listening out for it.

'Evie, what on earth are you doing?' Amy calls up the stairs. 'I told you not to go clambering around on things when you're alone in the house.'

'You told me not to use a chair. You said it wasn't stable enough.'

'I didn't mean you should start fiddling around on the stepladder instead! Evie darling, I know you're feeling much better now and it's wonderful, it really is, but you still need to be *careful*.'

She plonks her shopping down at the bottom of the stairs and comes up to help me close the stepladder.

'Why do you keep messing around in the top of this cupboard anyway? Grandma Suzie said that they had to ring the doorbell for nearly five minutes when they came over last weekend because you didn't hear them, though you know I told you they'd be here at four. What *are* you looking for?'

I shrug, looking away, and catch Paul's eye by accident. He grins at me, then pulls a face and ducks out to bring in the rest of the bags from the car.

I turn back to Amy, but she is staring up at the ceiling with a frown on her face. 'I suppose I should check the alarm while the ladder's out,' she says. 'I can't believe that battery hasn't run out by now.'

'It did,' I say.

Amy blinks at me, aghast. 'I never even heard it beeping. Evie darling, why didn't you *tell* me!'

'Because I got the spare from the drawer and changed it already.'

'Oh, Evie, you must be careful. And are you sure you

got the new battery all the way in? And did you press the test button?'

'We'll check it later,' Paul says firmly from the bottom of the stairs.

'But Paul darling...'

'If the house catches fire while we're awake, we'll know all about it. We can double-check the alarm before we go to bed, but I'm sure Evie's done it perfectly. Come on now. You can stand over me with a bucket in case I set lunch on fire.'

Amy heaves a huge sigh, but folds the stepladder up and carries it back downstairs. I traipse after her and collect her shopping, bringing it into the kitchen. 'Fire alarm aside, Evie, what *do* you keep looking in that cupboard for?'

I do the shrug thing again and busy myself with making tea, while Amy sets about putting the shopping away. She only gets halfway through the first bag before she stops and, gesturing with the tinned tomatoes, says, 'I don't like this climbing about on ladders right at the top of the stairs, Evie. Not when you're still healing. And why do you always do it when we're out of the house? I swear every time we've gone out for the last month...'

'OK, Amy,' Paul says. He puts his hands on her shoulders, kissing her cheek as she huffs a little sigh of frustration. 'I'm sure Evie's got the message now. Whatever it is she's trying to hide from our ancient eyes, I'm confident that if we set the stepladder up by the cupboard and then give her ten clear minutes while we go in the garden, it'll end up somewhere much lower down. And, in return for humouring us, we will *promise*,' he grins at me as he stresses the word, 'not to be nosy because everyone's entitled to a little privacy, and now that Evie's an official teenager, with a year of experience behind her, she's even entitled to the odd secret.'

Amy's face screws up in a mixture of worry and embarrassment. 'Evie knows I'm not trying to be nosy, Paul. No, really I'm not,' she protests as his arms tighten about her and he laughs into her hair. 'Of course she's entitled to her privacy . . .'

'And secrets,' Paul says, kissing her cheek again.

'Well, yes, of course, but only when . . .'

Paul laughs. 'I knew there was going to be a "but",' he says.

'Oh, Paul, don't be so difficult. Evie knows what I mean: that of course she should be able to have secrets, so long as they're not *dangerous*.'

'In which case, all bets are off,' Paul interrupts again.

Amy smacks his arm where it rests across her chest, starting to look truly annoyed. 'It's nothing to laugh about, Paul. We'd need to know if Evie were hurt or . . .'

They both go very still and it takes me a minute to realise that they're thinking about my keeping the ribs secret from them for so long.

'Evie's a brave, clever girl,' Paul says. 'She knows we love her and that she can tell us anything.'

'Yes, darling,' Amy says, her knuckles suddenly white where she is gripping Paul's arm, her eyes fixed on mine, 'of *course* we know you'll tell us anything we really need to know. We do know that. We'll let you move your little secret and I promise I won't ask you anything more about it.'

We all stand there, Paul and Amy staring at me and me staring at them until Paul clears his throat. 'Right. Come on, Evie love. Let's go put that stepladder back up, then Amy and I will have a nice cup of tea in the garden while you sort it all out.'

I trail after Paul, chewing at the ends of a loose curl of hair.

'Is that about right?' he asks, checking the stepladder to see that it's stable.

I nod at him, but he is staring up at the fire alarm.

'I'm going to get someone in,' he says suddenly. 'Have them set up one of those systems that are hardwired into the mains electricity. Get rid of these stupid battery-operated things before Amy drives us mad over them. Maybe I can get them to come this Saturday, while Amy's out at my parents'. Get it done as a surprise.' He sighs as he turns his attention back to me and finds me chewing my hair even more vigorously. 'I'm sorry, sweetheart. You know Amy doesn't mean to upset you . . .'

'I know,' I say. 'She didn't.'

'Evie, I was hoping . . .' Ms Winters trails off with a sigh. We've just put our books away for the day, so it's not like I don't know it's Talking Time, but I already have a bad feeling about where this is headed. 'I was hoping we could talk about something . . . difficult today. Since things are going so well . . . Well, I thought maybe this would be a good time to ask if you would tell me a little bit about when your . . . when Fiona decided to give you up.'

I shift my gaze to the window. Ms Winters isn't going to take the hint, not after that speech, but I stare out at the clouds anyway. In my pocket, my hand closes about the Dragon. The bone warms to my touch.

'We've talked a little before about how Fiona didn't protect you like she should have, but today I was hoping we could explore the possibility that maybe that was what she was trying to do when she put you into care.'

'Maybe if she'd done it when Dad died, before she took us to live with her parents,' I say, trying to make my voice dismissive, as if there's nothing further to say on the subject.

'Or maybe it was finding out how ill she was that finally gave her the strength to make the right decision.'

I wonder again just how much Amy and Paul have told Ms Winters. I can't make up my mind whether it's a good thing she knows so much or not. 'No,' I say firmly, pleased at how calm but definite it comes out.

'Well, perhaps she finally managed to persuade her parents that giving you up would be the best option for everyone when they understood how difficult it was going to be when she . . . as her illness progressed.'

I turn a flinty stare on Ms Winters. 'You're the one who told me they probably did the same things to her. You think they decided to let me go because they wanted to be able to look after her?'

Ms Winters sighs heavily. 'People are very strange, Evie. Sometimes ... sometimes they do things that are completely contradictory: that make absolutely no sense. Sometimes people can be caring in one way and terribly abusive in another.'

I shrug and turn my attention to the rug. It's a really ugly rug. I've always thought so. There's a series of misshapen blobs along the border and even after four years I've no idea what they're meant to be. Leaves? Sheaves of corn? They've got dots in the middle so I can never quite figure it out. I tilt my head to the side.

'What do you think happened, Evie? Why do you think they changed their minds?'

I shrug one shoulder.

'OK, maybe that's a difficult question. Let's start with why they changed their minds *then*. What prompted the decision?'

I meet Ms Winters's pretty hazel eyes, but part of me doesn't see her sitting on the other side of the kitchen table: part of me sees Fiona's mother's face, wide and frantic with fury and fear as she tows Fiona down the upstairs landing towards my room. She must have dragged Fiona up from cowering in the kitchen because Fiona still has a dishcloth in her hand.

'Go and clean it up!' Fiona's mother is shrieking. 'I told you to go clean it up!'

But Fiona is standing with her knees locked, staring at me.

'"Go and clean it up," I said!' Fiona's mother screams, pushing and pushing at her, but Fiona is heavy and stiff with terror, and the knowledge that her mother can't enter my room: can never bring herself to step past the threshold, no matter that she knows exactly what goes on in here.

Fiona's mouth is open. She gasps for breath as if someone has been holding her under water.

I shiver, jerking my head to the side, and close my eyes. *Just keep focusing on the blanks*, I tell myself firmly. *Life doesn't have gaps, only memories do.*

That day – that memory – is full of them.

I don't remember how I fit into the scene on the landing in Fiona's parents' house, though I suppose I must have been standing in the doorway of my old bedroom.

And I have no idea where Fiona's father was by then. Or when exactly they left the house, though with all that blood I know they must have gone to the hospital.

I do remember being downstairs in the kitchen,

watching Fiona take the rubbish out of the kitchen bin and lay it all out on the floor in a meticulous arc, every movement a study in precision. Once the floor is awash with cigarette packets and banana skins, she gingerly lowers the bloody cloths down into the bottom of the empty bin before piling the rest back in on top. She is whispering, whispering, whispering the whole time, though I can only make out the occasional word.

After that it's a blank. The next thing I remember is hearing the front door open and knowing that Fiona's parents are back. There's a murmur of voices in the hall, the sounds of people moving about the house . . . Then nothing. And it's not that I *don't* remember: it's that there is nothing *to* remember. Because by the time I hear the front door open, Fiona has locked me in my room.

She keeps me locked in there until I can show her that all my bruises have gone. It's the summer holidays so no one notices.

The day Fiona judges the bruises to be sufficiently faded to pass unremarked, she leads me out into the hall. Not to go to the bathroom – the only place apart from my bedroom I've been for what feels like years – but downstairs. Downstairs!

I think we must be going to the kitchen, but Fiona turns into the hall and we go to the front door. We go *outside*.

'Get in,' Fiona hisses, fumbling with the car keys.

And then we're driving, and I don't care where we're going. I just don't want to go back, even if it means leaving everything behind. If only we can just keep going . . .

But we stop in the car park of a big office building.

I close my eyes on the sight, concentrate on the feel of the wood-grain beneath my fingertips as I grasp the edge of my chair, fighting to hold myself steady. Fighting to remember *when* I am.

Amy and Paul's kitchen. Our kitchen with all the lights on and a pot of curry simmering on the stove, steaming up the windows. Ms Winters, sitting patiently on the other side of the table, is still waiting to see how much I'm willing to say.

'She went mad,' I tell her with a calm shrug and a tone that says *I'm sure Amy and Paul have told you this already. Do we really have to go over it?* 'Maybe it was the cancer drugs or something, but she just went mad. Totally bonkers. She drove me down to this office block. Probably Social Services. It's a miracle she managed to get there without killing us both. They took one look and knew she'd gone completely off her rocker and that was that.'

I remember the faces of the office staff as we came in, me first, Fiona trailing behind as if she couldn't bear to be near me, not even near enough to drag me inside to leave me all the sooner.

'Go!' Fiona gasps. 'Go. Keep walking. I said, "Keep walking."'

I shiver as her breath heats my hair.

I'm in Paul and Amy's kitchen, I tell myself, fixing my

eyes on the family photo Amy has pinned to the fridge. *I'm fourteen now. And Fiona is dead.*

The memory grows distant again: turns back into a story about the past.

'Go! Keep walking,' Fiona gasped.

Gasped, I repeat to myself, holding on to the tense: pinning down time.

I suppose we must have passed through some sort of reception area. And I suppose Fiona must have asked where to go next, but I don't remember any of that. I do remember the horror on the face of the woman nearest the door of the big open-plan office: I remember watching her look into Fiona's mad, staring eyes.

And just like that *then* starts to become *now*, rushing like floodwater into the present. The sides of the kitchen are being pushed inwards. The table is being squeezed, squeezed, squeezed, like when you screw your eyes up and the world compacts so you can only make out the things directly in front of you. To my right, there's a desk where the stove was and, on my left, another where the dishwasher should be. It's all dim and blurry, so faint beyond the bright vision of the kitchen in front of me, that perhaps it's just a trick of the light.

All I have to do is turn and look at that desk on the left – look at it straight on – and it'll vanish, I tell myself.

But I don't turn because somehow I know there's a photo frame on the left-hand desk and a plant on the right-hand one.

Just turn and it'll vanish ...

But what if it doesn't? echoes back because I can *feel* the desk there on my left. I can *feel* it.

And then Fiona is there. There, in the space where the back door should be.

She has put half her clothes on backwards and her hair is all clumped in peculiar ways: sticking out here, matted down there.

'I can't have her any more,' she gasps, staggering round to look at the people who have stood up from their desks to stare. 'I can't ... I can't ... I won't ... They said I can't ... They said they won't ...'

I stand there watching her until a woman kneels down next to me. 'Sweetheart, do you think you could come with me now?' she asks very kindly. 'Let's go and get you a nice drink while someone sees if they can help your mum calm down a bit.'

Just like that it's over. The office, the desks, Fiona – they're all gone. It's just me in Amy and Paul's kitchen with Ms Winters, and the memory of the way Fiona's voice rose and rose and rose until she was screaming things that even I couldn't make out. I'm not sure they were even words.

'She stood right in the middle of the office and started screaming,' I tell Ms Winters. 'Screaming and screaming. So I don't think she really made a decision about leaving me exactly. I don't think she was capable of deciding anything at that point.'

It isn't a lie. Fiona's parents made the decision, just like they decided I would stay safely locked up until the bruises were gone and no one would have to be any the wiser about what had been happening. I know it as surely as I know anything, even though I was locked in my room so I never heard the discussion that decided how things would be. But I didn't have to be there to know who was making the decisions. It had been a long time since Fiona had decided anything by that point and after that day . . .

Maybe the cancer and the drugs helped her along, but I always figured she lost her marbles the minute she started cleaning up the blood. All I know is that every time she brought meals up to my locked room she was just as hysterical as the last.

I'm surprised her parents managed to get her to take me down to Social Services, or wherever it was she left me. But perhaps by then they were as frightened of me as Fiona was: frightened enough to find a way. They must have realised there was no chance that anyone would suggest my going home with Fiona once they saw the state she was in.

'They took Fiona straight to the hospital,' I tell Ms Winters. 'I can't remember who told me, but I know that's what happened. Everyone could see that she had just lost it.'

'But something must have triggered it. Did she have a fight with her parents? Do you remember them having an argument . . . perhaps about Fiona's diagnosis and what would happen to you?'

I shake my head.

'Maybe your mother realised she couldn't leave you with them, once she had to be in hospital a lot. Maybe she wanted to make plans for when she died. After all, from your . . . from her parents' perspective, it might have been a lot . . . *easier* to have you to themselves, with her out of the way.'

'Fiona never got in their way,' I say. 'Not for anything.'

Ms Winters purses her lips together in the way that means she's sad but trying not to look like she pities me. 'Why do you think her parents let her send you away then, Evie?'

I think of the cream brocade of the curtains in my old bedroom and the slash of seeping spots of blood blossoming into the thick swirl of the fabric. I think of the warm slickness running down the cool sides of the glass that always stood on my bedside table so I could have a drink at night.

For a second, I feel blood collect in my palm once more.

'Do you remember how it happened, Evie? Did she just take you away one day without telling them?'

I shrug.

'Why do you think Fiona's parents didn't try to get you back?' Ms Winters presses. 'It probably wouldn't have been hard, since there wasn't any other family and no one realised then that you'd been abused.'

I flinch at the word. 'I expect they just said they couldn't cope with an eight-year-old grandchild *and* a daughter who was sick and mad,' I say to block out the echoes of that awful word, to move the conversation on before Ms Winters can use it again.

'Yes, but *why* did they say that, Evie?'

For a second I am back in my old bedroom, holding the rose-pattern glass.

I see it splinter as I smash the edge down on the corner of my bedside table.

I see surprise, morphing into horror, on Fiona's father's face.

It has always bothered me that I can't remember what happened next. But I just can't draw anything into focus. There are too many gaps, in all the important places. I have never been able to remember exactly what I did to create all that blood and that look on Fiona's father's face.

All I remember is how wonderful I felt.

And suddenly I remember the wisp of thought that danced out of reach when Ms Winters first talked to me about goals. I don't intend to tell Ms Winters the whole story – not now, not ever. But it's no longer because I'm trying to hide that thing I used to keep locked inside, all teeth and venom, thick and deep as oil. Somehow it just doesn't seem to be there any more. The place where I kept it, all secret in darkness, is full of light now. Whatever was there is gone: the Dragon has taken it away to guard it and keep it secret for me. And with it the Dragon has taken the fear that someday I will be careless and let it creep out into the open where even Amy would recoil from it. From me.

'Maybe Fiona's parents just thought I was as mad as she was underneath,' I tell Ms Winters. 'They always hated it when there was screaming. Everything had to be silent. As if then it didn't count.'

Paul grins at me as I trail into the kitchen and slump down at the table, yawning widely. 'I wouldn't bother trying to wake up,' he says as he pencils something into the crossword. 'Sounds like this soap opera marathon you've got planned with Phee and Lynne will just put you right back to sleep.'

'Not going. I texted Lynne already,' I mumble around another yawn, stretching awkwardly and then wincing.

Paul frowns. 'Is that wince you just gave something we should be worried about, Evie love?' he asks, making Amy turn abruptly from the dishes and begin scanning me from head to foot.

'No,' I say, sighing. 'Just a bit sore. Stiff. Think I slept funny.'

'But it's not like you to cancel plans with your friends, darling. Are you sure you're all right? We could pop down to the doctor ... We *should* pop down to the doctor if there's any *possibility* that something's wrong. Especially after everything that's happened recently with the pool and . . .'

'I'm fine,' I snap, then sigh, pulling an apologetic face. I make an effort to straighten up as I reach for the teapot, but Paul tosses the paper aside to pour for me.

'Honestly,' I say, struggling for a joking tone. 'I'm just a bit tired and . . . And I really don't feel like five hours of soap operas today.' I reach for a strand of hair and start chewing the ends. 'I'm trying to be interested in the same stuff as Phee and Lynne, really I am, but I'm just not in the mood today.' I look pleadingly up at them.

Paul smiles, though Amy sighs. 'Well, if you're sure you're all right,' she says. 'That's the important thing. You don't have to do anything you don't want.'

'Just this once,' I say. 'I'll go next time.'

'Well, since Evie doesn't need a lift, I think I might go over to your mum's now,' Amy says, absent-mindedly pulling the hair out of my mouth and tucking it behind my ear. 'I've been promising to help with pruning that japonica and it would be good to make an early start before the rain they've been talking about arrives. Now, are you sure you're OK for lunch?'

Paul rolls his eyes. 'She thinks I'm completely useless,' he tells the ceiling. 'We all know I make a better omelette than you do, so scram.'

Amy smiles as she bends down to kiss him. 'Evie will keep you in line and stop you destroying the house,' she says.

As soon as we hear the front door close, Paul pulls a face at me.

I pull one back, but then the front door opens again. There's rustling in the hall and Amy calls, 'Paul, have you still not brought the camera back?'

'Sorry, love!' Paul shouts back. 'I'm nearly done with it.'

We can hear Amy's sigh from the kitchen. 'And you've still got the torch too, I'll bet, so what we'll do if there's a power cut I *don't* know and for what? There's not been a hint of trouble over Ben's way for a month. Don't you think it's time the two of you packed it in with these night-time patrols?'

'Just another week or so, love,' Paul calls, rolling his eyes at me, 'but I'll get a spare torch in the meantime. Bound to come in handy and it won't break the bank.'

Amy shuts the front door by way of reply.

'Are you sure you should change the alarms without telling her when she's in this sort of mood?' I ask. 'Can't you call them and cancel?'

Paul sighs as he pushes himself to his feet, fetching himself a pop-tart from our secret stash behind the cereal boxes. 'The condemned man needs junk food,' he explains when I quirk an eyebrow at him. 'Look, I had a nice long chat with the lads who're doing the work. They've promised they'll be very neat and they won't muck up the plasterwork. It'll all be done and dusted – literally – by the time Amy gets back.'

I curl a new strand of hair around my finger and grind

the ends between my teeth.

'Don't look so worried, Evie love.'

'I like the old alarms,' I mumble.

'You don't care a hoot about the alarms,' Paul says, coming around the table to loop an arm about my shoulders. 'I don't know what's got you so worked up, but it's not a big deal, OK? Just a nice little surprise for Amy to cheer her up.'

I shrug one shoulder. Paul squeezes tight then releases me. 'What's really bothering you?' he asks, dropping into the chair next to mine. 'I promise not to nag or tell Amy.'

I spit the hair out of my mouth, wrinkling up my nose. 'Just out of sorts,' I say. 'Funny dreams. But I don't really remember them,' I add before he can ask. 'It just made me worried, I guess.'

Paul gives me another hug, then fixes us both pop-tarts with squirty cream. I trail around after him, helping clear up breakfast then get out the hoover and cleaning supplies (just in case). The alarm people are on time and set to work with neat efficiency, even though I'm now trailing after *them*.

'Can I pass this down to you, love?' one of them asks as I hover by the stepladder.

I take the old alarm and stand staring blankly as the workman starts doing stuff with the wiring in the ceiling light.

'Gonna use this to power up the new alarm, see?' he explains, smiling kindly down at me as he tucks a screwdriver behind his ear. 'That way we don't need to poke any holes in your mum's nice house or do nothing with the walls, like.'

I nod and turn my gaze to the alarm in my hands, picking at the catch until it pops open.

'Come on a minute, Evie, and give them some room to work,' Paul says as he comes upstairs to check on their progress. 'I'll make you some hot chocolate with marshmallows, huh?' he offers, as he pulls the strand of hair I've been chewing yet again out of my mouth. 'That'll perk you up, won't it?'

I nod, still looking at the alarm I'm holding, though I lean into him as he puts his arm around my shoulders. 'Can I keep this?' I ask, looking up at the line of his jaw and the tiny mole under his chin that is only visible up close, in a hug, by someone exactly my height.

Paul frowns down at me, bemused. 'The old alarm? Evie love, why would you want that? You can't be attached to it.'

I shrug, hooking my chin over the edge of his shoulder to meet his eyes. 'I want to see how it works. Because it will still work, won't it? It's just battery-powered, right? It's not plugged into anything in the ceiling, is it?'

'No. That's the whole point of the new system,' Paul says dubiously, turning to the alarm man. 'She can't get a shock from it, can she?'

The alarm guy smiles indulgently at me. 'Nah. 'S only nine volts that battery. Can't get much of a spark from that. And she's old enough to be trusted not to put it in water. Can't do no harm to have a bit of a poke about. Be a good learning 'sperience.'

Paul looks down at me, his mouth all bunched up to one side. 'Amy won't like it, of course,' he says, 'nine volts or no.' A sigh. 'How about this goes in your brand-new, super-secret hiding place and we just don't mention it to Amy?'

I beam at him.

Paul grins down at me. 'Good to know that next time you're feeling blue all I need to do is find some old bit of battery-powered junk to perk you up, though God help me if you end up a rocket scientist.' He shudders. 'Promise me you'll stick with nice low-powered electronics, OK darling? No explosives or setting fire to things. And definitely no rocket fuel.'

I put my arm around his middle and squeeze. 'No rocket fuel,' I promise.

Paul and I are sitting cross-legged on the floor, laughing over the Scrabble board. Neither of us likes playing the traditional way so we've made up our own rules. It's pretty much the same as normal Scrabble only you can't spell any of the words right: you have to spell them like they sound. Or you have to make up words that everyone agrees should be real. Like moronity or cretination.

'Now that's a good sound to come home to,' Amy says,

as she comes into the kitchen and jangles her keys into the dish on the sideboard. 'What have you two been up to that's put you in such a good mood?'

I look at Paul and lift my eyebrows.

'Show-time,' he says, pushing himself to his feet. 'We've been arranging a little surprise for you.'

'A surprise for *me*?' Amy says, smiling as Paul puts his arm about her waist.

'Just something to stop you worrying. Have a look up there,' he says, pointing to the new kitchen alarm.

Amy frowns in the direction of his finger. 'You've changed the alarm,' she says, puzzled.

'We've got a whole new system with the latest whatchamacallits and they're all hardwired into the mains electricity. No more batteries to check,' he says proudly, beaming as he leans down to kiss her.

But Amy steps away from him, her frown turning into a glare as she continues to stare up at the new alarm.

'They did a great job on them all, just like this one. No mess. Just a little wire between the light and the alarm,' Paul explains hurriedly. 'Nice and simple.'

But Amy is clenching her teeth together and she's flicking her thumb against her ring so fast that it clicks, like she's snapping her fingers, as she turns it and turns it and turns it.

'I thought you'd be pleased,' Paul says. I see his hand come up as if he wants to touch her, but he lets it fall and I realise that he's not disappointed but hurt. 'You've been fussing over those old alarms and . . .'

'Fussing,' Amy says quietly, but there's something not at all nice in her tone. It makes me pull back a step because Amy's voice isn't like that and her face isn't like that and I don't like the way she's snapping her thumb against her ring at all. 'You think it's *fussing* to want to be sure that my family is safe.'

'I know you want us to be safe. That's why I got you the new system,' Paul protests quietly. I can see in his face that he knows he shouldn't have said 'fussing'. 'This way the batteries can't go dead and there's nothing to worry about . . .'

'And what if there's a power cut?' Amy interrupts. 'Do they have a fail-safe? Do they beep like the old ones if there's a problem?'

'Amy . . .'

'And what if there's a power surge and they blow? That's exactly when there *might* be a fire, but will we have a single alarm that works then?'

'I'll ring them up tomorrow and ask. We can call them together and if you think we need something upgraded, we'll get it sorted, all right, darling?'

'There was nothing *wrong* with the old system,' Amy says in a voice choked with rage and the tears I can see in her eyes. 'It was just fine . . .'

'But you kept worrying about it, darling,' Paul says, reaching out to her, but she steps back again, bringing her hand up to grip her locket.

It leaves her standing there with her arm across her body as if to hold him away. Her cheeks have gone a strange colour, mottled red and white. 'Of course I worry,' she grinds out. 'And now I've got nothing I can *do* about it. I liked checking the stupid alarms. I liked checking that I was keeping my family safe. Why didn't you ask me? Why did you have to go and change things without asking me?'

Paul draws in a breath so heavy it sounds as if he's trying to do it underwater. 'Amy,' he says quietly. 'Amy darling, nothing's going to happen to us. We're going to call the alarm people tomorrow and ask all sorts of questions. As many questions as it takes to make you feel better.' He keeps his eyes locked with hers as he slowly, gently places his hands on her shoulders. She shudders, a full-bodied shiver as if his touch feels like ice even through her cardigan. 'And we'll take the car out to the garage and check the tyres and the oil and the water and everything we can possibly think of,' Paul continues, stepping forwards and slowly, slowly drawing Amy to him. 'And then we'll go all round the house and check all the appliances: make sure the wiring is good and the plugs are OK.'

I watch Amy's hands slowly come up to clutch at the back of Paul's shirt. Her face is pressed against his neck so all I can see is the curve of her cheek, still blotched with patches of red.

'We need to fix the gutter,' Amy chokes out. 'The

gutter above Evie's room. There's water and mud all over the patio under there every time it rains and half the time when it doesn't too.'

Paul kisses Amy's hair. 'We'll fix it, sweetheart. I'll even get Ben over to help so I'm nice and safe on the ladder. Then we can all go over to his house and check everything there too. We'll all be fine, Amy. We'll all be perfectly safe. You always do everything possible to keep us safe, right, Evie?'

I jump. Distracted by the whole gutter thing, I'd been making a mental note not to clean my shoes out of the window any more, then trying to figure out what to do instead. I'd just worked it out too: if I nick a roll of paper towels, Amy probably won't notice and that will do for now. Then, next trip to the supermarket, I'll ask for some wet wipes. Provided I put all the muddy stuff in a plastic bag rather than straight in my bin, I figure I'll be set. I am just in the process of congratulating myself for this clever thinking when Paul's voice jolts me back to the present.

I feel like cursing. Usually when Paul and Amy argue I wait until they've forgotten that I'm there and then slip quietly away. But it's too late: Paul is craning over his shoulder to look at me and he's taken one hand off Amy's back to reach out to me. I stare at him just a moment too long, until there is hurt as well as sadness in his eyes and he moves his arm to put it back around Amy. But that isn't fair because Paul and Amy have always, always looked after me.

I manage not to sigh as I get up and move around the table to put my arm cautiously, carefully around Amy on one side and Paul on the other. And when I look up at Paul, hoping that the hurt will be gone, I realise that his eyes are very red. But he looks almost happy too. He looks proud. And so I tighten my hand on his shirt and Amy's cardigan, resting my head against Amy's shoulder. Looking into Paul's eyes, I smile at him until he smiles back. He presses a kiss to my hair and when he pulls back, he doesn't look like he needs to cry any more.

It's Sonny Rawlins's first day back after his suspension. I expect him to glare at me every chance he gets, but he doesn't: instead, he ducks his head down and looks studiously away, though his mouth thins into a sulky line. I'm both nonplussed and elated by this, especially when the new gossip focuses entirely on him: there's not a word about me and how it's all really my fault for being a spoilt attention-seeker.

I find out why during lunch break, when Jenny comes up to us as we quick-march around the pear tree ('Because walking is good exercise for keeping our muscles trim that doesn't require any of that nasty sweating business,' according to Lynne). Apparently she's been reading about how important it is to exercise as well as eat healthily in order to stay thin and since Lynne can't stand actual exercise I foresee that Phee and I will be bullied into spending our break-times being circle-trained (or whatever Lynne called it) into vomiting.

'Evie! Evie, you won't believe what Fred told me.'

I'm surprised Fred managed to tell Jenny anything since they didn't seem to be coming up for air when we passed them in the cloakrooms earlier, snogging the life out of each other.

'Fred says that Sonny's been grounded for a month! *And* no pocket money!' Jenny whispers. She doesn't try to link arms with me, but skip-stumbles along, walking backwards in front of us. 'You know that big, fancy mountain bike . . .' Jenny trails off gasping and stumbles to a stop, making us halt too. 'God, what are you *doing*?' she asks.

'Evie needs a break,' Phee insists, towing Lynne towards the bench that's wrapped around the pear tree. We huddle together, shivering. 'What about Sonny's bike?'

'Well,' Jenny says, leaning forward eagerly, 'you know it must have cost an absolute fortune and everything. Top of the range . . .'

'*And*?' Lynne presses. She's red-faced and breathing hard.

'And it's wrecked. Completely trashed.'

'He doesn't look like he had an accident,' Phee says. 'More's the pity.'

'No. It was foxes. He was riding around, stuffing his face with a kebab or a burger or something, like always, and he got it all over his hands and then all over the bike, and the foxes just attacked it, like they tried to eat it or something as if they thought the whole thing was food. His dad's furious 'cos then the foxes got into the rubbish bin and made this huge mess all over their garden. Sonny had to clean it up. Fred says it took him four hours to get all the little bits of bin-bag out of his mum's plants. And his dad says he'll have to keep clearing up if the foxes come back expecting more food. He's so angry he's said that Sonny'll have to get a paper round or something to pay for the bike repairs himself to teach him to be less of a pig or at least a cleaner one.'

Phee, Lynne and I look at each other. Phee breaks into a grin, then we're all laughing except Jenny, though even she gives a little giggle.

'I shouldn't laugh really. He *is* Fred's best friend.' She grins all the same. 'But it is kind of funny.'

'It's brilliant!' says Phee. 'It's perfect. Just like something out of a book where the bad guy gets his comeuppance. I mean, he probably deserves something worse for nearly drowning Evie,' she says, giving me an apologetic nudge, 'but still . . . How often do things like that happen in real life?'

'And the best bit is that Fred says Sonny's dad is so cross he's told him that if he causes any more trouble, especially at school, then he'll make Sonny stay with his grandparents when the rest of the family goes off for their summer holiday, and you know they always go somewhere brilliant . . .'

'Wow. I *like* Sonny's dad. Who'd've thunk?' Phee says.

'You know, even Fred said that he couldn't really feel sorry for Sonny. He felt really bad about what happened to you, Evie,' Jenny says earnestly. 'He didn't think he'd better come and say anything to you about it, but he really did feel awful.'

'Well maybe he shouldn't hang around with someone so nasty then,' Phee says.

Jenny sighs. 'I know.'

'I mean, Fred's never been as bad as Sonny . . . but he's always there, sort of silently egging Sonny on,' Lynne adds. 'It's not like he ever tells Sonny not to be so horrible to people. I watched him one time when Sonny was picking on little Davey Perkins. Sonny punched him right in the face and Fred just stood there staring at his feet.'

Jenny looks down at her own. 'I know. But Fred's not really like that when he's not with Sonny. He's just . . . He's got this thing about being loyal to your mates, even when you don't think they're being very nice. He keeps going on about not judging people . . .'

'Bollocks,' Phee says. Jenny stares at her. 'Everyone judges everyone all the time. And we should too. How else do we pick who to be friends with? If you think someone's a nasty little git, shouldn't you judge them on that?'

Jenny pouts out her bottom lip in the sulky way that means she's actually thinking it over. 'I guess,' she says then shrugs. 'Fred's not really sure about the whole thing.

He just thinks it would be a bit rotten to start ignoring Sonny right when everything's going wrong for him. I think that's kind of … sweet. Fred really can be, you know.'

Thankfully the bell rings before Phee, Lynne or I have to find something to say about Fred's sweetness.

It's art next: the final lesson in the pencil-case series. And hopefully the end of Mrs Poole's dreaded textiles projects now that it's time to start on our GCSE coursework.

We all lay our creations dutifully out on the tables and then walk around them in a big circle, admiring each other's work. Several people snigger and point at my black rubber disaster. But that's fine with me: I'm with them.

Mrs Poole has a clipboard. We all try not to laugh (well, those of us who don't really care about Mrs Poole's pet obsession with sewing – Lynne is straining forwards, looking anxious) as Mrs Poole bends over each pencil case in turn and inspects it closely. Her glasses slip closer and closer to the end of her nose each time she bends down to peer at a new person's work. There's a collective sigh when she pushes them back up. Phee and I had been making Smartie-packet bets about whose pencil case they'd fall off on.

Then Mrs Poole tries to get the class discussing the merits of the different pencil cases awarded the highest marks. Phee folds her arms on the table and drops her head on to them. That would be too uncomfortable with my ribs (I still can't bend forwards very far), so I just slouch down in my chair and let my thoughts drift.

Then, to my great delight, we have a fire drill. Phee and Lynne spend it debating which of the sixth-form boys they'd be willing to snog and which they'd consider doing even more with: they have this whole system worked out for what stuff they'd be willing to do with boys once they're fifteen, sixteen, seventeen ... When they asked me, I just said that I'd worry about figuring it out when I met someone worth doing things with.

The sixth-formers troop past on their way back to class, to much giggling from Phee and Lynne.

'Do you honestly not like *any* of them, Evie?' Lynne whispers when I fail to offer even a single comment on which of them has the nicest butt.

I shrug. 'Not really.' Then, because we've been so close lately and the last thing I want to do is emphasise what we *don't* have in common, I add, 'I mean, what's the point of thinking about it when none of them have the slightest bit of interest in me? It's kind of depressing.'

Lynne sighs. 'I can't *believe* I'm going to turn fifteen next month without ever having had a proper boyfriend.'

'I can't believe Jenny's got a boyfriend and we don't,' Phee replies. 'Then again, Jenny's got Fred, so I can't really be jealous. Now if only Marcus Gilman were in our year ...'

By the time we get back to the classroom, the lesson is about to end. Lynne is feeling hard done by and hungry. She doesn't think much of our lack of appreciation for the importance of sewing. ('It's a really important life skill, you know, and don't think you can just come to me for the rest of your lives when you need help with loose buttons or taking up hems!') She stalks out ahead of us when the lesson ends. Phee rolls her eyes.

'I'll see if Mrs Poole has something I can cadge as a snack for her,' I say. 'You go and tell Ms Winters I'm in the loo. She won't mind.'

Mrs Poole smiles a little nervously as I hover at the end of her desk while she finishes congratulating Jenny on her pencil case. 'Lynne's not feeling very well,' I say as soon as Jenny leaves, because Mrs Poole is going all apologetic and I really don't want her to feel bad for giving me a low mark on my horrible pencil case. 'Is there something I can take her to eat?'

'Well, you're not really meant to eat in class, dear, but I did think Lynne was looking rather pale. How about a little piece of cheese? Very good for when someone's blood sugar is low.'

While Mrs Poole cuts and wraps up the little block of cheese, I fish in my coat pocket. Usually we're not allowed to wear coats to class but because of the ribs I'm meant to stay wrapped up when it's cold.

'There you go, dear. And well done for looking after your friends so nicely.'

'Here,' I say in turn, holding out the big, blunt needle. 'I hope you don't mind that I borrowed it. I don't need it any more.'

'Oh that's absolutely fine, Evie. It's wonderful that you're . . . you're so . . . *determined* to finish what you start. Very commendable. And very commendable that you'd bring this back safely.'

'All you need now is determination,' I say, smiling.

'Oh,' says Mrs Poole, blinking. 'Well . . . Well, yes, dear. I suppose you could say that. After all your trials lately, I suppose *you* really could say that.'

'I got it as a motto in a fortune cookie a few weeks ago,' I explain.

'Well, that's wonderfully appropriate! Now, that gives me an idea,' Mrs Poole says, staring off at the wall. 'Yes, what a lovely idea. We could all make fortune cookies and write some mottos . . .'

'Bye,' I say.

'Oh, yes, yes goodbye for now, dear.'

Ms Winters gives me a little nod as I sidle into the room and slip into the seat Lynne and Phee have saved between them. Across the classroom, Sonny Rawlins is glaring at the blackboard. He doesn't even look in my direction. Fred is giggling softly with Jenny, so no one comments on whether I was late on purpose to show how special I think I am. In fact, no one says anything.

I take the cheese out of my pocket and press it into Lynne's hand under the desk. 'Eat it,' I whisper out of the corner of my mouth. 'You're being a grump and you know you've walked off the calories already.'

Lynne shoves the cheese into her mouth. 'Maybe that

article was just a load of rubbish. There was one on that site the other day about computers giving you cancer. Maybe it's another one like that.'

Phee and I exchange a grin and high-five under the table.

Amy and I are in the kitchen making shortbread, while we sip from mugs of hot chocolate piled high with whipped cream, when the doorbell rings.

Phee is standing on the step, white-faced, tear-streaked and shaking.

We stare at each other for a moment.

'My mum's got cancer,' she says.

I don't usually hug people, though I don't mind so much any more if they hug me. But today I step forward and put my arms around her. She puts her head on my shoulder and leans into me, sobbing hot, wet air through the weave of my jumper.

'Evie sweetheart, who's . . .'

I look over my shoulder to see Amy come into the hall, drying her hands on a tea-towel. 'I'll make some more hot chocolate,' she says, and leaves us alone.

Eventually Phee raises her head from my shoulder. Her face is red now and sweaty. She brushes damp hair off her forehead and wipes her nose on the back of her hand. I leave her standing by the foot of the stairs long enough to grab my hot chocolate and the fresh one for her, then tug her up to my room. I push the clothes off the chair by the window and manoeuvre her into it, then settle on the edge of the bed.

Phee looks down into her mug. 'I . . . I wanted to ask you about your mum, Evie. I know you don't talk about her, but I really need to ask you some stuff.'

'OK,' I say.

Phee starts and looks up at me, staring into my eyes. 'My dad didn't come and pick me up from school yesterday,' she tells me. 'He just forgot. And I sort of get it. They've obviously known about it for a week or so. They said they just wanted to get a bit more information before they told me so that they could explain it properly. And Mum says that the doctor thinks she'll be fine. She told me all about what's going to happen and how long it's all going to take.' Phee takes a sip of her hot chocolate, then blinks, looking down at the mug as if she hadn't even realised what she was doing.

'And I don't want to sound like a brat, because I know Dad has a lot on his mind, but I just keep thinking . . .' She sighs and her face twists. 'Well, about your ribs. I mean, I know it happened on the way back from going to the hospital with your mother . . . and I know that she was very ill so everyone was really distracted, and then when you all walked away from the crash everyone just assumed you were fine too, but . . . but didn't your grandparents realise how badly hurt you were? I mean, I could sort of understand it if it was just for an hour or two or even a day, but how could they not notice *at all*? And so . . .'

She leans forwards, hunching over her mug, and I know that what's coming next is the thing that's really bothering her. 'I'm worried that my dad's going to get like that too,' she says, running the words together so fast it takes me a moment to grasp what she's saying. 'I'm worried that he's going to keep forgetting me and . . .' Her face screws up and the next words jerk with the hiccups of suppressed sobs. 'And I know I'm b-being s-silly because it was j-just once and it w-was only p-picking me up from school but . . .'

In my pocket, my hand closes around the Dragon.

'Your dad's not going to be like that, Phee. He loves you.'

'I know,' Phee says, screwing her face up even further and licking snot off her lip.

I pass her the tissue box, taking her mug while she blows her nose then mops her face.

'I know my dad loves me but your grandparents loved you too and I know old people are a bit dippy sometimes but . . .'

I lean forward and press the mug back into her hands. She frowns at me as she sips. 'Your dad isn't anything like my . . . like Fiona's family,' I say.

Phee doesn't get it of course. She frowns, and draws in a breath, and her shoulders go up as she prepares to get angry at me for being confusing.

'I didn't hurt my ribs in a car crash,' I tell Phee. 'One day . . . one day I'll tell you about it. You and Lynne. But you'll have to promise you won't tell anyone. I mean, I won't care if you tell your parents, but you'll have to promise not to tell anyone at school. Not anyone at all.'

'What do you . . . ?' Phee starts, looking even more confused.

It makes me smile, even as I ache. But I'm glad that Phee doesn't get it. She'll probably guess later, but it'll take her a while. And I love that it will, even though it makes me feel . . . I don't follow the thought any further.

How I wish I could un-know all the things that make me so very different from Phee and Lynne. Sooner or later, they'll have to learn about those things too – at least learn about them through other people's stories. But not yet. And I wish that even though I *can't* un-know any of it, I could at least remember what not-knowing was like.

'Anyway, that's not important now,' I say. 'It doesn't matter today. The important thing is that it wasn't my . . . it wasn't Fiona getting ill that stopped them from taking me to the hospital. It wasn't an issue of what they realised and what they didn't.'

Phee has gone rather still. 'Evie . . .' she says.

'Not today, Phee,' I say, and find that I've pushed aside my envy and my longing and that it's not as hard as I would have thought to say what Phee needs to hear. 'I know you'd listen, but not today. You can ask me all the questions you want about Fiona being sick, but I've told you all you need to know about the fact that your dad will notice if you come home ill or hurt: if anything happens to you, he'll notice. He might forget to pick you up a few more times, but you can always just come home with me or Lynne a bit more often.'

Phee leans forwards then and puts her hand on mine, weaving our fingers together.

'I need you to remind me how lucky I am, Evie,' she says in this strange tone that's all urgent and soft at the same time. 'I need you to remind me that my parents are great and so are my aunts and uncles and my grandparents. I've got lots of people who love me and would give me a new home if I ever needed one. And I'm not even going to, because my mum's going to be fine and anyway I've got my dad.' She gives me a smile that is weary with tears, but her eyes are calm and wise. 'I need you to remind me, Evie. Lynne will fuss when I need someone to, and God knows my aunts will smother me. But I need you to remind me.'

I don't think I can speak.

For a moment, the relief is scalding: *I'm not so different and distant from Phee and normal people after all.*

Then it runs cold.

Because I *am* different. Or I was, until a few minutes ago.

All I meant to do was help Phee to understand: to give what was in my gift . . . But Phee didn't know what she was asking. And I did. Because *that* is the difference between us. Or it was.

People get it wrong when they talk about innocence: they think it's something to do with ignorance about the facts of sex and all the nasty things that happen in the world. But facts don't change people: it's understanding how the facts *feel* that does.

Only stupid people think innocence is some weird state of not-knowing that children grow out of once they start to understand innuendo. Or maybe it's not that they're stupid: maybe it's just that in some weird grown-up way they *are* still innocent. Because otherwise they'd know better: they'd understand, even if they couldn't really explain it, that innocence is so much bigger. It's every aspect of the life you have before you know how precious and wonderful it is to be ignorant. It's all the time you spend rushing, rushing to *know*, never expecting to find grief waiting beside knowledge.

I just wanted to help.

But suddenly Phee and I aren't quite so different any more. I've closed the gap between us – at least a little – in trying to be kind.

I don't know why I am drawn back to the graveyard tonight of all nights, but I'm not even halfway across the golf-course green opposite when I hear shouts and see torch beams darting in the darkness. I hurry to the wall. Peering past the yew tree, I wonder if I dare move closer to find out which grave they're celebrating over. I'm almost tempted to go and ask . . .

No, commands the Dragon, breath warm on my ear. *We must not be seen.*

Still, I creep over to the gate and stare down at the mechanism, trying to figure out if I can open it without being heard. Only I realise then that the other people are in a different bit of the graveyard from last time. A completely different bit from where Adam and Aunt Minnie and Grandad Peter and Nanna Florrie's graves are . . .

Flash!

Flash! Flash! Flash!

I'm crouching behind the cover of the wall, gripping the edge of the gatepost with one hand and staring through the bars, before I've even registered the need to move. The Dragon's claws prick the skin over my collarbone.

The shouting is panicked now, fearful and angry.

Flash! Flash! Flash!

Camera flashes, I realise. Someone's taking pictures.

But it's not part of the group who were shouting earlier. They're running now, those people. Running and cursing. One of them has dropped his torch. In its light I see a man in a red bomber jacket snatch at the sleeve of a man in a black hoodie.

'There's only two of 'em! Come 'n' help me get them cameras!' the man in the red jacket is yelling, the beer bottle in his hand streaming glowing liquid as he gestures.

'We've called the police,' someone shouts from the darkness.

The man in the black hoodie curses, shrugging off Red Jacket's hand, and lumbers away across the graveyard.

Red Jacket stands swaying for a moment, then flinches away as the cameras flash again. He hurls the beer bottle wildly into the darkness. I hear it smash against a gravestone between the curses Red Jacket screams into the night. I watch him turn, slipping in the mud and falling to his knees before he finally scrambles away. The gate on the other side of the graveyard clangs.

The men with the cameras have turned their torches on now and are playing them across the ground as they move closer to where the group was sitting.

Flash! Flash!

A sigh. 'Doesn't look like that bottle's done any damage at least,' one of the cameramen calls.

Flash!

'Just the torch and some spray-paint cans here. They obviously didn't have time to really get started,' says Uncle Ben.

I can see it's him now in the light of the torch the vandals dropped.

I watch, frozen, as Paul joins him and together they stare down at the mess between the graves.

'Let's go, just in case they decide to come back,' Paul says after a moment. 'We don't want to lose the photos now.'

But they don't make any move to go.

'I don't like to leave it like this, even for the police,' Uncle Ben says, casting his torch about the ground. 'When you call the vicar to tell him not to clear up until the police have been, make sure you say I'll get them down first thing when I go to drop off the cameras. And tell him I'll stay after to put everything to rights.'

They sigh in unison.

'Right then,' says Paul.

I watch them turn away, the light of their torches fading. I listen for the sound of car doors slamming, an engine starting up. Only then do I set off down the path. My feet went numb while I was crouching by the gate and now, although I know I should hurry – should be sprinting back home as fast as my legs will carry me – the best I can manage is a shambling trot.

Finally, finally, I can see the garden through the woods and ... Yes! The kitchen light is off! No Paul and Uncle Ben at the table under my window ...

I've just reached the edge of the trees when the side gate opens. I throw myself to the ground in the shadow of the berberis, heart jolting against my ribs.

Footsteps on the paving stones. Two sets of footsteps on the paving stones. The dull scrape of chairs being pulled out from under the garden table. The jangle of keys, the click-putt of the lock and the faint squeak of the back door opening. Then footsteps again and the zisht-phut-scurr of a bottle opening. And another. A clink of glass against glass.

'To success against the odds!' Uncle Ben crows.

'And the triumph of hope over experience,' Paul adds ruefully, though the pride in his voice renders the words exultant. 'The police will be able to use the photos, won't they? You're positive there won't be any trouble with it, right?'

'You're really going to start worrying about that *now*?'

'I just don't want to get all excited over nothing and then . . .'

'You, my friend, have been married to my sister for far, far too long. It is obvious that whatever she has is catching. I can only hope that Evie takes after me in terms of resistance to this fantastical ability to worry over every possible thing under the sun.'

'So you still don't think we should tell Amy, even now it's over?'

Uncle Ben groans.

'No, be serious a minute, Ben,' Paul snaps. 'What if a police officer calls up about it?'

'That's why we're going to give them *my* number. Look, Paul, I know you've got this whole adrenalin-rush thing going on,' Uncle Ben says without a trace of deprecation, 'but please just sit there quietly drinking your beer and enjoying this.'

'It just doesn't feel right to keep it from Amy. She's got as much right . . .'

'Of course she does. That's not the point, Paul. The

point is that you don't honestly believe any good could come of telling my sister that the graveyard where Adam is buried, where our parents and my Minnie are buried, is a target for vandalism. That it has actually *been* vandalised. If you want your wife camping out every night over the graves to guard them, you be my guest, but you can't expect me to like it since she's my sister too and I'd rather she didn't get pneumonia, or have any more things to obsess over.'

Paul sighs. I lift my head just enough to see him drink deeply from his bottle. 'You know I agreed with you while we didn't have any certain way of stopping it, but now that we have the photos and the police can identify those . . . those *delinquents* . . . Now, it just feels like something I'm keeping from her.'

'For good reason. For God's sake, Paul. I was married too, you know: I get it. But keeping the odd secret from Minnie – especially about stuff that was only going to upset her – well, it didn't seem like anything more than what a sensible person should do to protect someone he loves. Secrets aren't bad in themselves, Paul. People don't need to know everything.'

'But it's our *son*, Ben. Ours. Not just mine.'

'See, this is exactly why I said you should talk to Evie. You have to know she'd tell you exactly the same thing. You just might believe it from her. And you know she can keep secrets. Evie can keep secrets better than both of us put together.' His voice trails off into a sigh. 'You need to be able to talk to someone about Adam, Paul. And if Amy's still not ready, then maybe you should consider the fact that Evie might like to know a bit about her brother.'

Paul makes a funny noise then: something I can't identify.

'Maybe she really would see him that way if you let her, Paul. If you told her about him, made him alive to her: let her help keep him alive for you.'

'Don't, Ben,' Paul says then, so softly I can barely make the words out. 'Don't.'

Uncle Ben reaches out to grasp Paul's shoulder. 'Amy's not the only one who lost him. And, yes, she needs to do what she needs to do. But you need to think about what you need too. Evie's a smart girl, Paul. Smart and brave and strong.'

'Evie has enough grief of her own . . .'

'Telling her about yours doesn't necessarily mean saddling her with it, Paul. Maybe it would do Evie good to see that you recognise how strong she is. Stop trying to protect her from everything.'

'I know exactly how strong she is, Ben,' Paul says and I've never heard him so angry. 'And don't you *dare* tell me that Evie shouldn't be protected.'

'Not from life, Paul,' Uncle Ben says quietly.

Paul sighs. 'We don't cosset her. Not really. I know Amy seems like she does, but she tries, Ben, she really does try to give Evie her space and the right amount of freedom. We're *careful* about that.'

Now it's Uncle Ben's turn to sigh. 'I know, Paul. I know how well you both look after Evie. I'm just saying that maybe she'd like to do just a little bit of looking after in return. Maybe you shouldn't deny her that opportunity.' Paul draws in an audible breath, but Uncle Ben speaks over whatever it was he was going to say. 'But I've said enough about it. Let's just enjoy our beer and our success. And then perhaps we'll even think about enjoying a bit of sleep!'

Paul gives an awkward laugh but it's enough for them to lapse into relatively comfortable silence, though they linger over their absurd celebration only long enough to tip back the last of their beers. Soon Uncle Ben is closing the gate behind him and Paul is relocking the back door. When the light goes out in the kitchen, I scramble to my feet and race up the garden, on to the table, on to the wall. Then I lean down and wipe my sleeve across the surface to remove the muddy footprints. Finally, I climb back up to my room, pausing halfway through the window. My hair is wet and slimy against my cheek, dripping mud down the side of my neck. My whole front is wet through to the skin.

The Dragon leaps from my shoulder to the dresser, flicking its tail so that a little glob of mud spatters against the mirror. I sit down on the window sill and take off my shoes one at a time, cleaning them on the rag in my pocket before tossing them into the corner. Then I pull off my socks and lob them towards the clothes hamper.

Next, I wriggle out of my jeans, giving myself a moment of heart-stopping fear as I nearly overbalance and topple backwards out of the window. I roll the jeans into a ball and set them down next to me, then ease off my coat, turning it inside out before I drop it on to the floor. My jumper and T-shirt follow. Shivering, I fetch the bottle of water from my cupboard, stick my head out of the window and start trickling it over my filthy hair, running my fingers through the strands to coax the mud out.

By the time I have towelled my hair off with my discarded T-shirt and pushed the bundle of wet, muddy clothing into my hamper, I am shaking almost convulsively, my teeth chattering so hard my jaw aches. The Dragon watches me silently as I wriggle into my nightie and dressing gown, then pull the duvet up around myself. I huddle against the headboard, arms locked across my chest and hand splayed across my ribs as if I can push the pain down deep enough for it to dull.

'So now we know,' I whisper into the darkness.

There is a funny sensation, like someone drawing a circle on my kneecap. When I look down, the Dragon is prowling in a tight circle, just like cats do before they settle. Finally the Dragon stops and sinks its claws down through the duvet to brush my skin.

Sometimes what you want is not what you need, the Dragon says.

'Very original,' I sniff.

Sometimes, the Dragon continues, unruffled, *what you*

. think you want is not what you truly want at all.

'What I want is for you not to speak in riddles the whole time. We've passed the point when it seemed clever and reached the bit where it's just tedious,' I retort. I feel my mouth start to quiver.

I try not to think of Paul and Uncle Ben clinking their beer bottles together, celebrating their bravery in the face of danger.

This was neither what you wanted nor needed, the Dragon says. *It was merely an easy thing to hope for. What would it really have solved?*

'Everything!' I hiss. 'Everything.'

The Dragon stares at me impassively. *You already know you are loved. You know that your family would move heaven and earth to protect you from any present danger. No, you are not truly sorry about what we have learnt tonight.*

The Dragon is right, of course. I didn't want Paul and Uncle Ben to do something awful. It would have ruined them inside . . . But if they had, they would have *understood* so very many things . . . Only then they would have been like me. Like me and Fiona and Fiona's parents. Not entirely, of course. But a bit. And I could never want that.

Only sometimes I do. Sometimes it feels like Amy and Paul and Uncle Ben and Ms Winters and Phee and Lynne are so different I must be one of those changeling creatures from a fairy tale. And I'm glad, glad, glad that my life with Fiona's parents hasn't reached out to touch

Paul and Uncle Ben and paint them with darkness, but still . . .

'What do you know?' I ask the Dragon, thinking my voice will be rough with anger. Instead, the words come out all bloated around a sob of jealousy so strong it is fury because I want to be disdainful over Paul and Uncle Ben's pitiful triumph: their self-important schemes, their 'courage' in photographing a couple of drunken yobs. But I can't. I can't, I can't. I want to fill my head with mocking words, but instead there is seething, wild rage and envy so strong I almost hate them, hate them, hate them for thinking *that's* danger.

How dare they think that! I want to scream. *How dare they not* know! And it's grief, grief and fury wild as a snowstorm because it's not fair, not fair, not fair that this is what they think, still, at *their* age and I can't even *remember* what it is not to know: I can't remember what that sort of innocence feels like. And right now I can barely remember that I love them because I hate them for not knowing when I've never had a time when I *didn't* and I want that, oh how I want that . . .

'What do you know?' I say again, choking the words out in a whisper that wants to be a scream.

The Dragon stands tall, head raised proudly, dark eyes reflecting the moonlight. *Everything*, the Dragon says.

'But I'm so tired,' I whisper, a thin quiver of sound. 'I've had enough. I'm tired of it all being so hard. Of everything being so hard. I'm tired of being strong and

gritting my teeth and getting on with it and bearing it and
... I've had enough now.'

No, commands the Dragon, and spreads its wings. Not
in a sudden flap, like someone shaking out an umbrella,
but a slow unfolding, like a flower unfurling new petals.
In the moonlight, the Dragon glows a strange blue-white,
the tracery of its veins and folds a faint lilac, blushing
purple. Out and out its wings stretch, rippling slightly as if
responding to the faintest hint of a draught in the stillness
of the room.

*Together we are strong enough to move the stars. But you
must make the right wish. You must wish for what you truly
need. That is why I am here. That is the fulfilment of the
wish that called me.*

Slowly, slowly the Dragon lowers its wings, folding
them back tight against its body and settling on to its
haunches.

*But tonight is another matter. Tonight is for weakness
before we gather strength once more. Sometimes it is no great
shame to give in, even to despair, provided that it is just for a
little while. Sometimes a little surrender is good for the soul.*

I gather the Dragon to me, cupped in my palms. Then
I press the globe of my hands to the pain in my chest,
double over so that my forehead is against my knees and
cry until the room is white with exhaustion. When I fall
sideways on to the bed, the burning skin of my face
throbbing against the cool of the sheets, I slip away into
sleep almost before I can think.

'Evie darling?' Amy says, sinking into the chair next to mine.

'Mm?' I mumble, mind on my homework.

'Can I talk to you for a second?'

Something in her tone makes me look up. 'Do you need a hand with dinner?' I ask, though I know that's not it.

'Evie darling,' she says, ignoring my question as she reaches out to put her hand over mine, 'I know I promised not to pry ... And I know Paul will say I'm being nosy,' her eyes flick to the garden window where we can just see Paul watering his way up the flower-bed by the house, 'but I need to know that you know that you don't *have* to keep anything secret from us. If there's anything bothering you, anything you need ... You know you can tell us, don't you?'

'I'm fine,' I say quickly, looking away from the worry in her face.

'It's just that when I came to help you change your sheets earlier, I thought I heard a strange noise, like a machine or something beeping. And I know we checked everything just the other day but ... Well, you've been so secretive this last month. And then when I knocked, you were obviously hiding something before you let me into your room.'

I heave a sigh, picking at a loose thread on my cuff.

'I just need to know that you're OK. That this secret isn't anything *bad*,' Amy says, reaching over to break the thread off for me. 'Because first it was all that stuff up on the stepladder, poking about at the top of the cupboard, and now it sounds like you're doing something with electronics and . . .' She catches herself then, realising that her voice has been getting louder and louder, the words coming faster and faster. I feel her take and release a breath that warms my cheek.

'I just need to know if I can help. Because if there's anything else . . . anything . . . anything like the ribs,' she finally gets out, 'if there is, Evie, I'll fix it, darling. I swear I will.' There's something like desperation in her voice.

My stomach turns over.

'It won't be like the court case,' Amy is saying. 'I promise it won't. Whatever it is, whatever you need, darling . . .' Her hand squeezes mine too tightly and now I can hear guilt and apology under the desperation.

'*Is* it about the court case?'

I jump at the sound of Paul's voice.

He's standing by the kitchen door. The hosepipe, lax in his hand, splashes water across his slippers. 'I know it's been disappointing and we've let it all go quiet. But we don't have to, Evie. We can find a new lawyer, or we can hire a detective. No, really, Evie,' he says, though I haven't rolled my eyes or, as far as I know, made any sign that I think this is a silly idea. 'We can do that. We just don't want you to be even more disappointed if it still ...' He stops and takes a deep breath. 'The one thing we can't do is promise it'll work. But we can keep trying, Evie. For as long as you want us to.'

Amy presses my hand. 'Is that what you were doing in the cupboard, Evie? Reading the file? You know we didn't put it away because we wanted to give up, don't you? We just wanted to ... to give you time to recover before we did anything else. But we don't have to wait, darling. You just have to say the word.'

I open my mouth, not sure what I'm going to say because my mind is blank, blank, blank, but I *have* to say something because I can't leave them thinking I don't understand that they're doing everything possible. I know they'd spend every penny they had if I asked, even though *they* know and *I* know that it's not going to make any difference. They've always done everything decent, law-abiding people can do. And it would be so, so wrong of me to let them think it's not enough.

I open my mouth and 'I was looking at the photos of Adam' is what comes out. I feel sick as soon as the words cross my lips.

They both stare at me.

'When we go to visit him, on the anniversary, you're always telling him what we've been doing,' I say, tripping over the words and my own wretchedness. 'But I don't know anything about him.' The millstone of guilt in my stomach pushes down so hard I feel as if I'm pinned to the chair, as if I'll never be able to get up under the weight of it again. 'I wanted . . . I just wanted . . .' I gasp, my throat going so tight it feels like I've swallowed liquid metal. The pain burns up into my ears.

Then Paul blinks. 'Evie sweetheart, why don't you make us all a nice cup of tea?' he says gently, in his usual soft, kind voice. 'I'm going to go and turn off the hose, and after that we're going to get all the photo albums down and we're going to have a nice look at them in the living room.' He's still talking to me, but now his eyes are on Amy. She is staring at the dishwasher.

The air feels heavy and dark. My head swirls with desperation and the beat of my blood, louder and louder until the chair beneath me, the floor under my feet, grows unsteady. There are not-sounds echoing in my ears. And things that aren't really there are stirring at the corners of my vision.

'I'm sorry,' I whisper.

Amy starts and looks up at me. She blinks a bit and her eyes go teary, but then she smiles. It's a wan little smile, but a smile all the same. 'Adam's not meant to be a secret, Evie. Especially not from you.' She coughs and blinks some more. 'Those albums shouldn't be shut away up in the cupboard where we never look at them.'

'I . . .'

Amy leans over then and puts her soft, warm hands on my cheeks. 'What on earth would we do without you to sort us out, Evie?' She kisses my forehead and my heart suddenly lifts and the air goes light again, like I'm coming up out of water. 'I'm really proud of you. That you've been . . . visiting Adam's photos. I should never have put them away like that, where they'd be . . . lonely.' She stutters over the word but I hear it clearly, despite the catch in her voice, because there's beautiful, blissful, ringing silence in my head and only whiteness at the corners of my vision.

'Now,' she says, sniffing, though her eyes are dry. 'Why don't you put the kettle on while I see whether we've got something extra-specially nice in the biscuit department.'

When Paul comes back in, Amy turns from the fridge with a smile. 'Can you get the photos down while we finish in here?'

He stops to kiss her as he passes. I can tell he means to kiss her hair, but she turns her face up to his and presses their lips together. They both smile.

In the end, it takes all three of us two trips up and down from the cupboard on the upstairs landing. We start with the photo albums, but then Amy takes a deep breath and says that we should bring everything down.

Soon the living room is strewn with albums and loose prints and drawings and school exercise books and certificates and scout badges . . . Hours later, we're still sitting there on the floor in the middle of the chaos. We've got our backs to the sofa and I'm in between Amy and Paul. I've got one of the albums open on my lap and Paul is telling me about Adam's first sports day. I look at the little boy with the curly brown hair bunny-hopping furiously across the grass, yards ahead of all the rest.

In the next photo, Adam, Paul and Uncle Ben have been caught in the act of arguing over how to carve the most enormous pumpkin I've ever seen. Adam has bits of pumpkin string all down his front. Uncle Ben is gesturing emphatically and Paul is laughing.

In the photo below, Uncle Ben is sitting on the floor with Adam between his legs, using his knees as an armrest, both dark heads close together as they pore over a board game. A pretty auburn-haired woman sits in front of them, at the feet of the person taking the photo: she looks as if she has just twisted around to smile for the camera. So this is Aunt Minnie.

On the next page, I see Adam's fifth birthday party. He's grinning, gap-toothed, from behind a huge chocolate cake. When Paul goes to turn the page, I stop him, still staring into the photo.

'Why a girl?' I ask, looking up at Amy.

She frowns, so I turn to Paul.

'Why didn't you adopt a boy?'

'We never really thought about it,' Paul says, leaning his head back against the sofa and reaching out to tuck a stray strand of hair behind my ear. 'We hadn't even decided whether we wanted to adopt a baby or a slightly older child, or even try to have another child ourselves. We'd just come in to talk to Social Services about the process. But then we met you there in the corridor and that was it. Minds made up. We hadn't even got back to the car park before we'd agreed that we wanted to adopt you. Of course we loved you even more once we got to know you, but somehow we loved you right from when we first talked to you. You were coming down the corridor, all covered in blue paint, with this look of absolute determination of your face. Do you remember? You asked me what the problem with painting the path was anyway since the rain would wash it all off sooner or later and at least it would be pretty in the meantime . . . Though what you were doing there that day, painting the pavement, I have no idea '

I frown down at the birthday-party photo.

'Penny for your thoughts?' Paul asks, elbowing me gently.

'It's just . . . I know my birthday's only two days after Adam's, but there must have been some boys the same age who had similar birthdays. Maybe four or five days' difference instead of two, but . . .'

Horror washes over Amy's face. 'Evie darling, you're not a *replacement*,' she whispers. 'We *never* thought of you as a replacement. We hadn't figured *any* of it out when we met you. But then we did and you seemed to like us too . . . Everyone commented on how you seemed to take to us that first day. I remember your social worker saying how impressed they all were with the fact that you'd bonded with us or they *never* would have *considered* pursuing an adoption match based on a chance meeting. I mean, we hadn't even registered to adopt, let alone been approved at that point . . . But it all just fell into place. So you see, we knew we loved you even before we had any *idea* when your birthday was or even how old you were. It just seemed so perfect when we found out. Like a sign that it really was meant to be. As if we were always meant to watch Adam grow to a certain age and then watch you grow from that point on. That's what it meant to us, Evie, your birthday being so close to Adam's: that we got to be parents through a whole lifetime, even if that life was divided across two children. But we never thought that made you a replacement . . .'

I stroke my fingers over the smiling faces in the photo.

'You don't really think that's how we see you – how we ever saw you – do you, Evie?'

I tuck one hand into hers and the other into Paul's.

'Do you think they would have liked me too?' I ask, turning my gaze to the photo on the page opposite: Amy's parents and Aunt Minnie and Adam smiling, smiling, smiling at the camera.

I have all their most precious things: Amy and Paul and Uncle Ben . . . And now I'm sharing their stories too I know all the things going back in time, just as Amy makes sure that they know all the things going forwards. I hope they don't mind too much. And I can't help hoping that they miss knowing me even half as much as I miss knowing them, even though Amy and Paul never would have needed to love me if they were still here. But I still hope that they miss knowing me, even if it's just a little, little bit.

Out of the mist come the horses. My breath catches in my throat. For a moment, I can't tell if they're even real. But there is steam rising from their nostrils, rising to embrace the mist.

I stand still, so very still.

They are all around me now. I watch the grey pony closest of all: the flick of his tail as it mingles with the mist like it is dissolving into it. The wind ebbs and flows, one moment sweeping the mist up into towering waves, cresting so high I have to strain my neck to see, then diving down at me, through me. It boils into angry eddies on the ground, then swirls away into whirlpools so real I wonder if I will be sucked down into the earth if I dare the currents twisting around me.

Thunder rips the mist apart. The horses throw up their heads.

Lightning.

For a minute the world glows blue and green. The horse nearest me neighs fearfully.

Then the rain comes down.

I am soaked in seconds. The horses vanish into the downpour. The ground turns to cloying mud, pulling at my trainers as I follow them.

Lightning. Ahead of me, the black and white world is spiky with the bare trunks and branches of winter trees.

As I reach the edge of the coppice a horse bolts away. Blinking rain out of my eyes, I realise that the herd has taken shelter under the trees. Some stand still, pressed disconsolately against each other. Others trot back and forth, running towards the open fields then snorting and jerking away as if whipped back by the rain.

Sometimes it is as important to touch as to stand and observe, the Dragon tells me. *You must not fear that clutching at your dreams will shatter them so they run through your fingers like sand. That way lies a life spent in yearning. But yearning is only a season of dreaming, for dreams, if nurtured, become strong. Like mist settling and turning to ice. So you must wait before you reach out to clasp your dreams. Wait just long enough, but no longer.*

Slowly, I ease forwards. Slowly, slowly, slowly. One of the horses trots away, but the white one stands and watches me. He huffs a hot, moist breath into my face as I grow near, then seems pleased when I do not start and jump away.

I raise my hand slowly, slowly, slowly. His nose is like velvet, so softly stubbled and textured with fine, fine hair. He pushes his head against my chest then, and whuffles into my neck: a billow of hot, white steam. I laugh in delight, though he snorts and pulls back for a moment before pressing his nose to my coat again. His neck is strong and sleek as metal as I stroke the wet hair.

He can smell food, the Dragon tells me.

'You want a mint?' I ask, reaching into my pocket. The

horse lips the sweets from my palm before I've even extended my hand to him. I give him more, then more again.

That is quite enough, the Dragon tells me.

This time, I tuck the mints into my inner pocket. The horse snorts his disapproval, but he lets me stroke his face and his neck and his side. He lets me lean into him. His flank warms me.

When the rain stops, I watch the steam start to rise from him until suddenly the horses turn as one and canter away into the darkness.

And I run with them. Run and am not breathless. Run and there is no pain. Just lightness and speed. As if I am flying with the Dragon. As if I have the strength of the wind. As if, unseen in the darkness, I am unstoppable.

With every exhalation, the lingering rage and hurt at Paul and Uncle Ben drifts away and dissipates into the night. The thick, cold, clean air of the fens fills me with calm.

I run on, back to the canal path, back towards home. When I reach the trees that mark the bottom of the garden, I pause to stare up at the moon. Then finally, *finally* I turn to the left and continue until, unseen, I pass beyond the boundaries of our town and the fens stretch out endless and empty around me. The weir is silent. The canal a road of tarnished silver, stretching into the distance. And all along is quiet and still. The longboats are gone now, downstream to Cambridge for the winter. The river is mine.

I draw to a stop, take in a deep breath of midnight air and stare down the canal.

This is far enough, says the Dragon.

I smile and turn towards home.

'I've got two new goals,' I tell Ms Winters before she's even had time to sit down.

'Oh?' she says, surprised.

'I want to learn to ride. I want to learn about horses,' I say.

'Oh,' says Ms Winters again, blinking in bewilderment. 'I never knew you liked horses.'

'I didn't. I just realised it the other day.'

'What made you think of it?' Ms Winters asks, so startled she hasn't even settled back into her chair yet but is still perched on the edge.

I find myself wondering if she'll fall off when I tell her what my second goal is. 'I saw some horses and . . . and I just realised that I'd really like to learn how to ride,' I say.

'Have you asked Amy and Paul about it yet?'

I wrinkle my nose. 'Amy says we need to check with Dr Barstow about whether it's OK for my ribs . . . or at least how long we have to wait before I can try. But we looked up stables in the Yellow Pages and everything, so I know exactly where we're going after Dr Barstow gives me the all-clear. Paul says that the exercise will be good for building up my muscles again and Amy says that maybe I can make some new friends at the stables, but Phee wants to come with me anyway. So now I've got something that's like D of E for Phee and Lynne: something that just two of us are doing together. I mean, I know Phee and I cycle to school together but that's only because Lynne lives in the opposite direction. It's just a matter of convenience really, so it doesn't count. But going riding together . . . That's a proper choice.' *Something special*, I add to myself, missing what Ms Winters says next as I hug the words close.

'. . . And you could have lots of little goals about different aspects of riding,' Ms Winters is saying approvingly when I turn my focus back to her. 'Excellent. I'm really impressed, Evie. So what's the other goal?'

'Well, Uncle Ben needs someone to love him: I don't think he ever goes out on dates. And he should get married again because he really should have kids. Kids of his own, I mean. Not just me.'

Ms Winters is smiling, but frowning a bit too. 'Well, that's a lovely thought, Evie, but that's a goal for your Uncle Ben, not for you.'

'No, it's not,' I say. 'Uncle Ben's not getting on with any of it. He needs my help. I don't think he's even thought about how to meet anyone who could understand him and what he's been through, so of course he's not going to have much luck finding the right person.'

'Evie ...' says Ms Winters in a warning sort of voice that makes me want to roll my eyes. 'Evie, it's lovely that you want to help your uncle and make him happy, but matchmaking can be a very tricky business. He might not appreciate ...'

This time I do roll my eyes. 'That's why I need to be subtle. Well, subtle-ish. Just to get him to meet someone nice and see if they hit it off.'

'Evie ...'

'Anyway, I had the best idea ever. And it sort of is a goal. I want you to go out with my Uncle Ben.'

Ms Winters's mouth falls open. 'Me?' she squeaks. She really does.

'Well, you said what a lovely person he must be one time when I was telling you about him ... and, well, you looked all *wistful*. And you're not married or anything, are you?'

Ms Winters closes her mouth and stares at me. Her right hand goes to her empty ring finger. 'Evie ... Evie, that's ever so sweet. It really is. But it's just not *appropriate*.'

'Why not?' I retort. 'You'd be able to understand all about Aunt Minnie. And you already know the whole family.'

'That's exactly why it's not appropriate, Evie,' Ms Winters says, trying to sound calm and collected and not managing it at all.

Though I keep my face eager and open, inside I can't help a thrill of deepest satisfaction that I've finally flustered her out of all recognition.

'I'm here to help you with *your* problems,' Ms Winters is protesting. 'And I'm your teacher … And that … that would cross all *sorts* of professional boundaries. It just wouldn't be *ethical*.'

'It's my idea,' I say. 'And *I* think it's a brilliant idea. And you're meant to be helping me. So help me with my goal. Go and have a coffee with Uncle Ben.'

'Evie, that is *not* what Amy and Paul were envisaging when they asked me to have extra sessions with you out of school,' Ms Winters says, not even trying to mask her exasperation.

I'm totally unmoved by it because she's also blushing down to her shirt collar. Plus it's clearly not the Uncle Ben bit of the plan that she objects to.

'I'm meant to be helping you with your schoolwork and with your own problems, not meddling in your life …'

'It's not meddling. It's just coffee.'

Ms Winters lets the following silence go on and on and on. I just grin because this time I know she's not waiting me out: she just has absolutely no idea what to say.

Besides, I've already figured out what to do if she does keep saying no. Uncle Ben hardly ever says no to *me*: if I tell him I want him to come over at particular times on particular days that just so happen to coincide with Ms Winters being here, he might be a bit confused but he'll do it. And then I just need to keep him talking once Ms Winters arrives so he doesn't leave right away or go off to another room. Of course, she'll suggest we make a start on our work, but she's too polite to insist in someone else's house. Plus I can always just *have* to duck into the loo or lie down somewhere for a few minutes if my ribs are aching. And then Ms Winters won't have any choice but to talk to Uncle Ben or be rude. And she'll never bring herself to be rude, so Uncle Ben will end up making coffee for the two of them to cover the awkwardness.

It's not exactly what I had in mind, but it'll do at a pinch. Like Ms Winters says, it can be a little goal on the way to a bigger one.

'Evie love, do you think you could come into town with me?'

I look up from my homework to find Paul standing on the opposite side of the kitchen table. Although his voice is cheerful enough, something about his tone isn't at all casual. And he's gripping the back of the chair he's standing behind. The tips of his fingernails are white.

Something in his face shifts. 'Sorry, love. Shouldn't interrupt your homework really, should I?' He says it as if he means to laugh, but he doesn't. 'And you've got plans with Phee and Lynne later, haven't you?'

He's nervous, I realise. He's afraid I'll say no. And he really, really doesn't want me to.

'Never mind then,' Paul is saying, pushing away from

the table. 'Maybe next weekend.'

And I realise that I'm frowning and he thinks it's because I'm cross, so I put a smile on my face and slam my book closed. 'Can we get flying saucers?' I ask, shoving my chair eagerly back from the table.

Paul starts then, just a little, but he smiles too. 'Whatever you want, love,' he says softly, his voice full of warmth.

I grin. 'Really? So we can get cheesecake and chips too and you'll explain to Amy why I can't eat lunch and why I haven't finished my French?'

Paul takes a step back, widening his eyes and forcing a huge gulp. 'Couldn't I just buy you a Ferrari?'

I tilt my head to the side for a moment and then screw my eyes nearly closed. 'Perhaps I'll settle for a cheesecake to bring home,' I say.

Paul pantomimes wiping sweat from his forehead as he drapes his arm around my shoulders and leads me over to the coat rack.

'Don't you want your blue coat, love?' Paul asks. 'I thought that was your favourite.'

'Nah.' I wrinkle my nose. 'Can't be bothered to go upstairs for it.'

'Then stop keeping it up there!' Paul scolds, rolling his eyes as he pulls my scarf snug about my neck.

We stop at the garage first and get the promised flying saucers. We always do this together. Amy won't let me have them. She's says they're nothing but nasty chemicals and she's probably right. But I still like them and so does Paul: it's one of our little things together.

Paul punches the radio on to our favourite channel, but he doesn't sing along like he usually does. And he keeps looking over at me, though he doesn't say anything. Because he doesn't, I don't either: I don't even ask where we're going.

We park in the supermarket as usual and walk through to the high street. When he stops for a moment and takes a deep breath, I slip my hand into his and squeeze his fingers. He smiles down at me and squeezes back. Then we turn into the art shop and he leads me over to the wall display made up of the corners of different types of picture frame.

'I want you to help me pick out something special,' he says.

And I know from his tone that this is what we're here for, but I can't for the life of me work out why it's such a big deal, these little bits of wood.

'Is it for a present? For Grandma Suzie's birthday?' I ask when Paul doesn't say anything. I know that's not it, but in the absence of even a single idea, a stupid question seems as good a way to get Paul talking as any.

He squeezes my fingers, but though his face is turned to me, somehow his eyes don't meet mine. 'It's for us,' he says quietly. 'For you and me and Amy. Something to go in the living room.' He pauses and his eyes drift back to the frames. 'I want to put a big photo up on the wall. And then I want to get two smaller frames to go on the coffee table.' His eyes move from the bits of frame on the wall to the shelves of standing picture frames. 'I want to put that photo the waiter took of Uncle Ben and the three of us at your adoption birthday up on the wall,' he says, but then he goes silent and just stands there staring blankly at the frames: just stands there and stands there.

I lean into his side and my weight seems to push the next thing out of him. 'And I want a photo of Adam on the coffee table,' he says. 'I want a photo of my son. And the family one that Ben took just before the accident. I want photos of my kids in the living room.'

I feel the tears in his voice in my eyes and hug his arm tightly.

'I want you to pick the frames, Evie,' Paul tells me softly, and I realise he is looking down at me now: really looking at me and seeing me, instead of gazing vacantly as he has all morning while he thought this through.

'But shouldn't you and Amy . . .'

'You know the sorts of things Amy likes. You won't pick anything she'll hate,' Paul says, and there's something a little sharp in his tone. 'So it'll just have to be good enough, because I want to pick it with *you*, Evie. I don't want to talk about it and discuss it and negotiate it. I want photos of my kids. And I want my daughter to help me pick the frames.'

I stare up at him but don't know what to say. His eyes soften.

'Amy won't mind,' he tells me quietly. 'It'll give her a start but she won't ...' He draws in a deep breath and looks away then, but his hand comes up to stroke my hair. 'This last week she's talked about Adam. You've let her talk about him, Evie. And look at his pictures without ...' He takes another breath. 'She couldn't do that before. She just couldn't. So I couldn't. I couldn't talk to her about him. Or to you. Even though Ben kept telling me I could. That I should. Smart man, your Uncle Ben,' he says, making a funny gulping sound I know was intended as a laugh. His hand is slick with sweat in mine.

'This week we've talked about our son. With you. With each other. And ... And that's how I want it, Evie. I want you to know all about your brother. And I want us to have his photo and your photo together in the living room where I can see them all the time. That's what *I* want.'

I stand there, leaning into him, until his breathing settles and he presses a kiss to my hair.

'You did that, Evie,' he says fiercely. 'You fixed that. And I want you to pick the frames for the photos of our family.'

'I've been thinking ...'

'Kind of the point when we're doing homework,' Phee says testily. I sigh. So does Phee, tossing her pencil to the side. 'Sorry,' she says.

I bump her shoulder with mine and she grins at me wanly, then crosses her arms on the table and drops her head on to them. Her mum's in hospital because of the operation to take out her tumour. Phee says she's doing OK, but there's still the radiation therapy to come.

'I was thinking about what we could do to help your mum when she gets out of hospital,' I say. 'And I think we should cook.'

Phee blinks up at me. She opens her mouth, closes it and then opens it again. 'But we can't cook,' she says as if she thinks I've somehow forgotten this. 'I mean, neither of us can. We're rubbish.'

'Yes,' I agree. 'But Lynne isn't.'

'So we're going to turn Lynne into a kitchen slave?' Phee says slowly. The contemplative look in her eyes sharpens into something mischievous and infinitely less sad.

'I was thinking we could do a blog together,' I try to explain, but my mind's not really on what I'm saying as I grin at Phee's grin. 'A blog about cooking for teenagers who want to help their parents out for whatever reason. And we could make it all about cooking really healthy food.'

Phee frowns. 'And why would any of us want to do this?' she says dubiously. 'I was just going to keep doing the hoovering and washing and stuff when Mum comes home. And Dad's getting the shopping delivered. Why would we want to cook when we can just get microwave meals or take-out or call my aunt?'

'Because we could write all about cooking so you can eat healthily.'

Phee rolls her eyes. 'You said that already. And I bet there are a million webpages that do that already anyway.'

'But think about it: we could all work on it together.'

Phee drops her head back down on to the table. 'And?' she prompts.

'And we can write about Being Healthy.'

Phee sighs. 'I got *that* bit. What I *don't* get is why you think this is a good idea.'

'Maybe if Lynne thinks about teaching other people about healthy eating – about meals that aren't low-cal because they need to be good for people like your mum who need enough calories, but they're healthy for normal people who don't want to get fat, like your dad – maybe we can get her to start, you know, focusing on Being Healthy. Not dieting, just eating things that are good for you. But we could make it about teaching other teenagers how to do that.'

Phee rolls her head so she's facing me again. 'Your pitch stinks,' she says. She yawns and sits up, stretching her arms above her head. 'But the idea's good,' she concedes. 'We get her to do it to help me . . .' Phee tilts her head to one side and then the other. 'I wonder if we can make it count for that public service bit of our Duke of Edinburgh thing. It's about the only way I'm ever going to finish. I mean, I was going to do some volunteering on Mum's ward, but it's just too depressing. Plus I don't really care about it any more to be honest. Lynne's never going camping ever again, so it's not like we're going to do our Silver and there's not much point just having a Bronze level.' She wrinkles up her nose, then nods. 'OK. We'll cook. If Lynne's helping, it'll be decent and that'll be good for Mum.'

'And Lynne will have to eat if we're doing all that cooking.'

Phee does the head-tilt thing again, but this time it worries me. There's something calculating in her expression. 'You're feeling good, aren't you, about all this? Keeping me company when I'm stressed about my mum. And trying to help Lynne with her eating thing.'

I shrug, frowning. 'I like helping, if that's what you mean. It's not like I want you guys to be unhappy though, just so I can feel useful.'

Phee rolls her eyes. 'Duh,' she says. 'The point is that it makes you feel good, helping us, right?'

'*Duh*,' I return, making a face at her.

'So when do we get to feel good for helping you?'

I stare at her. 'You started cycling to school every day just because you knew Amy would only agree to let me if we went together. And you're going to come riding with me next week. And you and Lynne took me out after the thing with Sonny Rawlins . . .'

'So?' Phee asks. 'I've got to get to school somehow. And I *want* to go riding. And as for the Sonny Rawlins thing, we took you out *one* time.'

'But I don't need . . .'

'Evie,' Phee says and it stops me dead. 'It's really nice that you want to help. But friends tell each other things. They share their secrets. I know you feel left out sometimes: we *know* that,' she stresses when I open my mouth to interrupt, 'but the reason you feel left out is that Lynne tells me everything. And I tell her everything. And you never tell us anything important.'

In the pause Phee gives me to respond, I open my mouth again but nothing comes out.

'The reason it's sometimes me-and-Lynne and then you on the side is that you know everything about us but you don't trust us to know anything about you.'

'You know about . . . about Adam, and about me being adopted and . . .' I trail off at the look of exasperation and hurt on Phee's face.

'Evie,' she says, '*you* know about when my dog died when I was four, and when Lynne's gran died when she was seven.'

She opens her mouth to go on, then stops, closes her eyes and takes a deep breath. When she opens her eyes again, the exasperation is gone, replaced with determination. 'You know about how we used to think it was "good tidings we bring to you and your king" instead of "kin". You know what my first My Little Pony was. Maybe we can't help much 'cos it's all stuff that's really serious and we wouldn't know what to do. But maybe it would just be nice if your best friends knew things like why you were so upset when you broke that stupid glass at Lynne's birthday party that you went and cried behind her dad's shed for an hour and then pretended you'd just been in the loo. Or why you freeze up if one of the teachers comes and looks over your shoulder at your work and then you can't concentrate for the rest of the lesson. Remember that time you didn't realise Mrs Poole was standing right behind you? You shouted at her. And you never shout at people, Evie. We know that. What we don't know is why things like that upset you so much.'

Phee reaches over then, and takes hold of my hand. 'Maybe your best friends should know about all those everyday things that just aren't normal for you. Maybe we'd be able to help. Just like you and I know when Lynne's upset because she thinks she's somehow got fat in the space of an hour, and how to calm her down when she decides that something she ate is going to make her put on a stone by tomorrow.'

The doorbell goes then. I'm so relieved that I almost miss the look Phee and Lynne exchange when Lynne pops her head around the kitchen door. It takes me a minute to figure out what it is: it's the look I would have given Phee if Lynne had arrived just after I proposed the blog idea.

Phee just grins when I break down in giggles.

'What?' Lynne asks, hands on hips, looking disgruntled. 'What did I miss?'

I am watching for the look on Ms Winters's face when she realises that Uncle Ben is in the kitchen. Although by the time she turns to me she has wrestled her face into something that I think is meant to be disapproval, that's only after I've seen hope and pleasure, perhaps even excitement, in her eyes. In any case, the failed attempt at disapproval soon shifts into something that is closer to resignation.

She turns to greet Uncle Ben, who's come into the living room to say hello, and there's a sudden intensity in both their eyes. That sense of recognition that isn't quite recognition. And it's nothing like when Phee sees that guy from the Lower Sixth she says she'd do *anything* with if she had half a chance, or when Lynne pauses the TV to ogle an actor she fancies like crazy: it's not an avid look they're exchanging. There's just something shared there: not exactly heated, but strong all the same. They keep trying to force their expressions into normal, polite, slightly disinterested friendliness, so I can't quite put my finger on it, but I suppose that doesn't really matter.

'Just going to the loo,' I say, grinning at Ms Winters.

Her face says she thinks she should glare or take another shot at the disapproval thing, but all I get is something fretful and uneasy: it's in her hands, playing with the knot of her string belt, as much as in her face.

I smile as encouragingly as I can, giving a little quirk of my eyebrows before I hum my way down the hall to the bathroom. I stand in front of the sink for as long as I can bear it, grinning at myself in the mirror.

I thought about saying something encouraging to Uncle Ben before Ms Winters arrived, but I'm saving that for later, when I can fish for information. Not that it's really necessary. Whatever that not-recognition thing they've got going is, it's obviously significant *and* not just a one-off.

I expect Ms Winters will try to make things difficult but, for once, I rather think she'll be a bit half-hearted. That's not usually her style at all, but her failure to pull off disapproving or embarrassed in favour of resignation seems fairly definitive to me. Besides, Uncle Ben's pretty single-minded when he wants to be. I figure if I explain it to him and make it clear just how happy about the whole thing I am, then it'll all come right. I've just got a feeling about it.

I mean, I know these things don't usually work like that . . . and it's not like I think it's love at first sight exactly: it's that recognition thing, whatever it is. There's something about it, and the fact that they both have it, that tells me that whatever's going to happen is going to be relatively straightforward. Once I set Uncle Ben straight, he'll sort the rest out. I just know he will.

I wink at myself in the mirror then hum my way back down the corridor to find Uncle Ben leaning against the kitchen table, sipping from a mug and saying, 'I'm sure Evie won't mind delaying your lesson for five minutes if there's one of my world-renowned triple chocolate caramel brownies in it for everyone,' while Ms Winters frets at her belt with one hand and her bracelet with the other.

So of course I say, 'Hand it over then. No way I can concentrate now.'

And what can Ms Winters say to that?

I've had a funny sense of anticipation all day. I have no idea why. It made me so distracted I got told off by four different teachers. Sonny Rawlins started sniggering at one point, but *Fred* told him to shut up, so it was a really good day even though I was so preoccupied by the afternoon that Phee asked me whether I was sad about Fiona and her parents or something and whether I wanted to talk about it. Of course I told her that school lunch break wasn't exactly the best time – and the cloakroom certainly wasn't the best place – to have any sort of serious conversation at all. I know she meant well but then I was distracted about that too.

Phee and I had riding after school and I felt calmer after that. It helped that between getting cleaned up and having dinner there wasn't time for Amy or Paul to notice that something was up with me.

I went to bed early but here I am, still lying awake two hours later, listening to my audiobook for the second time.

Finally the Dragon comes leaping off the bedside table on to my chest and sits regally down like a sphinx, staring at me just as cryptically.

Tonight is the night of our dark moon.

'Where are we going?' I ask, moving to sit up.

The Dragon sinks a claw through my nightie. I feel it scrape against my skin.

You are going to sleep now.

'But . . .'

You must go to sleep now, the Dragon repeats.

'But can't you tell me . . .'

That, says the Dragon, *would violate our contract.*

I roll my eyes. 'I hate it when you talk about our contract. You never make any sense.'

I make as much sense as is good for you and no more, says the Dragon.

'But I don't understand any of it!' I protest.

The Dragon smiles. *That is precisely the point.*

'Urgh,' I say. I am tempted to roll over but know that the Dragon would not appreciate the insult at all.

Remember that night in the rain and thunder spent among the horses, says the Dragon. *Remember the horses in the storm and the mist.*

I see the mist curl up around the horses' legs. I remember the velvet-soft nose against my palm. I smile, on the cusp of the fall into dreaming.

'This is the third dark moon since I wished you,' I whisper to the Dragon. 'When's it going to be our special one? When will we have done enough planning and preparing that we can do something important?'

The Dragon smiles down at me. *Three is a very special number.*

'Third time lucky?' I mumble around a yawn, the mist from the dream welling up around me, thickening as it drags me down into sleep.

When you have planned so carefully, there is no need for luck, says the Dragon. Sleep now. *Our dark moon is nearly upon us and you must be dreaming when it comes.*

The mist creeps out of the darkness and wraps around me, but, as I sink down, I dream that I am throwing back the covers and sitting up, while the Dragon sails across the room to the window and crouches there, looking back at me.

Come, the Dragon commands.

'Evie? Evie darling, are you all right?'

It is morning. Bright daylight.

I hear the bedroom door creak open as I roll my head to the left. Amy peers in at me.

It's a school day, I realise.

I sit up, yawning, feeling limp and wrung out. I ache,

but oddly it's my legs that are most sore. My legs and my arms. I try to remember the Dragon waking me for our dark moon adventure, try to remember what special thing we did that has left me so stiff and achy, but nothing comes. I remember my edge-of-dream vision of the Dragon launching itself into the air like the night it ate Sonny Rawlins's bike. But then the next image that pops into my mind is a glimpse of my bike. For a second, I remember the feel of the handlebars shuddering against my palms as I bump over the tree roots at the bottom of the garden. The sound of crumbling concrete grinding under my weight as I turn on to the canal towpath. And I remember my heart pounding, pounding, pounding like when you're being chased in a nightmare . . .

And a sudden thrill, like jumping through ice and soaring from the top of a mountain at the same time.

I frown, but even these vague memories are making me feel sick to my stomach somehow. I push the lingering images away.

When I move to stretch, I find myself wincing. Before the Dragon, I used to have nightmares all night long and wake up feeling like this: like I've been running all night from the things in my head, some of them memories and some just normal nightmares. Often they get mashed together, one nightmare running into another. It all drifts away like smoke after a fire has gone out when I wake.

'Are you feeling OK, darling?' Amy asks, perching on the edge of the bed and reaching to feel my forehead.

'Think I had nightmares,' I say around a huge yawn.

I'm tireder than when I went to bed last night. And grumpy. Because it's been weeks, months even, since I've felt like this. It's the first time I've slept badly since I summoned the Dragon with my wish.

'Why don't you come and have some breakfast, then we can talk about whether you should go to school today or not,' Amy says, patting my knee. 'How about some bacon and eggs to get you going?'

'Please,' I say around another yawn, stretching hugely like a cat – or a dragon, I think – as I go to brush my teeth.

Over breakfast, I realise that Amy is watching me eat, and then I realise that I'm stabbing my bacon. I sigh and start eating properly.

'Do you want to go back to bed?' Amy asks. 'I'm happy to call Ms Winters . . .'

I shake my head. 'Phee's mum's having more radiation stuff today. Lynne and I got a present for her. I need to take it.'

Amy's smile is proud. For once, she doesn't argue.

'Everyone has the odd bad night, you know,' she says as I put my plate and tea mug in the dishwasher. 'It doesn't mean you're going to go back to having nightmares all the time, darling.'

I give her a tight little smile and drag myself off upstairs, wondering why last night of all nights the Dragon didn't wake me. Especially after all that rubbish about it being the third dark moon: our dark moon.

Maybe that was where my nightmares came from: too much mystery, too many hints at dark magic.

There's a police car parked on the street when I arrive back from school. The front door opens before I'm even halfway up the path.

Paul has come home from work early. 'Evie darling,' he says, taking my bag from me.

There are people talking quietly in the living room.

'Let's get your coat off,' Paul says.

I let him help me. He keeps a hand on my shoulder as we go into the living room. There are two police officers there, sitting on the sofa: a man and a woman.

'Hello, Evie,' the woman says. 'Do you mind if we call you Evie?'

I shake my head.

'Evie sweetheart,' Amy says, coming forwards and towing me by the hand to the other sofa. She sits down so close her leg is pressed to mine, my hand pressed between hers. Paul perches on my other side. 'Evie sweetheart, this is Sandy and Brian. They've ... they've come to give us some ... some news.'

She waits for me to ask. I don't.

'Evie, your ... Fiona's ...' Amy casts an uncomfortable look at the police officers and changes what she was going to say. 'Your grandparents' house burned down last night.

They ... they died in the fire.'

I turn to stare at the police officers. The woman nods regretfully at me. 'We don't think they suffered at all,' she says. 'They probably died from the smoke long before the fire got to them.'

I consider her silently. I have no idea if she is lying or not.

Paul squeezes my shoulder. 'I'll go and get you some hot chocolate, sweetheart, OK?'

I turn my gaze to the policeman. He doesn't seem to know quite what to do with his face. I realise that he must be rather younger than the woman. Perhaps this is the first time he has gone to tell someone news like this.

'It'll take a while before we know for sure – there's always an investigation after house fires involving fatalities – but preliminary indications are that someone left a cigarette burning on the edge of an ashtray on top of a stack of newspapers.'

I see a photo-flash of their living room, all the old, familiar furniture and ornaments.

'It's very common,' the policewoman is saying. 'You wouldn't believe how many house fires start that way.'

I see the ashtray tipped at a precarious angle by the newspapers stacked underneath.

'Unfortunately, they didn't seem to have checked their smoke alarm lately. Lots of people don't.'

I see the old alarm box on the wall by the kitchen door, right above the back of the armchair, within easy reach.

Amy laughs nervously. 'Paul had ours wired up to the mains only a month ago so I wouldn't keep worrying about changing the batteries.' She gives him a tight-lipped smile as he comes back in with a tray of steaming mugs and a plate of biscuits. 'I didn't think it was necessary at the time, but I guess I should have been more appreciative.'

The policewoman nods sagely. 'It never hurts to be on the safe side, though battery-operated alarms are very reliable if people check them often enough.'

I look at her, but see the long fringe of the table lamp just dusting into the ash on Fiona's parents' coffee table.

'Now, your parents . . . your adoptive parents, that is, have told me that your grandparents didn't have any other family,' the policewoman says, turning back to me. 'We're still trying to find out if they had a will or a lawyer, but we'll be in touch as soon as we have all of that figured out to help you start the process of . . . well, sorting out the funeral and stuff if there aren't already arrangements in place.'

But I'm barely listening as I stare into an image, frozen out of time, of our old sitting room: behind the lamp, I can see the old curtains, faded into yellowness, with the faintest trace of a pattern of meadow flowers. But now I see the flame take hold there and the pattern blazes out, suddenly bright, as if newly printed. Then it is swallowed by the advancing black as the fabric turns to ash, as the fire devours its way upwards, up and along . . .

'Anyway, we're here today to acquaint you with the

process of what happens in these sorts of situations: to see if we can offer you any help in dealing with your loss,' the policewoman says. 'Brian's going to tell you a bit about what we can offer, while you have your hot chocolate, if that's OK with you . . .'

The policeman gulps and nods. 'Uhm,' he says, and clears his throat.

The policewoman's smile turns frozen for a moment and I see her foot twitch as if she wants to kick him. 'Just remember that you can interrupt any time you'd like to ask us questions: any questions you want. We're here to try to make things just a little bit easier for you, Evie, so you stop us whenever you need to, OK?'

When Amy closes the door after the police officers, I sigh and push myself to my feet.

'Is it OK if I go to my room for a bit?' I ask Paul.

'If that's what will help,' Paul says, giving me a kiss on the forehead.

'Evie darling, are you sure you want to be alone?' Amy asks as she comes back into the living room. 'We could play a game, or watch something nice on TV. We don't have to talk about it if you don't want to.'

I smile. 'Maybe later. I just want to think for a little bit.'

Amy starts twisting her wedding ring: a sure sign that she thinks it's a bad idea.

'Let the girl have some peace, Amy,' Paul says, getting up to put his arm around her waist. 'You and I can go and make something nice for dinner, and Evie can have a little time to herself.'

Amy twists the ring anxiously in the opposite direction. This means she is about to give in. 'You *will* call us if you're upset, won't you, darling?'

'I'm not going upstairs to cry,' I tell her. 'I just need to think. I promise to come down and find you if I decide to do the weepy thing instead.'

Paul grins, but Amy starts plucking at the ring as if it's a spinning top, turning it faster and faster. 'Maybe I should just come upstairs with you for a moment,' she frets, wrenching at the ring so violently Paul moves to capture her hand in his.

'Our Evie's perfectly capable of deciding what she needs,' he says firmly. 'And if that's a couple of minutes' respite from the two of us, then that seems quite reasonable to me.' He jollies her shoulder with his. She makes an attempt to smile: although she fails, she does let Paul usher her into the kitchen and doesn't call me back as I start up the stairs.

Although it is daylight, the Dragon's head turns to follow me as I close the bedroom door behind me. Once I'm settled cross-legged on the bed, the Dragon leaps across to join me, sitting neatly down on my crossed ankles and smiling smugly up at me.

'Was that why you never woke me up last night?' I ask.

The Dragon doesn't answer, but its smile deepens. A wisp of smoke curls up from its nostrils.

'We've got to be careful,' I whisper. 'We've got to be very, very careful.'

I went up to bed too early tonight. Now I am tired of my audiobook, but it's too early to go out with the Dragon. As I shuffle down the hall towards the stairs, thinking that a second helping of dessert is just what the situation calls for, something of the conversation below quiets my steps. I creep forward to crouch unseen on the top step.

'Don't get me wrong, Ben. I'm not saying that I don't think it's all worked out rather well. Lady Justice taking a hand and setting things to rights. Or at least as far to rights as they're going to get.'

'Purifying,' Amy says quietly, with a thoughtful satisfaction that makes me start. I grip the banister with sweaty fingers.

'Well, the world's certainly a better place without such *scum* in it,' Paul says, biting out the word. 'And I'll be damned if I apologise for feeling glad about the whole thing. Evie's taking it OK so . . .'

'I think she's relieved,' Amy says softly.

'Well, she would be, wouldn't she? Seeing as how they're not all that far away in real terms. Well . . . weren't that far away.'

'Yes, but that's exactly it. Why do you think the police aren't even curious? Not a question about where any of us were . . .'

'Don't be a twit, Paul,' Uncle Ben interrupts.

Paul gives a sigh and I hear a dull sound as if he's knocked into the table in the process of getting up to pace. 'It just seems odd, that's all. That perhaps they're trying to . . .'

'To what? Lull you into a false sense of security so that they can catch you red-handed doing what exactly? Burying empty petrol drums in your garden? Amy, you're usually the nitwit: tell your husband not to be such an idiot.'

A murmur from Amy and a grumble I can't make out from Paul.

'Look, I'm sure they'd have been round here like a shot if there were anything suspicious about the fire. But there's obviously nothing fishy going on: they know how the fire got started and there's clearly no sign of anything sinister. They must be able to tell that the doors weren't forced. No windows broken from the outside. No petrol or lighter fluid sprayed about. No sign of anything other than two horrible people quietly putting an end to themselves by accident. The police are probably no sorrier about it than we are.'

'Maybe so,' Paul says, heaving a sigh I can hear from the stairs. 'Maybe they were glad to see no sign of anything suspicious so they could write it off as an accident right from the start.'

'You got a guilty conscience worrying you that they'll find stray fingerprints, Paul?' Uncle Ben teases. 'Or have you never heard of plastic gloves?'

'Ben, don't be awful,' snaps Amy.

'Not that your conscience would need to prick you if you had.'

'Don't be stupid, Ben,' Paul says.

I can practically hear Uncle Ben roll his eyes when he says, 'I'm not the one fretting over the fact that, for once, things have worked out like they should. Besides, I know you'd have called me over to help if either of you had even considered it. And you both know I would have come.'

There is silence below. I see Amy reach out to the coffee table and pick up the smart brass picture frame that holds the last picture of Adam, taken only two days before all chance of further photos was lost for ever. Amy wipes her sleeve across the glass one way, then the other. It's a nervous habit, like twisting her ring: there's never any dust on the photo. She and Paul both take it up too often for any to settle.

'But you didn't and I didn't . . . And thank God that our collective cowardice has been rewarded. We've got what we want – what Evie needs – and none of us even had to get our fingertips dirty.'

'I just can't help feeling like we've still not seen the end of it yet,' Paul says, with a weary sigh. 'Like we're waiting for the other shoe to drop, as the Americans would say.'

'For God's sake, Paul. Just be happy about it. It's practically a fairytale ending. What more do you want?'

I creep down one step, then two, leaning forwards until I can just make out the matching picture frame at the other end of the coffee table: a portrait of Adam's family, everyone present and accounted for. Behind it, on the wall, I see the picture of my family.

In the kitchen, on the fridge, my latest drawing is taped next to one of Adam's: I press my hand against his sometimes, just at the corner so I won't ruin it, just to feel … I don't know what exactly, but it's a good feeling that has nothing to do with jealousy. And I'm proud of myself for that. Proud and happy. Somehow that picture makes the house feel full.

Paul collapses back on to the sofa, his hands clasped white-knuckled between his knees. 'It just feels like there's a price to be paid.'

'Oh for Gawd's sake,' says Uncle Ben impatiently. 'Don't give me any rubbish about karma. If it's karma, then it's just what's coming to them. Don't you think Evie's paid any price ten times over? This is just settling up the score. Balancing the scales. Why do you have to worry over the best thing to happen since she came through the operation such a star?'

Paul's hands come up to rub at his temples. After a moment, he slumps back so that his head is tilted up to the ceiling over the sofa back.

'Maybe some things are too good to be true.' He sighs,

and then rolls his head to look at Amy. 'If you made chocolate mousse tomorrow, I might be persuaded that you were one of them.'

I return to bed, smiling.

It turns out that Fiona's parents didn't leave a will. No one can even seem to work out if they had a lawyer. I'm their only family so it's been decided – I don't understand exactly who did the deciding, but it seems to be something Amy and Paul's lawyer arranged – that I inherit. They had a bit of money in a bank account and then there's the insurance on the house. I don't really care about all that. The important bit was that the lawyer asked me what I wanted by way of funeral arrangements and so forth. So I got them cremated and the ashes put in a plain wooden box. Amy offered to get something nicer for them if I wanted, but I said that I knew exactly where I wanted the ashes to go and so they wouldn't be staying in the box for very long.

We're with the lawyer now, in his office, and they're all watching me carefully: Amy with worry, Paul with pride and the lawyer with rather excessive sympathy.

'Well . . . Well, I'm sure it's all been a bit trying for our young lady,' the lawyer says, smirking all over his big, fat face. 'Maybe we should . . .'

'If there aren't any wills and that means it's all up to me, does that mean I can change something?' I interrupt.

'What sort of thing were you thinking of changing?' the lawyer asks, looking puzzled.

'Fi— my ... my mother's grave,' I say, refusing to let myself dwell on the words. 'If ... if my ... grandparents,' I get out, 'put something – an inscription – I don't want, can I change it?'

The lawyer opens his eyes as wide as they'll go and blinks. 'Well ... Well, I suppose it would be possible. Provided that your mother didn't leave a will specifying any of the arrangements that you would like to ... er ... undo.'

I smile. I know that Fiona can't have left a will – at least none that was honoured. The grave must have been her parents' idea. I might talk to Ms Winters about that, actually. It would be interesting to see if she thinks they knew it was the last thing Fiona wanted.

The day before we went to live with her parents, Fiona took me out on to the fens and we scattered Dad's ashes. We walked for hours and hours, scattering a bit here, a bit there. I nearly cried at first because I had a horrid image of the ashes being blown about the fens, trying to reunite into my father. I remember asking her if it would hurt him to be all divided up like that, but Fiona just smiled and took my hand and guided it into the little wooden box.

'It wouldn't hurt him at all,' she said. 'He loved to feel free. He would want to be spread out so he could be in lots of places at once. Then, if his ghost decides to come back, he can wander around, all over the fens. He won't have to be trapped. Stuck in just one place. That's why we didn't get him a grave. He would have hated that. Being stuck in a box: being put down into the ground in a box. Being trapped there in the dark.'

Her face is haunted and pale in the sunlight. I tilt my head back to look up at her. The sun is like lightning in a white sky. In the glare, her eyes glow like glass. I turn to follow her gaze, to see what she is looking at that is making her face so sad and desperate. Almost as if she's afraid. Tightening my hand around hers, I wonder if she is seeing ghosts: other people whose ashes have been scattered here and are walking through the fens with us. But there is nothing. Just the golden late-summer grass and the dazzle and shimmer of water glinting through the reeds.

'She didn't leave a will,' I tell the lawyer. 'I'm sure she didn't.'

The lawyer sighs. 'Well, I don't doubt you're right, but I'm afraid that we'll need to establish that as fact. We'll need to prove it,' he explains, as if I'm five *and* stupid.

'So *can* you find out?' I ask. Then I suck in a breath. 'I want you to find out,' I amend. 'And when you do and you *establish* that there's no will or anything then I . . . I want the grave to just have her name and the dates. I don't want anything else. Not even "RIP". Just her name and the dates. If it says anything else, then I want it taken off or the stone changed or whatever has to happen, but I just want the name and the dates.'

'Evie dear . . .' says Amy, putting her hand on my knee.

'That's what I want.'

Amy looks up at Paul, her face a picture of worry, but Paul is looking steadily into my eyes. He nods. 'If no one said anything in a will about what has to go on the grave, then it's up to you, Evie.'

The lawyer looks deeply uncomfortable. 'It is a most . . . unusual . . . request . . .'

'There's more than enough money in the estate for the work, and for whatever changes are necessary to effect the result my daughter wants,' Paul says firmly.

'I don't want to know, though,' I say quickly. 'I don't want to know what the grave says now: whether you have to change it . . . I don't want to know.'

Paul squeezes my shoulder. 'I'll take care of it, Evie.'

And he does. One day, I come back from school and Paul is home early.

'The grave's exactly how you want it, Evie,' is all he says.

And I say, 'Can we go and visit?'

So here we are, standing at the church gate.

'Can you wait here for me?' I ask.

Paul puts an arm around Amy's shoulders as she opens her mouth to protest. 'Call when you want us,' he says, and leads Amy away up the path.

I smile as she strains over her shoulder to stare back at me and see her sigh then smile in return before she turns away.

I go through the gate.

There's no one in this part of the graveyard. On one side is a tennis court, but no one is playing there. I know that the grave is at the far end, on the third row. It doesn't take me long to find it. When I get there, I kneel to stare at the stone. Just her name and the dates. If anything had to be removed, it doesn't show. Pulling my bag off my shoulder, I take out the trowel and start digging. I go deeper than I need, but no one disturbs me.

Amy offered to get flowers of course, if I wanted: 'But only if you want, darling. You will ask, though, won't you, if you *do* want anything?'

But all I wanted was my school bag. Amy stared a bit when I came out to the car with it, but Paul just gave me a one-armed hug and reminded me to put my seatbelt on.

I don't talk to Fiona. I thought about it, but it seems wrong to talk to her like Amy talks to Adam, even though I'd say such very different things. But now I am here I find I don't feel the need to say anything to her at all.

Instead I take out the wooden box of ashes, unlatch the little clips and reach down into the hole to tip it out. Then I pile the soil back in and punch the whole thing down with the trowel again, and again, and again.

I wipe my hands on the grass until most of the dirt is gone, then take the bottle of water from my bag and use it to rinse the rest of the mud off before picking the last flecks out from under my nails and wiping my fingers dry on a tissue. I inspect my hands – all clean again – then get to my feet.

The muddy trowel goes into a shopping bag and then back into my school bag. The box stays in my hand. When I let myself back through the gate, I detour away from the church towards the tennis court. There's a bin there, right by the fencing, and I push the wooden box into it. Its fall is cushioned by the rest of the rubbish and makes no sound, as if it has just dropped down, and down, and down into nothing and beyond.

I thought about just tipping the ashes in our wheelie bin the day the lawyer handed them to me. Instead, Fiona and her parents can rot in the dark together.

As I walk back up the path towards the church, I see Amy twisting her scarf anxiously about her hands. She says something to Paul that makes him hug her to his side and kiss her hair. Then he glances back and sees me, bends to tell Amy. She comes hurrying down the path so fast she is almost running, while Paul strolls behind, grinning at her.

I stop and smile as I watch them come towards me. Amy slows to a walk and smiles too, her face alight with relief, and with love.

They put their arms around my shoulders, one on either side, as we walk back to the car.

'Ms Winters did say she would come over tonight, didn't she?' I ask as we crunch across the gravel.

'Of course she did,' Amy says softly, smiling down at me. 'She's very proud of you for coming here today. We all are.'

I got Amy and Paul to invite her. And I made sure that they went on and on about how important it was to me: how much it would mean for all the people who understand the significance of my going to see Fiona's grave to be there tonight to support me . . .

Although I know she must suspect the real reason I want her to come is that Uncle Ben will be there too, I figured she'd agree anyway because she *is* proud that I came today. And that's the perfect excuse for her to give in because I know she wants to see Uncle Ben again. And over a family dinner she's not just my teacher or even my not-counsellor but a friend. Someone who's slowly becoming part of *all* of our lives. I mean, I know that it's mostly because of me right now, but I doubt that's how it'll turn out in the end.

She can talk about it 'not being ethical to develop a romantic connection' (as she puts it) all she likes, but she was always quite clearly and purposefully *not* my counsellor: that was the whole point. So she can't have it both ways, can she?

And what's the harm in my favourite teacher dating my uncle? There aren't even any rules against teachers dating parents. Oh, I don't doubt she'll fret and stress over it for a while yet. But I'll just keep reminding her that she's hardly letting me down since it was my idea in the first place. Maybe I'll even volunteer to see a real counsellor for a bit, just to make her and Uncle Ben happy. And maybe I can even get the counsellor to report back to Amy (who can report back to Ms Winters and Uncle Ben) that I'm really and truly happy about them being together. I've never understood the whole fuss she's making or how she could think that going on a date with Uncle Ben would cross 'ethical and moral boundaries', but I figure she'll get over it in time as happiness smoothes everything over into contentment and laughter.

They're laughing as they spill into the hall this evening, having arrived at our garden gate at exactly the same moment. They laugh as they shed hats and gloves and scarves and coats and inner layers. And then all of us are laughing together as we collide in the kitchen trying to set the table and finish cooking. More laughter as we eat.

I wait until after dinner, when Amy, Paul and Uncle Ben are finishing up in the kitchen, then ask Ms Winters to come and lay out the mah-jong set with me.

I fetch the case while Ms Winters clears the table, then I tip the tiles out in a roar like monsoon rain. We both laugh awkwardly at the noise as we bend to pick up the pieces that have spilled on to the floor. The conversation ahead is heavy in the air.

Suddenly I am struck with the urge to be wicked. It's partly because of the tension and partly because there's something I've been wanting to know for months now. I sit back on my heels, abandoning the fallen tiles. 'Do you and Uncle Ben know each other from somewhere?' I ask. 'I mean, had you met before that day when Uncle Ben bought me the Dalí book?'

'Oh,' Ms Winters says, blinking at me as she redirects her thoughts from Fiona's grave. A smile gentle with pleased surprise comes across her face. 'I've been thinking about that myself, actually, and I don't know,' she says. 'I just don't know. Sometimes it seems like I must have met him before – several times I've felt like I recognised him and he me – but I just can't put my finger on it. Perhaps we talked one day over oranges in the supermarket. We both live and work so close by, I suppose it would be surprising if we *hadn't* met in passing or at least seen each other on the street one day, but . . .' She shrugs.

I return her smile then turn my attention back to making sure all the tiles are face down. But when I glance up, Ms Winters is looking away towards the window with that same expression of wistful tenderness I wondered about before, though now it's mingled with curiosity and humour. Then suddenly the line of her jaw tightens and something else enters her eyes: something a little like hope and a little like wonder. I watch it mellow into longing before I look away, busying myself with the game.

'So I went to Fiona's grave today,' I say, as I straighten the wall of tiles I'm building.

Then I wait until Ms Winters sighs. I know that however she feels about possibly 'muddying the waters' by *talking* to me outside one of our not-counselling sessions, she can't resist this invitation. After all, she's not just my teacher now. Not after tonight. Not even before tonight. She's a friend and one day she'll be family. She's not sure of that yet, but that's OK. I can be sure enough for all of us.

'I was pretty surprised when I got Amy's call about your plans, but I expect you've been thinking about it for a while,' she says eventually and I smile, wondering how long Amy and Paul will make me wait after she and Uncle Ben start dating before they let me ask if I can be a bridesmaid.

'I hope you weren't disappointed with how you felt afterwards,' Ms Winters is saying cautiously, feeling her way through the words even as she sinks back into the sofa cushions now that we're ready to play the game. 'I know how easy it is to build up all these hopes and expectations, and then find that real life just doesn't match up to your imagination.'

I meet her concerned look with a smile. She smiles tentatively back.

In my pocket, I cradle the Dragon in the palm of my hand. 'Sometimes it does,' I say. 'But sometimes there's not such a difference between imagination and reality after all.'

That night, when I go to bed, I find the fortune-cookie message sitting on my alarm clock.

I quirk an eyebrow at the Dragon. 'Did you put that there?' I ask.

The Dragon puffs smoke into the air. It does that now sometimes. I'm still not quite sure what it means. Perhaps something like purring. I doubt I'll get an answer if I ask.

Sighing, I pick up the little piece of paper and pull out the storage drawer under my bed to tuck it back into my secrets tin. Of course, I end up sitting cross-legged by the bed, going through all the special things I keep in there. And then I come to the little matchbook from the Chinese restaurant. Only it's crumpled and a little dirty. The bit where you strike the matches is marked. I open the book and see that three of the matches are missing.

I turn to the Dragon, frowning.

'What on earth did you want with the matches?' I ask. 'Why would a dragon even *need* matches?'

The Dragon sends a tiny puff of smoke into the air and smiles.

Author's Note

Before moving on to more important things, I have one factual note to mention. As plant-lovers (and poisoners) are probably aware, the botanical name for deadly nightshade is *atropa belladonna*, though it's often referred to simply as *belladonna*. In Italian it means 'beautiful woman'.

Before any book-related thank yous, I want to give special thanks to Jill Shields, Ian Gavin Wright, Emma Beddow and Neal Evans for all their help with potting ribs. And for a great deal more kindness than anyone could ask for, but for which I am very grateful.

Among the many, many wonderful people who have helped, directly and indirectly, with the writing of this book, particular mention must go to my 'first reader', the fiercely wonderful Pat Neal, for never being anything less than completely supportive and, in this case, for loving my wicked little book, including its ending, before anyone else had reassured me that other people might like it too. And to Riccardo Bennett-Lovsey and Frances Housden for reading and commenting even when frantically busy (and for providing me with one of the best things ever: a real bone dragon), James Wildman for also somehow finding the time to provide a wealth of ideas and act as a sounding board, Tony Barry for listening and talking and standing around in a swimming pool coming up with new scenes (the smoke-alarm stuff turned out rather well!), and Sarah Goldsmith for tips on dialogue. My parents provided, among many other things, a room of my own and, thus, the means to pursue a very, very stupid career choice. Thanks for letting me be dumb and only saying 'We told you so!' about the good stuff.

Huge thanks to Michael and Malsi Foreman, Irv and Dena Schechter, for always reading my work and encouraging me. To Jacob Bauman for giving me confidence when I was most afraid I'd never get there. To Fionnuala Duggan and Steve Kanis for their super-quick responses to pleas for advice. To Jonathan Davis for taking the time to read and personally pass the manuscript along. And to Susan Schonfield for her medical expertise and tips about the carving of bone and cartilage, and Claire Preston for helping me find my way about the Cambridgeshire fens.

Many, many thanks to Lizzie Hasnip-Hill and Guy Brandon for many, many dragons over the years. To Dany Khosrovani (my wonderful godmother), Jens Turowski, Neil Rickards, Andrew Shepherd, Krysia Szurlej, Clare Reed and Jenny White, and the Anglo-Italian hordes for making me feel good about life. To Fauzia Rahman,

Janine Oliver, Heather Steady, Chris and Carmel Siggs, and especially Katie and Peter Gray for believing I could do it. To Jimmy Nederlander, Michael Codron, John Packer, David Good, Bobbie Wells, Jonathan White and Shohini Chaudhuri for all the opportunities and encouragement. And to Maureen Cooke, for giving me the words.

Last but by no means least, I wish I had the words to express how grateful I am to the many wonderful people who liked my book and helped get it into print. My first thanks must go to agent extraordinaire Claire Wilson, who is not only brilliant but amazingly kind and patient; she not only gave superb advice and feedback, but gave it with such understanding of what mattered most to me about the book that it made the initial editing process far, far more fun than I ever realised it could be. Huge thanks and heartfelt gratitude are due to Rebecca Lee, my fabulous editor at Faber & Faber, who took such tremendous time and care over the edits that I was in the ideal situation for any author – able to actively enjoy revising the manuscript through sensitive comments that helped me produce the book I'd hoped to write. Lucie Ewin project edited at the speed of lightning and made the process unbelievably calm and organised. Eleanor Rees, copy-editor par excellence, did the most brilliant, meticulous job on the manuscript, especially with hyphens and repeated words (where did they all come from?). Many other people contributed to the book including (in strictly alphabetical order) Luke Bird (design), Lizzie Bishop (rights), Marta Gala (sales and publicity), Susan Holmes (marketing), Laura Smythe (publicity, including the first little piece in *The Bookseller*), Leah Thaxton (Children's Publisher), and Dave Woodhouse (sales). I am sure there will be other people who I've missed out because we hadn't met at the time of writing, but many thanks to you too! I shall update this note in the paperback, I promise.

So many well-deserved thank yous: what a very lucky writer I am.

Along with all these thanks, there's just one thing I want (for obvious reasons – see the ending for further details) to state for the record. I do have a rib in a pot, but I am not Evie: I am three full rib-points ahead of Evie with a grand total of four potted ribs (well, four pieces of rib since we're not talking entire ribs here). I'd always planned to make the first rib into a necklace ornament (of a Dragon, of course, engraved with eldritch symbols) and then I figured I'd get not only earrings but a bracelet out of pieces 2-4. No such luck: they were stolen by medical science. However, if there are any critics reading this note and feeling particularly critical, please bear in mind that I *do* still have one very nice rib-in-a-pot just waiting to become a *Dragon*.